# Passion of Sleepy Hollow

# Passion of Sleepy Hollow

## LEXI POST

# Acknowledgments

To Bob Fabich, my real-life hero and everyday champion. And for my sister Paige Wood for her tireless support and keen insights.

Donn Brous, thank you for delving into the Dutch side of our family. Your help was invaluable!

This story came to life under the sharp eyes of Marie Patrick, the detailed focus of Grace Bradley, and the support of Jill Marsal. What an awesome team!

# Passion of Sleepy Hollow

Recluse Braeden Van Brunt is not happy to be the Headless Horseman…until he meets Katrina Van Tassel, owner of the Sleepy Hollow Inn, whose allure bewitches him from the front desk into the bedroom. When he discovers Kat and the village of Sleepy Hollow are cursed to exist only in the present day for one weekend a year, he realizes the sacrifice he must make if he wants to keep her.

Katrina Van Tassel lives between slivers of time. She thought she was through grieving her betrothed's death, but her dreams flare to life when his mirror-image arrives requesting a room. Drawn to Braeden, she is taken to greater heights of intimacy than she ever imagined, but she can't be sure if her heart is with him or with the love from her past.

Knowing he must conquer both time and ghosts to keep the only woman he's ever loved, Braeden must put the past to rest. But the dead won't rest in Sleepy Hollow.

*Passion of Sleepy Hollow* was previously published in 2014.

# Author's Note

*Passion of Sleepy Hollow* was inspired by Washington Irving's short story, *The Legend of Sleepy Hollow*, published in 1820, featuring the famous schoolteacher Ichabod Crane. Despite his abject fear of the dark and obsession with ghost stories, Ichabod's attraction to the beautiful Katrina Van Tassel drives him to trek to her father's party where he discovers the bountiful farm Katrina is destined to inherit. Though well aware of "Brom Bones" and his long relationship with Katrina, Ichabod puts in his bid for her hand. After what appears to be a rejection, Ichabod leaves the party late at night only to be chased by the Headless Horseman, who throws his head at Ichabod. The next day Ichabod has disappeared with nothing but a smashed pumpkin left upon the trail. Irving suggests that Brom may know a bit more about the disappearance than he allows. In the end, Katrina accepts Brom's proposal.

But what if Ichabod had the last laugh by initiating a curse upon the village of Sleepy Hollow and luring Brom away from Katrina forever?

The current town of Sleepy Hollow does indeed hold multiple

Halloween events every year and many of the landmarks from the original story can be found there. However, the geographic description and events of the present day in *Passion of Sleepy Hollow* are fictional.

# Chapter One

### Present Day, Sleepy Hollow, NY

B rom." The tortured whisper escaped Katrina Van Tassel as she stared at the back of the man waiting by the reception counter of her inn.

He must have heard because he started to turn in her direction.

Panicking, she retreated two steps and swung around the corner of the hallway, plastering herself against the floral wallpaper. Her heart beat faster than the wings of the monarch butterflies of summer, and she folded her arms across her stomach as a chill filled her soul and tears blurred her sight.

It couldn't be him. He was dead. Long dead. It was someone else, a Newtimer, that's all. But his build was so exact that she didn't want to see the front. What if he looked just like Brom? She would faint. Yes, she was sure she would. No, she wasn't. She'd never fainted. Of course, there was always a first time.

Brom had been her first, her only, her intended.

Her gut twisted at the remembered pain of sitting on the church steps realizing something terrible had happened. That was long ago. Too long ago. She needed to get a hold of herself.

Ignoring her agitated pulse, she stepped away from the wall, tucked stray hair back into her braid and straightened her shoulders.

This man was probably lost. That's all. No reason to make a mountain out of a molehill. She brushed down the apron on her cotton dress.

The little bell on the counter rang again.

"Well, hold your horses," she murmured under her breath as she strode around the corner to face her visitor. Her feet slowed of their own accord. The striking man with amber eyes and the build of the only man she ever loved tapped his long, blunt fingers on the counter. He looked so much like Brom, and yet not.

Irritation with herself and him brought her heart back on track. Stepping behind the counter, she nodded once, her lips refusing to smile her usual welcome. "How can I help you?"

"I need a room."

She ignored his smooth baritone and the goose bumps it sent along her arms. "I don't have one."

He had the audacity to raise one eyebrow. "Really. I see three rooms right here."

"That would be the parlor, the breakfast room and the kitchen." She glanced down, searching for the stool she used when dusting, wishing she could step on it now to meet the man eye to eye. She settled for craning her neck and catching his gaze. "I'm sorry. I thought you wanted a bedroom."

His brows drew downward, giving him a menacing look, but he didn't say a word.

She didn't even blink. She hadn't been running the Sleepy Hollow Inn by herself since her grandmother's death because she backed down from a little conflict. Besides, staring at him was pure pleasure. Like her former betrothed, his face had all the right masculine angles from his straight nose to his lightly bearded chin. His dark brows, lowered as they were, set off warm, amber eyes, and his wavy black hair gave him a polished air that Brom never had. The fact that this man was just as tall and broad as her only lover proved she still found that physique attractive. More than attractive, if the warmth suffusing her body was any indication.

The man's mouth quirked to one side, causing her heart to stutter. His lopsided grin could melt ice. "I *am* looking for a bedroom." He sighed and ran his hand through his hair. "But I can sleep in the parlor if I have to."

Oh Lord, he needed to stop being nice or she would be ready to give him the whole darn inn. She shook her head. "I'm sorry. I'm full, but you can find a room in town or even try Tarrytown. That's just down the road and they have a lot of inns."

"No. I already checked. They're full too. I didn't know this festival thing was such a big deal." He rubbed one side of his face with his large hand.

He had no calluses. Just another way in which he was different from Brom. She simply had to keep finding differences until he left, and he needed to leave soon. His continued presence was shattering her nerves. She pulled out her reservation book. "It's always this busy. That's why people book rooms so far in advance." She turned the page. "If you like, I can check to see if I have a room available for the next festival."

His hand came down hard next to hers, effectively covering all the names listed there. "I need a room tonight. Just tonight. I have to play at being this stupid Headless Horseman at midnight."

She snapped her head up, her voice barely a whisper. "The Headless Horseman?"

At her undivided attention, he squirmed and glanced away. "Yeah. Stupid, I know. But my brother asked me and since he can't do it, I promised him I would."

Kat's hand on her book gripped the pages into a crumpled mess as she croaked, "You're Stephen's brother?"

"Hey. Are you all right?" He covered her hand with his, its warmth relaxing the muscles between her fingers, as well as those around her heart. All she could do was shake her head.

He took her hand and kneaded it. "You aren't going to faint on me or anything, are you?"

"Is Stephen hurt? I know he loves being the Headless Horseman. He wouldn't miss it. He'd move mountains to get here. Something must be terribly wrong." She squeezed the man's hand like she wrung out the laundry, but she couldn't help it.

Stephen's brother wouldn't meet her gaze, but his face had definitely closed off that conversation.

"What's your name?"

"My name?" His eyes found hers again and his devastating smirk returned. "I'm Braeden Van Brunt, temporary Headless Horseman, only as you can see, I have my head."

She dropped his hand. "Braeden Van Brunt?" Brom Van Brunt. "But you look nothing like your brother." Not even slightly. Yes, his brother had dark hair and was tall as well, but that was where the resemblance ended. Stephen had a softer face, was small-boned and very thin. Even his eyes were hazel, which had made her think he was a distant cousin of her Brom. But Braeden, even in the loose garment he wore—

"Yeah, we get that a lot. He takes after our uncle and I take after our dad." He stood straighter, his whole body stiffening. "Stephen had open heart surgery and asked me to fill in. I'm guessing no one will mind who rides tonight as long as there is a Headless Horseman."

Kat's mind tried to grasp Braeden's words, but her heart beat too loudly for her to focus. Stephen's heart? Kind, sweet Stephen's heart was bad? His brother, Braeden, so like Brom. She didn't want this. To feel like this again for him. No, not for him. For Brom. For—Argh. His baritone words finally penetrated her thoughts.

"I have to stay here. There isn't enough time to find another place." Braeden ran his hand through his hair again.

"Fine." The word was out of her mouth before she could stop it.

"Fine?" His voice softened. "You'll let me stay?"

She shook her head but refused to meet his gaze. "Wait here." Without checking to be sure he remained, she spun on her heel and headed down the hall to her room. She needed to remove herself from his presence to find her brain again.

Once behind her closed bedroom door, she looked around. *God in de Hemel*, what was she doing? She had no rooms available. Her inn was filled with Oldtimers every festival because Newtimers simply couldn't stay at the Sleepy Hollow Inn. But Braeden was the Headless Horseman. If she turned him out, the festival wouldn't be complete. He had only asked for one night. One night shouldn't hurt. As long as he didn't want to stay Sunday night, it would be fine. After midnight Sunday the whole village disappeared. That secret could never be revealed to a Newtimer, or so it was said.

Kat glanced around her room, the only room not occupied— well, not by a guest. Worrying her bottom lip, she took a shrewd inventory. She could have the room made up in an hour.

Then what? How could she let a Newtimer, who reminded her so much of Brom, stay in her room? How could she let a descendant of Brom sleep in her bed?

How could she not?

Braeden leaned back against the check-in desk, his elbows resting on the wooden surface. The diminutive innkeeper was his biggest surprise of the day. At least a foot shorter than his six-foot-five frame, she had the curves of a larger woman packed into a concentrated package, easily assessed in her historical outfit. Her pale golden hair didn't like to stay in the loose braid she wore and it teased her round blue eyes as they danced with her changing emotions. Too bad he couldn't tell if he irritated her or attracted her, though he had a hunch it was the former. That in itself was strange. He couldn't remember the last woman he irritated, not counting his mother. After high school he'd found his ridiculous muscles attracted women. He hadn't minded that until he'd lost his best friend, or rather half of his best friend.

Why hadn't his brother suggested he stay here? Because it was always full? He could sleep in his car tonight if he had to, but he'd be sore tomorrow. He hadn't ridden a horse in over a year.

Braeden surveyed the tiny interior of the inn. He doubted it had more than eight bedrooms. The parlor had two settees and an armchair. The breakfast room, as she had called it, was only set for six. The entire building was like a dollhouse. He straightened. Maybe the beds were small too. He'd never fit anyway.

"Just great." He glanced at his Rolex and tensed. It was already past nine. He wanted a shower before putting on the costume Stephen had designed. He still couldn't believe he'd let Stephen talk him into this. If his brother hadn't been in the hospital, he would never have caved. But seeing his brother sitting in bed, wearing that crappy hospital gown with his wife and four kids all in the room with them, he couldn't say no. He might not see his brother in person very often, but he'd do anything for him, even be the Headless Horseman for a night.

"I have made the arrangements." The innkeeper's voice had him turning as she strode up the hallway toward him, hips swaying with purpose in the full skirt of her dress. "You can have a room in one hour. If you want, you can go next door to the pub until then."

Not likely. His bulk tended to challenge smaller men, especially while they were drunk, and the last thing he needed was a fight tonight. He glanced at the parlor as a possible place to wait, but when he looked back at his hostess, it was clear she wanted him out. Not wanting to push his luck, he nodded. "Great idea. I'll be back in an hour, Miss…"

Silence greeted his polite inquiry. If she pursed her lips any tighter, they might just disappear altogether.

She glowered. "Do you want a room or not? Now go while I get it ready."

He turned away before she caught him smiling at her. It wouldn't do for her to see he found her interesting. She appeared immune to his physique, a breath of fresh air for him. That was at least one bright spot in his day.

Striding out the door without looking back, he walked by the building next door and glanced in the window. The bar was dimly lit, but even so, it was clear there were plenty of people inside. Ignoring the inviting feel of the place, he continued along the darkened dirt road.

He didn't like having to be out among so many people. Luckily, not many strolled around the village. Most seemed to be at the other end of the road where tall lanterns shed light over stalls and tents. He should check in with the stable. His brother had told him where to retrieve the horse, but never said how much it would cost.

Braeden strode farther down the road until he spotted a wooden sign touting a horseshoe. Since his brother had been playing the Headless Horseman for years, the least the organizers could do was provide a horse free of charge, but since Stephen had a soft heart, Braeden doubted the man ever suggested it.

Stepping into the wide opening of the wooden stables, he stopped and took a deep breath. Despite his best intentions, the scent of hay and old wood had excitement growing in his chest. Anticipation built at the remembered feel of a horse beneath him. It had been too long.

"Do you need somethin', sir?" A bulky man with a balding head and a large nose emerged from the shadows to the right of him. Some kind of suspenders held brown knickers up over a white shirt with the sleeves rolled up to the elbows.

Braeden turned and the man stopped, both hands out in front of him, shaking his head. "No, don't come no closer. I be a good man."

Braeden looked behind him to see what caused the man's fear, but there was nothing. "What are you afraid of? There's no one there."

The man lowered his hands and stepped forward hesitantly, squinting. "Who are you?"

"I'm Braeden Van Brunt. My brother Stephen rides as the Headless Horseman?"

The man broke into a smile. "Ah yah, Stephen is a good man. You are his brother, huh?" He took a lantern off the hook and brought it closer, holding it high. "Hmm, I don't see much 'semblance."

"Yeah, I know. We look different. I understand I don't have much time, so I thought I'd better make arrangements to pay for a horse to ride tonight."

The man reached out his hand. "I'm Ludo Van Ripper and you don't pay for the horse. You just ride it. You know how to ride, yah?"

Braeden shook Ludo's hand, the hard calluses on the palm telling him this was a hardworking soul. "Yes, I do."

"Good. Come. You need to meet Daredevil."

Braeden followed Ludo down a short row of stalls. The man lifted the lantern and pointed. "This here's your mount."

The huge black stallion lifted its head high before bringing it down in short bounces.

The blood sped through Braeden's veins at the sight of the beauty walking toward him. The horse lifted its head over the stall door and sniffed him. Braeden didn't blink. Now, *this* was a horse. Braeden stepped forward and lifted his hand slowly, so as not to spook the animal. When the horse nudged him with its nose, he stroked its neck.

"I'll be a barn swallow's baby, I never seen Daredevil take to no one like that except his master."

Braeden continued to stroke the majestic beast, sensing its need to run. "We'll be out soon, boy. Just a bit longer." He gave the horse a final pat and turned to Ludo. "Didn't my brother ride Daredevil?"

The older man shook his head. "Nah, he couldn't get near him. He always rode Gunpowder."

Braeden followed the man's nod to see another black beauty across the way, but that horse stood at least a hand shorter and was smaller-boned than Daredevil. Daredevil took the opportunity to nudge Braeden's shoulder. He grinned and gave the horse another stroke.

"Yah, *that* is the horse you need to ride tonight." Ludo ambled away. "Yah, it's a right match, it is." His chuckle hung in the air and despite his loose cardigan, Braeden felt a chill.

Zipping up, he returned his attention to the horse. "We'll have a great ride tonight, Daredevil. I promise."

Kat examined her room one last time, her gaze resting on her armoire. Buried in the back of that piece of furniture was the wedding dress she'd worn on what was supposed to be her wedding day. Seeing Braeden reminded her she had yet to sew it into something else. It was such a waste of material to be sitting in there, but somehow, she just hadn't done it. Closing the door to her room and straightening her back, she made her way to the kitchen. It was just one night. It couldn't be wrong to help the village's Headless Horseman so he could do his work, surely. The more she reassured herself, though, the more doubtful she grew.

Setting a pot of water on top of the two-opening stew stove, Kat jumped when the kitchen's outside door flew open.

"Kat, Kat, you've got to see what they've invented now!"

Kat put one hand to her chest and another to her hip. "Maxwell Vandend, you just about scared the life from me. What do you think to come into my kitchen like a witch on a broom?"

Max's shoulders fell. "But Kat, I always come in this door, and you have to look at this." He held out his ever-present sketchpad. "Kat? Is everything all right?"

She quickly dropped her hands and pulled a bowl off a shelf. Max must think her a bit touched to be so surprised by his entrance. It was her nerves and her conscience telling her nothing good would come of her good deed this night. "I'm fine. I just can't be expected to know who is coming through my door."

He lowered the pad and her stomach clenched. Now who was being a witch? "I'm sorry, Max. I had a bit of a surprise already tonight. Let me see what crazy new invention the Newtimers brought with them this time." She smiled encouragingly.

Max suffered the most of all the villagers. Though a strapping young man of twenty, his curious mind longed for the excitement of invention instead of the local young ladies. A situation much bemoaned by not a few mothers.

His mercurial mood rose as he stepped closer to show her his sketch. He always shared his discoveries with her. Not only did it help her keep abreast of the Newtimers' culture, but it gave him someone to share his excitement with. His grandmother wanted no part of Newtime.

"What is it? What does it do?"

"This is the dashboard in one of their cars." Max pointed to his drawing. "Irwin said he tells the car to do something and the car answers and then does it."

"No. How can that be?"

She grinned as Max proceeded to tell her how it worked, a regular routine for them. When he was done, his cheeks were flushed with his enthusiasm. His youthfulness made her feel older than her twenty-eight years. "That is astounding. Have you—"

A shadow fell over them. A very large shadow. Kat looked up to find Braeden in the doorway, his body overwhelming the opening and his face serious. "Excuse me. I rang the bell but no one came. Is my room ready?"

Her tension returned full force at Max's quiet gasp.

"I'll be right there."

Braeden nodded and retreated.

Kat spun. "Max. You mustn't tell anyone." She grabbed his arm. "I had to let him stay because he is the Headless Horseman tonight."

Max's face grew paler as he moved his gaze away from the door to meet hers. "That was Brom." His voice was barely above a whisper.

"No, it wasn't. It's just one of his descendants. He's Stephen's brother."

Max's color started to return. "That is Stephen's brother?"

"Yes. I know it's hard to believe, but he is." She glanced toward the closed door. "He's only staying tonight so he can be the Headless Horseman for us. Stephen is not feeling well and asked him to do it.

You know Stephen would never let us down, so I couldn't send his brother away."

Max suddenly looked his age. "But Kat. That's against the rules."

"I know." She latched on to his arm. "But what could I do? If I didn't let him stay, we would have no rider tonight. Please. Don't tell anyone."

Reluctantly, he nodded. "Very well. I suppose it will be all right for one night."

She moved her hand from his arm to his cheek. He was truly becoming a man. "Thank you. Now I better show him to his room. He doesn't have much time."

"Right. I'll be by tomorrow."

As Max strode to the back door, she untied her apron and headed for the front counter. But Braeden wasn't there. "Now where did you go?"

"I'm in here."

His soft-spoken voice came from the parlor, but she didn't see him. Walking into it, she found him looking at a painting on the wall shared by the entryway and the room. No wonder she hadn't seen him. He stood with his arms behind his back, contemplating the scene with the Catskill Mountains rising above a stream where two men fished. His build, so much like Brom's, had her heart aching again. But Brom would never have stood still long enough to study a painting. Hanging on to that fact, she steadied herself. "I can show you to your room now."

He turned his head to look at her—no, study her. From the top of her head to the bottom of her dress. She swallowed, wishing she could fan herself. She raised her hand to put her hair back in place but stopped herself, placing it on the top of the settee instead.

She hated that he could rattle her so easily. "Are you going to want breakfast in the morning?"

He cocked his head, as if he wanted to determine if there was more meaning to her question. Finally, he stepped away from the painting, walking toward her like a bear bent on his prey. "No, thank you. I just drink coffee in the morning. So where is the room you were able to conjure up despite being full?"

She glared at him before spinning on her heel to lead him down the hall. "If you must know, it's my room."

His hand on her arm stopped her cold, or rather hot, as heat streaked from the place where he touched her all the way to her toes. "Your room? I can't do that. I'll sleep back there."

She pulled away and he let her go. Putting her hands on her hips, she focused on her irritation instead of the heat building in her belly. "Oh no. You are not staying in my parlor. First of all, in case you haven't noticed, you're big. My biggest settee could sleep an eighteen-year-old at best. Second, I just spent the last hour making the room ready for you, so you will use it. Understand?"

His mouth started quirking at the corner again, and she quickly turned. She needed to stay mad at him for at least another twelve hours. She strode down the hall quite confident he was right behind her. His weight alone on the old wooden floorboards made that clear enough, but even without the creaks and moans, her body was well aware of his presence. When they reached her door, she thrust it open before she could change her mind. "Here you are."

She stepped back while he walked through, directly to her bed. The thought of him in there, naked, asleep, had her body warming all over again.

He turned slowly and looked at her. "That's a large bed for such a small lady."

She shrugged, trying for nonchalance. "It was my grandparents'. I saw no reason to change it." She brushed by him to the washstand. "There is a pitcher here if you want to wash before your ride. This village is set in the 1790s and we keep everything authentic. That's why you won't see any electric lights here. Just turn down the lanterns before you go to bed. Now, is there anything else you need?"

He was still staring at the lantern by the bed when she asked the question, but his gaze found hers and it was filled with curiosity. "No, I'm good."

"Good." She started back through the room, anxious to shut the door behind her, but he stopped it from closing.

"I need to retrieve the costume from my car. Is there a key to the room?"

"A key?" She lowered her brows. Why would he need a key? Oh, right. Theft was common in Newtime. She looked up to find him gazing at her hair. He was only a foot from her and she stepped back. It was easier to meet his eyes while standing farther away. "No, I'm afraid I have no key for this room. But don't worry, your baggage will be safe." She turned to leave but his hand on her shoulder stopped her. His palm covered her entire shoulder easily, just like Brom's.

"Wait, I need to thank you."

She didn't want to turn and look at him. He would have a friendly smile for her and she'd melt completely.

"I don't even know your name." His low voice caressed her nerves, making them settle.

Ducking out from under his hand, she forced herself to walk away even as she spoke over her shoulder. "I'm Katrina Van Tassel, proprietor of the Sleepy Hollow Inn."

Braeden watched Ms. Van Tassel's ass as she stalked down the hall, the hint of roundness beneath her skirt making his body come to attention. The name, Katrina, seemed too dainty for her. He liked "Kat" to fit her confident personality. He grinned in amusement. She reminded him of the yellow shrub rose, small, curvy, natural, and full of thorns. She was a contradiction in so many ways. She'd obviously taken an instant dislike to him and yet had been kind enough to give him her room. She made it clear she wasn't happy to be in his presence, and yet he would swear she might be just a bit attracted to him. Maybe it was wishful thinking. She probably couldn't wait for him to leave. Actually, he couldn't wait to leave as well.

He headed for the front door, watching for his hostess, but she was nowhere in sight. He let himself out into the dark night and made short work of the long trek back to the dirt lot where his car was parked to retrieve his bag and the costume.

Stephen had outdone himself. The costume was ingenious and a spark of excitement hit Braeden's gut. He might be doing this as a favor to his big brother, but after seeing Daredevil, he was anxious to take the ride that would culminate the night's activities. There was quite a bit happening at the center of the village. From the dirt road, he could see the flames of a newly lit bonfire, and fiddle music played on an outdoor stage. Tent stalls were selling food and drink, lots of drink from the way the shadows swayed of the people who danced.

Returning to the inn, he slipped into his room unseen. Discarding his loose-fitting sweats and sneakers, he put on a pair of black leather pants he'd bought for the ride. His brother had insisted on him wearing exactly what he wore. He pulled on a black tank top and a wide-sleeved black silk shirt that buttoned at the wrists. Sitting on the edge of the bed, he slipped on the riding boots. Their familiar feel had his excitement climbing. Looking around the room for a mirror, he found none. Now, what woman didn't have a mirror in her bedroom?

There had to be a mirror somewhere. Maybe the closet, but there was no closet either. A large armoire stood in the corner. That had to be the closet. He opened one door and the scent of brownies greeted him. Brownies? The last time he smelled that scent he must have been about eleven. Why would Miss Van Tassel have brownies in her closet? The feminine clothing exuding the homey scent invited him to touch. He reached out.

What the hell was he doing? He pulled his hand back as if he'd been caught with it in the cookie jar and yanked the other door open.

Ah, now here was a mirror. It was oval in shape and ran the full length of the door. Its intricate engravings didn't fit the rustic décor of the rest of the room. Perhaps that's why his hostess hid it away. She was proud to portray life as if it were the 1790s. He grinned at her small nod to vanity, but then his reflection caught his attention. "Shit. I look like a damn Zorro. All I need is the mask and sword."

Grimacing at the image, he stepped away and lifted the top frame of the costume from the floor. He unscrewed the wing nuts and carefully slid the shoulder mounts to the farthest width. Tightening them again, he grabbed the chest drape from the bed and settled it over the metal framework, making sure the slits for his arms were lined up as Stephen had explained. Then he pulled the black cape from the bed where he'd laid it and hooked it on the top, around the neckline. He found the Velcro tabs that kept the cape to the side. His brother had said those were important for him to be able to see.

After donning the black leather gloves, another purchase his brother had insisted upon, he lifted the Headless Horseman's chest and mounted it on his shoulders. Cinching the straps under his arms, he tightened another strap across his chest only to find there was less than an inch of leather left. He hoped it stayed on. The whole contraption was very light, and he had full range of movement.

He stood in front of the mirror, but had to take a number of steps back to get the full effect of the costume. A chill raced up his spine. He could see perfectly through the black drape. The Headless Horseman in the mirror was eerie. He grinned in spite of himself. This could actually be fun.

He glanced at his watch. Already half past eleven. Taking his Rolex off, he laid it on the nightstand and grabbed the plastic bag with the fake jack-o'-lantern. It was a Halloween prop that was battery operated, so he switched it on, lighting up the eyes. Not as convincing as the rest of the costume, but good enough.

Quickly, he made for the stable. As he passed the pub, he noticed no one remained there. They must be along the route already.

His long strides brought him to his destination within minutes. "Hello? Ludo?"

There was no answer. He headed for Daredevil's stall only to see the stallion, saddled and ready, tied to a hitching post just outside the back doors. The horse neighed and tugged at his reins. "Whoa, wait for me, Daredevil." Braeden scanned the old plantation saddle and double-checked the cinch strap. With a practiced hand, he untied his mount.

Daredevil snorted and stomped his feet, but he remained still until Braeden mounted and his foot found the other stirrup. Then, without warning, the horse took off.

Braeden laughed loudly and gave the horse his head, one hand holding the reins, the other gripping the jack-o'-lantern.

# Chapter Two

Daredevil sped up the street, straight toward the revelers. Braeden tightened his knees and pulled the reins to direct the horse between the two lines of onlookers.

The bonfire burned brightly on the far side of the crowd and the loud partying had gone silent. He glanced at a reveler as he flew by and the man's face was in such open-mouthed horror that Braeden couldn't help himself. He laughed aloud at his success.

Through the village they galloped, the horse and he as one. Finally, they hit the wooded lane where only a few brave souls dared to watch. The adrenaline rush fueled his euphoria and he laughed again. The sleek strength of his mount beneath him made it feel as if he had wings. In little time, they left all the revelers behind, but Daredevil sped on.

He missed this. Not the people. Never the people, but the freedom of the ride. When he returned home, he needed to ride more. He'd make time for it. One day a month outside his penthouse couldn't cause too much trouble.

The dirt lane soon turned to a path, the elm tree branches overhanging so low that he pulled Daredevil to a walk. Still, he had to duck regularly for fear of the costume being torn. In the distance, the path appeared brighter, revealing an opening in the forest. It must be the church his brother had mentioned. It was the three-quarter marker.

He and Daredevil stepped into the clearing when a flash in front of the church spooked the horse and he reared. Braeden dropped the pumpkin, grasped the reins to control the horse and tightened his legs to keep from falling. The horse came down hard and immediately raced through the clearing toward an old wooden bridge.

Movement to Braeden's right caught his attention and his blood froze. Unclear—and yet clear—was a mirror image of himself racing on a white steed alongside him. It couldn't be. It had to be another trick of the festival. Yet even as Daredevil hit the bridge, Braeden watched in fascinated horror as the apparition disappeared.

He pulled on the reins while laughter floated on the air around him. Finally, Daredevil stopped, though he continued to prance in triumph over the white horse. Braeden looked back toward the church. Nothing moved. The only sound the quiet gurgle of the brook they'd left behind under the bridge.

He should go back to investigate, but even as the thought surfaced, Daredevil pulled hard, and he let the horse start the walk back toward the stable. He'd have to ask around. It had to be a trick of the organizers, but he couldn't shake the feeling he was dead wrong.

When he arrived at the barn, having completed the two-mile loop, Ludo walked out and crossed himself. "Mother, Mary and Joseph, you look like the real Hessian."

Earlier in the evening Braeden might have laughed at the idea, but after his encounter in the wood, he was less confident in the fun of the event. Still… "How would you know what the real Hessian looked like, Ludo? Especially without a head?"

Ludo grinned as he finally approached to take Daredevil's reins while Braeden dismounted. "That be a good point, Van Brunt. Did Daredevil do you well?"

Braeden uncinched the strap at his chest and those under his arms and lifted the horseman chest from his shoulders. "Daredevil was great. He raced through town and the wood as if the devil were on his heels. But he's a smooth ride."

"He didn't throw you or nothin'?"

"Hey, it takes a lot to throw me." Braeden slapped the man on the back carefully as Ludo led the horse into the stable. Setting the costume on a sawhorse near the entrance, Braeden divested himself of the gloves and silk shirt. His brother had been right, the shirt had blended well with the drape. He should have known Stephen had thought of everything. It was his way. Still, he'd rather not be seen in it. Being the Headless Horseman for a night was one thing. Dressing like some swashbuckler was another.

Ludo came out with a bottle of whiskey. "Would you like a nip before you turn in?"

Braeden grinned. "Am I the Headless Horseman?"

Kat wrapped her full-length shawl over her shift and dragged her quilt to the longest settee. Dropping her pillow at one end, she made her temporary bed. "It's just for one night. I'll be up before anyone wakens anyway."

While that was true, she still had to wait until Braeden returned. He was a grown man and could find his own way to his room, but the thought of him seeing her sleep made her body flush. She'd wait until he settled in for the night before closing her eyes.

Once her bed was made, she sat on the settee across from it

to watch the door. She could have witnessed Braeden's ride through the village as she had Stephen's many times, but when she'd peeked out from the kitchen to see Braeden leave the inn, a shiver of dread raced up her spine. He made the costume appear too real, and when he bent low to allow the specter through the front door, her memory of Brom ducking his head through that very door had knocked the air from her chest.

Brom had been gone four years now and she still missed him. The change in time had started when he disappeared, though none of them had realized it at first. It was one Oldtime year later before those in Sleepy Hollow discovered their little village was on a different timeline than the rest of the world. She'd noticed a young version of Brom come to the village, which at the time celebrated Halloween. The tall, lanky young man held a baby boy with the same dark hair he had. After a brief conversation, she began to have an inkling, but when old, drunken Kolbus Van Bueren went missing and was found the next weekend, or rather his skeleton was found just past the border of Sleepy Hollow village, Maxwell's grandmother had pronounced their dilemma at a town meeting. For every week of Oldtime, a year passed in Newtime. They only had this one weekend in common.

So Braeden was not Brom, but he had to be a descendant of his. That meant Brom, trapped in Newtime, had found another love, married and had children. Everything she and he were supposed to have had. Brom was no more, but she still loved him. Braeden, being so similar physically, dredged up powerful feelings for her, but they were for Brom. Luckily, Braeden planned to leave in the morning.

The grandmother clock in the hall toned one. The short Dutch-made clock had been a gift from her cousins. They had visited her when she was young. She loved the clock as it kept her on schedule, ringing its chimes every fifteen minutes. She wouldn't get much sleep this night if Braeden didn't return soon. Tomorrow, all her other guests would rise early to work the festival for the last afternoon, and then at midnight, Sleepy Hollow village would remain in Oldtime while the rest of the world continued.

The door to the inn opened and Braeden entered. Her breath caught at the sight of him. Unlike the loose clothing he'd worn earlier, his black shirt exposed his large, muscular arms. It was also tight against his body, showing a wide chest and narrow waist that fit snugly into black leather pants and riding boots. The rush of heat that hit her cheeks had everything to do with the pure sexuality the man exuded and nothing to do with the temperature in the room. Her body came alive, sensitive even to the light brush of air as he turned to close the door.

The sinews in his shoulders flowed with his movements, and she wrapped her arms about her as if that would help her ward off the desire hitting her full force. Tearing her gaze away before he noticed her distress, she looked at her hands to study a nail that had grown too long.

Footsteps halted before drawing near, and she looked up as if just noticing him. She kept her gaze on his face and it was easy to see he was disturbed. "Was your ride uneventful?"

He stood in the opening to the parlor, his brows furrowed. "Why do you ask? Did you expect something to happen?"

Taken aback by his suspicious tone, she shook her head. "No, but I do know Gunpowder doesn't take to everyone the same."

"I didn't ride Gunpowder. I rode Daredevil."

"Daredevil?" She couldn't stop her intake of breath at her shock over him riding Brom's horse. "No one has ridden Daredevil except Ludo and—Are you all right?" She took the opportunity to scan his arms for scratches, but soon lost track of why she examined him as desire rolled through her like a sudden thunderstorm.

He leaned against the wall and crossed his arms over his broad chest, making it hard for her to ignore the massive tendons he displayed. "I'm fine. I didn't know you cared."

That brought her gaze up, and her back. "I don't like to see anyone hurt, and Daredevil has been known to throw many a rider. It's nothing personal."

"I'm sorry." He stroked his hand through his wavy black hair again and stood away from the wall. "It was a weird night."

A shiver raced up her back at his puzzlement and effectively cooled her blood. "What happened?"

He stepped into the parlor to sit on the opposite settee, but when he noticed her blankets, he stopped. He glanced at the chair, guessing as she did that it wouldn't hold him, and sat next to her instead. Not exactly comfortable, but not uncomfortable either.

"I'm not sure what happened. The ride through the village was perfect. The costume did the trick and people were duly frightened. And the ride through the wood was exhilarating."

Kat was mesmerized by his eyes as they glowed with his excitement. Their amber depths turned a golden yellow near the center.

"But then I came to the church and…" He looked away and leaned his elbows on his spread knees.

She placed her hand on his arm, surprised by its unexpected warmth. "You came to the church and what, Braeden?"

At the mention of his name, his gaze returned to hers. "I'm not sure. I saw something, I think." He shook his head. "It was probably just the moonlight playing tricks on me."

"There was no moon tonight. If you were by the church, you

may have seen something. You would not be the first. Here in Sleepy Hollow, it is not so strange." She smiled, needing to reassure him that he was not crazy. It was hard enough with Oldtimers, but for a Newtimer to witness the supernatural, that had to be difficult.

He studied her face. His intense gaze made her stomach feel like fireflies danced inside it.

"I thought you didn't like me. Why are you trying to make me feel better?"

She widened her eyes. "Not like you? Why do you think that?"

His hand covered hers on his arm. She looked down to see her small pale fingers engulfed by his darker ones. Her arm tingled as he gently enfolded her hand. "Because you always seem to be irritated with me."

She continued to stare at their joined hands, unwilling to look into his eyes. If she did that, she would surely be lost. "It's not you. The festival is always a trying time and my patience is not what it should be."

"So it had nothing to do with my demand for a room?"

She looked at him then to find his mouth quirked up to one side in that lazy grin that made her heart melt. She shook her head.

"I'm glad. Because there is something about you that I like."

"Really?" Her cheeks flushed, but she couldn't look away.

He pulled his arm out from beneath their clasped hands and stroked her cheek. "Really. Mostly, I like that you didn't come on to me as soon as you saw me. That in itself is a relief."

"Come on to you? What do you mean?"

"You know. When a woman is trying to get a guy in her bed."

Kat pulled away hard. "What? Why would I do that?"

His surprise turned into a chuckle. "Exactly."

She folded her arms over her chest. "Are you saying women,

they try to, I mean, they—they…" He grinned a heart-stopping smile that had her stuttering to a stop.

"Yes, that's exactly what I mean. I'm not being egotistical. It's these muscles." He held his arms out straight as if that clarified everything. "In fact, I think of them as a curse. That's why I don't interact with people in person. I do all my work from home through my computers and phones. I learned a long time ago that being super strong can cause major—well, the point is, you aren't like that. You talk to me as if I'm a person and not a muscle man and I appreciate that."

She wasn't sure what he meant about a muscle man, but she did understand what he was saying. That he was attractive was true, but she found it difficult to believe women threw themselves at him simply because he was big and she let her skepticism show by raising an eyebrow. "I'm glad I could be of some help."

He chuckled again, a warm sound that settled around her like a fur blanket. "You don't know how good it is to hear your doubt, but trust me, it's true. Maybe I can show you tomorrow."

"I thought you were leaving tomorrow."

As his smile disappeared, she wanted to pinch herself for making it go away. Why was she reacting this way to a complete stranger? *Because he seems so familiar.*

"You're right. Speaking of tomorrow, I should let you go to sleep." He stood, towering over her. "Are you sure I can't sleep out here? I hate to think of you on your couch while I'm sleeping in your bed."

She rose too. Looking up at him when standing was enough to give her a kink in her neck, never mind while sitting. "No, please. Sleep in my bed. Honestly, it would save me buying new furniture because I don't think these settees could hold you tossing and turning on them."

"I think you may be right. Guess I owe you one."

"I guess."

He remained where he was, studying her again, making her body heat.

"Did you need something else?"

"Yes, I think I do." He stepped closer. "I need to thank you for listening to me."

She tried to put volume into her words, but they came out in a whisper as she gazed up at him. "You're welcome."

One large hand cupped her cheek and his face drew closer to hers.

Enthralled, with her heart beating faster than a woodpecker at work, she could only watch.

When his face was but an inch from hers, he spoke. "Thank you." His lips brushed against hers in the gentlest of kisses.

Before the kiss truly began, it was over, and he nodded once before turning around and striding to his room, grabbing his costume from the table by the front door on his way.

Kat stood frozen in place and brought her finger to her lips. They still tingled from the pressure of his kiss. *God in de Hemel,* what was she doing? Spinning around, she pulled the quilt aside and threw herself on the settee. She covered herself to her chin and closed her eyes.

Immediately she felt his lips upon hers again. Opening her eyes, she gazed across the room to the painting he'd originally stopped to view and tried to focus on the calm scene. Braeden was not Brom. He was different. He was gentle and concerned. Brom had been boisterous and a bit self-centered. She could admit that now. Then again, Braeden thought every woman wanted him for his brawn. If that wasn't egotistical, what was? Besides, he had the exact build of

Brom with his large shoulders, height, dark hair and well-defined muscles, but his amber eyes were nothing like Brom's gray ones. Brom was her one true love.

None of it mattered anyway. Braeden would leave tomorrow, and she'd go back to her routine of having no Brom, no Braeden… no excitement.

~~*~~

Kat stopped mid-step as she came through the kitchen door. Braeden, in a snug gray t-shirt, blue jeans and some kind of brown hiking boot, sat in her parlor, one leg crossed over the other as he balanced a computer on his lap. She'd thought him long gone when he didn't make it to the breakfast service. To see him still there sent her usual calm out the door.

His brows were furrowed as he frowned at the machine.

Taking the bull by the horns, she strode into the parlor. "Would you like coffee?"

He glanced up with irritation before he smiled crookedly. "I'd love some. Don't you have internet here?"

"In the 1790s? What do you think?"

His bafflement was obvious. "But that's the theme of the festival. Aren't there towers nearby?"

She shook her head as she turned, talking as she headed for the kitchen. "No. There is nothing modern in Sleepy Hollow woods at all. That's the point."

When she returned with his coffee, he'd closed his computer and put it on the side table. She handed him the cup, which based on the size of his hand would take him no more than two swallows to finish. Oh well, her inn was perfectly sized for Oldtimers. She wasn't about to change things for one Newtimer.

He took a sip and put the cup down. "I was trying to find out more about America in the 1790s. I always enjoyed history in school but didn't keep up with it after college."

Tension filled his face at the mention of college. What could have happened then? Oh no, she wasn't learning more about him than she already knew. That path was not safe. She smiled politely and turned to leave.

"Can you tell me a bit more about this era? I'm sure you are a walking encyclopedia on it. Your inn is authentic, and I imagine your clothes and food are as well. Right?"

She stopped, unable to retreat without being rude. Turning to face him, she was struck once again by his size and his similarity to Brom. The difference was Brom would never sit still long enough to have coffee and conversation. "Actually, everyone who works the festival is very knowledgeable about this time period. Maybe you should take a walk around and visit the stalls and demonstrations. You could learn a lot."

Having handled that little interruption, she spun again and retreated to the kitchen. Once in the relative safety of the room, she simply stood there. She had cleaning and bed making and many chores to accomplish, but she didn't want to go about the inn until she was sure her most recent guest had left.

She strolled to the window and checked the sky. It was clear blue, and bright sunshine shone on her little vegetable garden in the back. Her potatoes were probably ready to be pulled. She could do that until—

"I was hoping I could get some more coffee?"

She looked over her shoulder to find him standing in the doorway, or rather, just inside the doorway as his head rose above it. She hadn't even heard him bump his head yet, which meant he must be used to ducking. "Of course." She walked to the stove where the pot of coffee sat, the embers of the fire beneath keeping what was left warm.

He put his cup on the wooden counter. "Here, let me."

As he reached for the coffee, she seized his arm. "No!"

She clung to him though he stared at her as if she'd grown devil horns. Releasing him, she moved to the hook on the wall and grabbed the cloth towel that hung there. Wrapping it around the hot handle of the coffeepot, she poured him more coffee and handed him the cup.

"Thank you." He grinned sheepishly. "I guess I have a lot to learn about the 1790s."

She put the coffeepot back on the stove and hung the cloth before meeting his gaze. "The festival only goes until dusk tonight, so you will want to get started on that learning."

"Come with me."

"Huh?"

He wiggled his brows. "Be my guide. Show me how much I obviously don't know."

Oh Lord, being in his presence made her head spin. She couldn't do that. "I have a lot to do here at the inn before this evening. You may not be staying another night, but I have to make the beds of the other guests and fill water pitchers and a dozen other chores. If you're as irresistible as you say, I'm sure you will find a willing woman to enjoy the festival with."

He took a sip of coffee and simply studied her, a habit of his that made her uncomfortable. It was as if he tried to see inside her mind.

"Tell you what." He put the cup down. "You be my guide through the festival, and I'll help you with your chores when we get back."

"What? You can't do that. You're a guest."

"Okay, so consider me an employee. I'll help you with the chores and you can pay me by not charging me for my room."

His arrogance at having solved the problem so easily goaded her. "That's all fine, but I don't go walking with people who work for me. That would be inappropriate."

His smug look disappeared and his voice softened. "Then come with me as a friend, and I'll help you as a friend."

Her heart skidded to a halt before it decided to start pounding again. She couldn't resist the tone of his voice or the pleading look in his eyes. Why was it important that she go with him?

"Besides, I need someone to protect me from all those willing women."

Ugh. The man had a large dose of conceit in him. Well, good. This would be the perfect opportunity to prove his ego wrong. "Fine. Let me get my shawl and we can go. But not for long as *we* have chores to do."

Braeden watched Kat leave in a huff, her bristling reminding him of a porcupine. When had he decided he liked to play with porcupines? When had he decided he liked to play with anyone? He'd avoided most human contact once he graduated college, his sole goal to make enough money to support Reed as a poor attempt to make up for what he'd done. He'd even limited his visits to his own family.

It must be the place. Sleepy Hollow.

His brother had tried to tell him it was different. Even Kat admitted to strange occurrences, though he still wasn't sure if that included spirits, but he'd be damned before he'd admit to seeing himself in ghost form. Of course, he was still alive, so it couldn't have been a ghost. It had to be part of the festival. A magician's trick of some kind. He wouldn't put it past the organizers. The more realistic the spookiness, the better the reputation, and the more people came back next year. Except no revelers watched at the church.

A door closing sounded at the other end of the inn. Kat must be gathering her wrap from the closet with the Victorian mirror. He liked the idea of her in his bedroom, or rather hers. Was she fixing her hair for him?

What was he thinking? She most likely grumbled all the way down the hall about how pushy he was. If she only knew how unusual it was for him to go out in public.

Maybe he should throw on his sweatshirt and cover his body more. He meandered over to the front bay window. The sun shone brightly and people were wearing tanks and t-shirts. He'd sweat to death if he added any more clothes. Indian summer was late this year and for once, he would enjoy it. Somehow, having Kat with him made him more comfortable with braving mankind. He was less likely to cause someone a problem with her at his side.

"Let's get this done so we can get back to work."

Braeden turned to find Kat had donned a cap and a pale-pink wrap that set off her soft skin. He smirked at the wisps of hair that remained outside her braid. Nope. No primping for him at all. He stepped to the door and opened it. "After you."

Kat breezed by him, leaving a whiff of warm chocolate cake behind, and he took a moment to enjoy the scent before closing the door. He wanted to offer his arm, but something about the way she held so tightly to her wrap made him refrain. "So where to first?"

She appeared startled by his voice, probably going over her to-do list in her head, but she didn't face him. "I suggest we visit the village center. There you will find stalls of food, goods and animals."

"Animals?"

She turned toward him and met his gaze. "Yes, animals. Mostly chickens, cows and pigs. I do believe there's a batch of baby chicks this weekend."

He liked the way her face softened when she talked about the animals. They were obviously a favorite of hers. "Please, lead the way."

They strolled toward the village center where most of the visitors gathered. Kat explained the festival setup and how each booth was arranged strategically to avoid unwanted smells. They were almost there when a group of three women left the center and sauntered toward them. Braeden silently groaned, but Kat was blissfully unaware.

"I know you didn't eat breakfast, but I believe Janna has waffles for sale. Or if you prefer, Ria is selling koekjes this morning."

The three women approaching were almost upon them and Braeden tensed. Maybe it would be different in Sleepy Hollow. He could certainly hope so. "Which treat do you recommend?"

As Kat pondered her answer, the women stopped in front of them, halting their progress. The tall one with long black hair and a tank top that read Laconia Bike Week addressed him. "Hi, I'm Lea and these are my friends Tina and Stacey. We were wondering if you wouldn't mind showing us around. We heard the wooded path to the church is beautiful, but we're nervous about going out there by ourselves. Having someone who is strong with us would make it feel safer."

Braeden glanced at Kat to find her back ramrod straight, but he couldn't see her face because of the ruffles on her cap. Frowning, he wished they'd go away. "I'm sorry, ladies, but I'm being given a tour myself. I'm sure the three of you would be more than a match for any possible ghosts."

The blonde next to Lea sidled up to his side and grabbed his forearm. "But it would be better if you came along."

Kat turned at that, hooking her arm through his other arm and placing her hand on her hip. He warmed at her touch, bending his elbow to hold her against him.

"I believe the gentleman said no. Now if you will excuse us, we are touring the festival and you are *not* welcome to join us." Kat stepped forward, so Braeden moved with her as she directed them between two of the women.

He was admiring her forthrightness when one of the ladies hit his butt. "Ouch." He stopped and looked back. The blonde wasn't happy.

Kat tugged his arm. "What's wrong?"

He should ignore the episode, but an imp he didn't know he possessed had him confessing. "One of those women slapped my ass."

"What do you mean?"

"I mean exactly what I said. She slapped my backside."

As the truth dawned for Kat, she looked affronted, but then she turned, ready to battle all three women at once, and he was fairly certain she would win. To avoid the confrontation, he scooped her into his arms and strode toward the village center.

"Ah! What are you doing? Put me down. This is highly improper."

He smiled but continued walking.

"Braeden. I will not say it again. Put me down now."

He stopped, amused that she had her arms crossed and gave him her best angry look. The problem was, she had such a cute button nose that her lowered brows combined with it to make her look like a five-year-old pouting.

"What are you waiting for? Put…me…down."

She hadn't raised her voice, but her tone was so stern, he had no choice. Dropping her legs, he carefully set her on her feet.

She straightened her clothing and rewrapped her shawl before looking at him. "Now why on earth did you do that?"

"Many reasons. First, I was afraid you were going to do bodily harm to those women. Second, I wanted to feel what it was like to hold you in my arms. And third, I saw more people approaching, so I kept you in my arms longer to discourage them from interrupting our stroll."

"Oh."

Proud of himself for having struck her silent, he offered his arm. When she absently threaded hers through it, contentment seeped into his soul. "Now which treat were you going to recommend I try?"


After eating the koekjes, she'd chosen the strawberry jam cookies, and perusing the many wares of the goods stalls, where Braeden bought her a new coffeepot that came with a wooden handle, they approached her favorite area. She tried to shake off her guilt at the surprised and questioning looks she received from the villagers. They had marked Braeden's likeness to Brom and were understandably concerned, but they didn't say anything directly. After all, it was clear Braeden was a Newtimer and no village secrets were spilled in front of strangers. She ignored her own confused feelings at being held in his arms. They didn't bear examining as he would be leaving soon. Instead, she was determined to enjoy the day, something she never did during festivals.

They strolled to the fenced-in area where the chickens were for sale. Unhooking her arm from his, she leaned on the sturdy wood. Below was a small wooden crate with baby chicks making a lot of noise. She sighed, engrossed in the cute yellow balls of downy feathers. "I love baby chicks."

He leaned his forearms on the fence next to her. "I think you like anything smaller than you."

She turned her head to respond but her words stuck in her throat. His position put his head next to hers, and she didn't have to look up for once. Unfortunately, that gave her a full dose of his sculpted profile and in particular his masculine lips. Heat rose to her face as she remembered his kiss from the night before. She wanted him to kiss her again.

"Katrina! There you are. I've been looking everywhere for you."

At the sound of Irwin Crane's nasal voice, she straightened and looked over her shoulder, more irritated than usual with his presence. He moved through the crowd like a runaway rooster, complete with wings flapping, only instead of a red comb, his was black. The red t-shirt he wore added to the image.

Braeden, still bent at the fence, spoke into her ear. "A friend of yours?"

She shook her head to hide the shiver of excitement his breath sent along her skin. "No, just a regular festival attendee who is as nosey as my neighbors."

They turned around to watch Irwin's approach, Braeden's arm resting on the fence behind her. She stepped closer to him. Not just to give Irwin the wrong idea, but also because she liked the feel of Braeden next to her.

He glanced down, one eyebrow lifted in question. She raised her chin, unwilling to acknowledge her movement toward him, but then his hand left the fence and found her shoulder. She wanted to purr like a well-fed alley cat, especially as Irwin stopped before them.

# Chapter Three

"Hello, Irwin. I'd like you to meet Braeden Van Brunt. Our latest festival participant."

Braeden extended his free hand. "Nice to meet you."

Irwin glanced upward before finally focusing on Braeden's face and shaking his hand. "Van Brunt? I've heard that name before."

"I'm here for my brother, Stephen."

Irwin nodded quickly, like a chicken pecking at the ground. "Yes. Yes. Stephen. That's where I know the name. You're his brother?"

Kat held up her hand before Braeden could speak. "Yes, he's Stephen's brother. Are you enjoying the festival?"

Again, the nodding ensued. "Wonderful! The bonfire last night was amazing. Why aren't you at your inn? I stopped there to find you but no one was there."

She shrugged. "I like to enjoy the weekend too, not just work all the time." She smiled to take the bite from her sarcasm. "Did you bring anyone with you this year? I thought you said you had met a special someone."

Braeden's squeeze on her shoulder made her take her eyes off Irwin for a moment. She didn't like that two women approached, smiles wide, hips swaying.

Irwin put his hand on the fence next to her, boxing her in. "I did, but I learned they don't allow dogs on the grounds. I really wanted you to meet Summer."

"Summer?" Kat kept part of her attention on the two brunettes as they sidled up next to Braeden.

"Summer is my new husky. I just know you'd love her. Here, I have a picture on my cell."

As Irwin concentrated on his phone, Kat gave her full attention to the women. One placed her hand on Braeden's bare forearm. Kat saw red. Before the woman could say anything, Kat stepped in front of Braeden and pulled the woman's hand off him. "Excuse me. But I don't think you'd enjoy a strange man touching you like that, would you?"

The woman raised her brows. "I would if he was as strong as that."

Kat turned and grabbed Irwin's arm. He tripped as he moved forward, bumping into the woman's chest. "Oh, excuse me."

"You jerk. Get away from me." The woman recoiled, disentangling herself from Irwin's ever-present hands.

Kat crossed her arms. "I thought you didn't mind strangers fondling you."

The woman glared. "Come on, Liz, let's go check out the oxen pulls. This is obviously not the 'strongman' we heard about."

Kat stayed where she was, breathing hard. How dare they? Braeden wasn't an oddity from a traveling show.

Two large hands on her shoulders transferred the vibration of quiet laughter from the man behind her, but before she could give him a piece of her mind, he bent down and whispered in her ear, "Thank you."

The light kiss he placed on her neck before he straightened had her whole body flushing.

Irwin stopped ogling the women and turned back to face them. "I said I was sorry. Guess they're just uptight bitches."

Braeden's voice came from over her head. "That's not the right language to use in front of a lady."

"Oh, it's okay. It's just Katrina."

Braeden started to move from behind her and she quickly placed her hands over his on her shoulders and caught his gaze. "How about if we get those chores done now. I think you have learned enough for one day. And so have I."

His face was taut with anger, but he nodded once before pulling her arm through his. He turned them back toward the inn.

"Bye, Katrina. See you later." Irwin's voice followed them and she sighed. She hoped not.

As she and Braeden made their way through the crowd, she caught the gazes of many of the villagers. There would be a lot of questions to answer come tomorrow.

~~*~~

Braeden leaned back on the settee, keeping his eye on the door to the kitchen where Kat had disappeared to once again. After an afternoon of sweeping, hauling in logs and emptying wash bowls, he was thankful they used outhouses in the 1790s, but he wasn't tired. Far from it. As usual, the physical labor energized him.

Kat had insisted she make him dinner before he left. Since he'd found himself in no hurry to make the two-hour trek home, he'd been pleased to accept, never expecting her to disappear into the kitchen, leaving him to eat alone.

She was a puzzle in a sexy package that she seemed completely unaware of. Her feistiness told him she had a passionate nature, but did that extend to the bedroom? Why did he think about the bedroom? He needed to go home, back to his computers and the stock market and making his clients happy.

The splashing noises of dishes being washed had long since stopped coming from the kitchen. He would bet she hoped he would leave while she was in there. He smirked. Maybe he should stay another night, just to rile her. He enjoyed challenging her and then defusing her irritation with a little charm. He had to admit, it was an addictive pastime and made his errand in Sleepy Hollow bearable. No, more than bearable. Pleasant.

Hmm, if he stayed another night, he'd be putting her out of her bed again and that didn't sit well with him. He'd seen how hard she worked. She was no delicate flower. Maybe they could share her bed. He locked his hands behind his head at that possibility. Though she wasn't impressed with his physical bearing, he could always entice her.

Voices from the kitchen had him standing. Kat shushed someone, but he distinctly heard a male voice. He didn't like it. He didn't care why he didn't like it. He just didn't and strode toward the kitchen.

"Katrina. What were you thinking? You can't let him stay here."

"Don't you tell me what to do. This is my inn and I decide who stays here."

Braeden grinned at her spunk.

The deep voice wouldn't take no for an answer. "People will not be pleased. Do you really want to face them?"

"I'm not afraid of anyone. Now go."

"You have to make him leave. Do you understand me?"

"Stop it, Jurgen. Let me go. It's fine."

Braeden pushed the door open wide. A blond man with streaks of brown in his hair and a few inches taller than Kat gripped her shoulders. The muscles in the man's arms bunched, showing the strength with which he held her. Every nerve in Braeden's body tensed. "I believe the lady asked you to let her go."

The man turned with a scowl, but in seconds his face changed as his mouth dropped open and his eyes grew wide. His arms fell to his sides.

Braeden looked behind him, but found nothing there. When he turned back, the man was at the door and giving Kat the evil eye. "Nothing good will come of this. Mark my words."

"You're being dramatic, Jurgen!" Kat yelled as he strode off. Closing the door, she faced Braeden. "That man is a pain in my, well, he is a real bother."

"Come here. Are you all right?"

"Of course. Why wouldn't I be? He's just a nosey neighbor."

Braeden liked that she moved toward him as if she didn't even think about it. When she was close enough, he gently ran his hands over her shoulders and down her arms. "Did he hurt you?"

"What? Oh, no. I'm made of sterner stuff."

"I'm glad to hear that. Do you think he'll run to all your neighbors if I stay here another night?"

She stepped away and stared hard at him. "Stay another night? I thought you just needed to stay the one night. I'm still full if you're wondering if a room is open, and I don't do breakfast on Monday mornings and the festival will be gone and—"

He put his finger over her lips. "Please?"

Her blue eyes, so full of life, looked everywhere but at him as multiple emotions crossed her face. He didn't want the one that meant he irritated the hell out of her. She was like a roulette wheel and he needed it to stop so the ball fell in his favor. Lifting his finger, he replaced it with his lips.

Just a gentle kiss, like the night before. But her intake of breath parted her lips and he couldn't resist. Not wanting to scare her off, he slipped his tongue inside slowly to explore.

When her hands came to rest on his waist, he deepened the kiss, moving his hand behind her head to hold her in place. A tiny sound escaped from her throat and his cock came to life. He needed her closer.

Suddenly, she pulled away and stared at him. "Fine."

"Fine?" Nothing was fine. He wanted to keep kissing her. What was she doing?

She brushed past him and opened the kitchen door. "Fine, you can stay. I need to get my quilt and pillow from my room."

The door shut solidly, leaving him to stare at the wooden grain. "What the hell?" He ran his hand through his hair and shook his head. Obviously, he had no skill with the opposite sex anymore. His long abstinence since the debacle with Reed had taken its toll.

His blood cooled at the thought of his best friend. He should know better than to get close to people. He was better off behind the screen of his computer where it was safe. Kat was not safe. But God, she was fun.

He opened the kitchen door and strode down the hall to her room, his room…their room if he had his way.


Kat closed the door to her room and leaned against it. Her heart raced so fast it could beat a squirrel up a tree. Licking her lips, she closed her eyes. Braeden's kiss brought back all those wonderful feelings she used to have with Brom. The ones where her toes curled inside her buckle shoes and her body quivered.

She crossed her arms over her stomach. She hadn't had those with anyone else since. Not even slightly. What was she going to do?

She'd been desperate to get away, and now he would be staying the night. She opened her eyes. Staying in her room. Oh Lord.

Moving to her chest at the end of the bed, she pulled out a pillow and threw it on the floor. She'd already changed the sheets because he was supposed to leave. It had been so hard not to bury her face in his unique scent. It reminded her of the forest after a rainstorm, musky, comforting, making her want to snuggle in for a winter hibernation.

Ugh, what was she thinking? He was Stephen's brother, a Newtimer, and he would leave tomorrow.

Oh no. The village would be long gone by then. What would happen to Braeden then? She glanced toward the door, listening to the floorboards creak under his weight. Quickly, she pulled her quilt from the chest and grabbed the pillow.

Too late.

The door opened and he ducked inside, obliterating the opening from her sight. He stood stock-still, studying her once again. The lantern light softened his features, proving how different he really appeared from Brom.

Straightening her shoulders, she stepped toward him. "Your room is all set. I'll just make my bed in the parlor."

He didn't move, and she couldn't go through the door unless he did.

"Braeden? You need to step aside for me to leave."

"And what if I don't want you to leave?"

Her breath caught in her throat as tingling sped from her head to her toes. She swallowed hard. "What do you mean?" She turned away to give herself a moment without looking at his handsome visage. "Did I forget something?"

The floor creaked behind her and she stepped forward to

inspect the water pitcher. If he touched her again, she'd be lost. She turned to review the bed. "I assure you these are clean sheets."

The door closed.

She spun and the quilt knocked the pitcher off the table onto the floor with a crash. "Oh no." She knelt, suddenly wanting to cry, though the pitcher wasn't anything special. In fact, it had a crack along the handle and was bound to break soon anyway.

"Come. It's okay." Braeden's hands on her arms helped her to stand and sent fire through her already taut nerves.

Gently, he enveloped her in his arms. Her heart slowed as a feeling of rightness settled through her. With her face against his chest, she could hear his strong heartbeat.

"Kat." The soft-spoken word came from deep within him and she met his gaze. "Don't be mad at me."

The loneliness she glimpsed in his eyes undid her. Before she could think about what she did, she hooked her hand around his neck and pulled him forward for a kiss. This time, she breached his lips and explored his mouth, tasting the red wine he had with dinner.

Heat pounded through her limbs as he pulled her tighter to his body. One hand held her head to the side so he could fully devour her while the other cupped her arse, pushing her into him. His erection pressed against her belly, causing excitement to race to her core, which made it difficult to breathe. She held his face and pulled back to nibble at his lips while she gulped in air.

He bent and scooped her up in his arms and laid her on the bed. He followed her down, lying on his side, and swept stray hair back from her eyes. "I can never tell if you're attracted to me or irritated with me."

She gave him a shy smile. "You mean that kiss wasn't enough of a clue?"

He chuckled. "You're a very unique woman, Kat."

"Is that good or bad?"

"Oh, it's good. Very good." He held her head and kissed her again, his tongue tangling with hers.

She ran her hand through his hair, enjoying the silkiness of the strands as she pressed her body closer to him.

He moved his chest on top of hers.

"Ow." She broke their kiss, pushing against him.

He lifted. "What do you have on under that dress?"

"They're my stays. They have whalebone inside them."

"Whalebone? Hunting whales is illegal." His brows drew together as he stared at her chest.

Heat rushed to that area. "If it offends you, I can leave." She rose onto her elbows and his gaze fell to her breasts as they pushed upward.

"Offended?"

His mind was obviously not on their conversation. He lowered his head and kissed the tops of her breasts. She inhaled slowly as streaks of pleasure raced from there to her stomach and lower.

He grinned before he licked, forcing his tongue between her shift and her skin. He ran two fingers along her neckline, then dipped them beneath her dress, stays and chemise to push her breast up and out.

She watched as his mouth moved lower and his tongue encircled her nipple, lapping at her hardened peak. Pulling back an inch, he blew air across it, causing it to grow painfully hard. Tension shot from that point to the juncture of her thighs.

"Now I see the advantage of these stays." He gazed at her leveraged breast and her quim grew moist. His hand once again burrowed inside the neckline and pushed her other breast over the edge. With excruciating slowness, he gave that one the same attention. She nibbled at her lower lip to keep from moaning.

When he pulled back to gaze at his handiwork, her breathing quickened. The desire in his eyes made her tighten her legs.

"Beautiful." He ran his palm over both nipples, sending more hot sensations to her core.

She couldn't help watching as he played with her exposed breasts, tweaking first one nipple and then the other, pinching, twisting until she gasped from the pleasure that built inside her.

Braeden lowered his head again and laved at her nipple before he sucked it into his mouth. As his teeth began to bite, she let her head fall back and moaned. She felt like a maiden sacrifice, giving her breast to a lustful god. And that god didn't disappoint as he moved his talented mouth to the other nipple while his hand kneaded the first.

"Oh Braeden. What you make me feel."

He spoke against her nipple. "What do I make you feel, Kat? Tell me."

"You make me feel as if lightning is buzzing through my body."

"Hmm, lightning. I like that." He punctuated his statement by sucking as much of her breast into his mouth as he could.

When he removed his hand, she whimpered in disappointment, but then her skirts lifted. "Braeden?"

His mouth left her breast and he stared into her eyes. "Yes?"

"What are you doing?"

His crooked grin returned. "I'm pleasuring you. Do you feel pleasure?"

Oh Lord, did she. She nodded, unable to speak while he watched her so closely. His hand moved along the inside of her knee, just past where her stocking was tied. His fingers against her bare flesh made the tension inside her build. She wanted that hand to continue to the moistness waiting for it.

"Lie back."

She trembled at his command and willingly let her elbows collapse. He leaned over and kissed her neck, her chin, the corner of her mouth even as his hand crept slowly up her leg. He licked at her lips just as his finger touched the wetness of her opening.

Something changed in him. She sensed his playfulness disappear.

She opened her mouth to his tongue and it explored her teeth while his fingers surveyed the moist folds between her legs. She spread her legs wider. She wanted more.

He gave her more. A lot more. His tongue delved into her mouth at the same time his large finger pushed inside her. Her hips rose to take it. It had been so long she'd forgotten she could feel this way. His tongue wrestled with hers as he pulled his finger out and added a second.

She whimpered. Her world began to spin. She held on tight to his shoulder as his fingers pulled out and pushed back in while his mouth ravaged hers. She wanted both. All. Everything. She wanted him.

With her other hand, she cupped his butt and tried to pull him toward her, but he didn't budge. Instead, he increased his rhythm between her legs, her wetness making it easy for his fingers to glide.

She broke the kiss, needing air, and his mouth moved to her breast. His tongue played havoc with her nipple as he bit and sucked it, causing new sensations to travel to where his fingers worked. The combination had her lifting her hips, pressing against him, begging for release.

Then his fingers plunged deep inside her and halted all movement. His thumb brushed lightly across her sensitive nub, rubbing and circling.

Her breathing stopped as muscles in every part of her body went taut and pleasure streaked through them to her quim. She exploded. Ecstasy rocked her body, causing her to tremble, the lightning breaking her apart. She held tight until her breathing calmed, relaxing back into the bedding.

Braeden kissed a trail from her worked-over breast to the side of her temple. He eased his fingers from between her legs.

"Kat." His deep whisper sent a shiver across her skin and she opened her eyes.

He brought the fingers he'd had inside her to his lips and kissed them. She stared, surprised by the jolt of sexual excitement his simple act sent through her. Then he thoroughly licked each finger clean.

By the saints, he was beyond sexy. He was downright sinful.


Braeden enjoyed pleasuring Kat. She wasn't a taker. Not like other women he had sex with in his past. Kat was fresh, a small bundle of potent passion. Just the thought of her tight sheath as it sucked on his fingers had his cock pushing the limits of his jeans. He wanted to be inside her.

He bent his head and kissed her cheek, hesitating to kiss her lips after savoring her sweet juices. She was so tight, probably inexperienced, and that might be too new for her.

She pulled her arm from under his and cupped his chin with her palm. "That was wonderful."

He grinned at her honest response. No playing coy from her. Her reddened lips and flushed cheeks attested to the satisfaction he'd given her. He wanted to see more of her. Was her pussy the same rosy hue as her nipples, which still remained propped above her dress? He just couldn't resist and kissed each tight peak. Her hips moved against his groin and he jerked up.

"What's wrong?" Her brow furrowed with concern.

"I'm so hard for you that your movement actually caused me pain." He tried to grin, but the best he could do was grimace. He needed to release his cock from his jeans soon but wasn't sure how she would take that.

Her gaze moved downward even as she leveraged herself up on her elbows again. "Oh." She nibbled at her lower lip, making him want to join her there. "Can I see?"

His gaze flew to hers. Uncertainty was clear in her eyes. They probably had the same thought. He was a big man, but she was not small-boned. In fact, she was filled out nicely in all the right places.

"Yes, I'd like you to see." With one hand he unzipped his jeans and pulled out his cock. Her eyes rounded as she stared, but then she licked her lips and he grasped the base to gain control of his need.

She sat up, her breasts propped up by the stays she said she wore. Shit, she was so hot.

"May I?"

He returned his gaze to her face, her interest in his cock so intense, he groaned in anticipation. Rolling to his back, he put his hands behind his head, hoping he would be able to control himself. "Be my guest."

She straddled his leg, her layers of skirt keeping him from feeling anything beneath. He needed to get her out of her clothes eventually. Hell, they both still had their shoes on. Not a great first impression, but she wasn't complaining.

He started to smile but froze as she touched his cock. Her fingers explored every bump and crevice. He gripped his hands together behind his head to keep from throwing her back to the bed and pushing himself inside her. He wanted her comfortable with his size before he did that.

Her fingers on him were hot and trailed heat wherever they wandered. This was not what he was used to. She finally enveloped him in her hands and stroked down. His balls tightened and it took all his strength not to tilt his hips up into her soft hands.

He tried to focus on her beautiful breasts, but all he wanted was to suck them. Not able to satisfy his craving, he brought one hand up and cupped a heavy globe.

She stilled. "You like my breasts."

"Absolutely." He grinned.

"I like your manhood."

He stared for a moment before swallowing his chuckle. She wasn't kidding. "Is that what you call it?"

Her hands began to stroke again. "Yes. What do you call it?"

"I call it a cock."

She giggled. Actually giggled. "You mean like a rooster?"

"Does that look like a rooster to you?" He dropped his hand from her breast.

Her smile faded and she licked her lips. "No."

He wanted to be inside her. He wouldn't last much longer and there was still the issue of her clothes. How the hell they ever had sex in the 1790s was beyond him. Maybe they approached their women when they were bathing and already naked.

"I want to taste you, your…cock." Her husky voice had his entire body paying attention.

"Then do."

She lowered her head and licked his tip. He hoped to God she did more than that. As if she heard his thoughts, both her hands encircled him and she enclosed the head in her mouth.

A tightness shot from his balls up into his spine, causing him to clench his ass. Her movements were tentative, making him crave so much more, winding him tighter.

He buried his hand in her hair, wishing it was free of the damn braid. To have the golden silk between his legs would be the epitome of eroticism.

Her mouth drew down farther and he held his breath. He wanted to encourage her but held back. Something in his mind tested her, compared her to other women and their need for his body to satisfy themselves.

Would she bring him to the brink and then straddle him like most?

Her movements were jerky and he found himself guiding her with his hand on her head. She developed the rhythm he craved and randomly pressed her tongue against the underside of his cock as she sucked upward.

It was too good and air escaped through his gritted teeth. He was going to come.

She cupped his tightened balls as she took him deep into her mouth again and his hips lifted of their own accord.

Little moans in the back of her throat as she sucked him in and out caused small vibrations along his shaft. He couldn't hold it. It was too good. It was— He came, his seed spurting into her mouth, his tip pounding her throat even as he held her in place with his hand.

As the last vestige of his orgasm left him, he released her hair and dropped his arm to the side, spent. He opened one eye to see if she was okay and caught her stretching out her tongue to lick him clean. "Oh God. You're amazing."

She didn't respond, intent on her clean-up, and he drifted off to sleep, the soft laps of her tongue following him into dream land.

Kat smiled wide as she carefully rose off Braeden's leg and stepped onto the floor. Her legs, though, started to give way and she grabbed the bedpost to stay upright. She shouldn't be surprised. It wasn't every day she had sex like that. The last time she had sex was with Brom just before he disappeared.

Her smile faded. Brom had been big like Braeden, not just in stature but also in his manhood or rather his cock. Thick and long and incredibly pleasurable, not that she knew what it would feel like if Braeden entered her, but from the look…

Shaking her head, she reprimanded herself. "Stop woolgathering. The poor man is still completely clothed." Without another thought, she went to work taking Braeden's shoes off. The ties on his boots made it a lot easier than the boots Brom used to wear. After divesting him of his socks, she tried to remove his pants.

"Ugh. You could help a bit. It's not as if you're drunk."

"Huh." Braeden didn't open his eyes but he did lift his legs, so she shimmied the thick material past his knees before his legs lowered again and his breathing evened out. It was easy enough at that point to lift each leg and take the pants off him. She'd had practice. Brom had occasionally imbibed too much.

She stood looking at Braeden's naked bottom half. He was a big man. His thighs were thickly muscled and his calves as hard as the plow. His hardness made her feel even more womanly soft. She liked that. She'd seen his arms, but had been denied the pleasure of his chest.

Biting her lower lip, she contemplated removing his shirt. He was too big to take it off completely, but he shouldn't sleep in his clothes. She shrugged and carefully climbed on the bed again. Gently, she tried to wriggle the t-shirt over his stomach. When she uncovered that piece of artwork, she halted. He had four rows of hard bumps that were irresistible. She placed her palm on his abdomen and stroked upward, enjoying the feel of his rippled muscles. As her hand swept to the side, he jolted upright, grasping her wrist.

"No tickling."

She swung her gaze from his hardened waist to his face. "You're ticklish?"

He rolled his eyes. "No, I just don't want you to keep touching my naked body."

She met his sarcasm with her own. "You're only half naked, so I can only touch half of your naked body."

He rubbed one side of his face before staring at her. "All right." Dropping her wrist, he pulled his t-shirt off and threw it across the room. "Is that better?"

She stared at his mounded chest with the taut nipples and suddenly wanted to suck them like he had hers. Would he enjoy that? She'd never done that before, but they almost begged her to, the way they stood up from such large muscles.

He made one side of his chest move and then the other, the varying tension making the taut planes look like a children's seesaw. She couldn't help giggling at the sight.

"What? You laugh at me?" He lowered his brows and tried to look stern, but the corner of his mouth kept lifting, spoiling the effect.

"Maybe. Do you mind terribly?" She gave him a coy smile, loving the way he teased her.

"Not at all. In fact, here." He lay back and threw his arms wide. "Feel free to do anything you want to me."

# Chapter Four

Kat stared at Braeden's hard, naked body and long-dormant fantasies surfaced. She licked her lips. "Anything?"

"No, not anything. I don't trust the way that mind of yours works."

She laughed fully at that. "You're a smart man, Bro—Braeden Van Brunt." She bit her lower lip at her mistake. Braeden. This was Braeden. He studied her again and she moved her gaze to his hard abdomen, but was distracted by another hardness that had sprung to life. Pride warmed her that he so quickly responded to her even when she was clothed.

Refusing to give in to his manhood's blatant bid for attention, she drew closer to Braeden's chest and satisfied her own curiosity. She bent and flicked her tongue across one of his nipples. It hardened immediately, bringing the skin around it to a tight, pebbled appearance. Was that how her nipples looked to him when they were hard?

Braeden's hand touched her back.

With that bit of encouragement, she licked the nipple again. This time she swirled her tongue around it and sucked it into her mouth, thoroughly enjoying its hardened texture. Braeden's hand on her neck encouraged more and she took the hard peak between her teeth and gently bit.

"Kat. You make me so hard."

She raised her head to view the length of his large body and found his cock, as he called it, standing upright. Moving her hand across his chest, she indulged herself in the pleasure of feeling every contour, every edge of each muscle until she passed over his rippled abdomen and reached the juncture of his thighs.

With her hand firmly around the base of his erection, she reclined on top of him and brought her lips close to his. "So exactly what are the limits on my 'anything'?"

Braeden's arm encircled her, pinning her to his chest. "Anything I want." His lips found hers and she moaned into his mouth as her own filled with his tongue stroking hers. She caressed his hardness, touching his tip with her thumb.

He broke the kiss, his breathing faster. "You have too many clothes on."

"No, I don't. I'm not going to bed. You are." She smirked.

"Oh yes you are." He fairly growled at her as he rolled them over, his naked body pinning her to the bed from the waist down. "Now how do we get this damn fish skeleton off you?"

She laughed. "They are called stays and they are tied in the back."

His growl of frustration just made her laugh more. "They were determined to protect their women back in the 1790s, weren't they?"

"Yes. Women protected their virtue because it was all they had. And the harder it was to have some randy young buck get them out of their clothes, the better the chances they had to stay pure." She smiled innocently and lowered her lashes.

"Randy buck? I'm not some deer in heat. I just want to dive into your sweet, beautiful body with my now-aching cock."

She caught her breath at his words and felt heat rush to her face, even as an ache started again between her legs. He watched her so closely she was sure he could read her mind because a slow grin of triumph spread across his face.

"You like to hear what I want to do with your body, don't you?"

At his words, a shiver of need raced through her. She did want to—

The grandmother clock in the hall began to chime. She froze.

"Kat, what is it? You look as if you've seen a ghost."

She stared into his warm brown eyes and her vision blurred. "I can't do this."

"What?"

"Let me up."

"Kat, it's okay."

She struggled to move her legs. "No, it's not."

"Okay, okay. Hold on." He carefully untangled his legs from her skirts and rolled off her to sit on the edge of the bed. "What is it?"

She leapt up to put space between them, cooling space. She crossed her arms over her stomach and leaned against her armoire, three paces away from him. "You will be gone tomorrow."

He nodded, his eyes never leaving her face. "Yes. That's true."

"And at the next festival," she swallowed hard, "next year, your brother will return as the Headless Horseman."

"I hope so because that will mean he has recovered fully from his surgery."

"Then there would be no reason for you to come here."

"I see. You're right." He pulled his hand through his hair and looked away. In that one movement, he validated her decision.

"I can't couple with you and then forget about you. It will be hard enough as it is with all we have shared this weekend. I'm sure you will find a woman who pleases you." Jealousy flared unexpected and had her tightening her grip to stop her stomach's twitches. "I'm not like that. I'm sorry."

Braeden stood in his naked glory and stepped toward her.

She shook her head and tried to burrow back into her armoire, but it was a sturdy piece of furniture and it stopped her retreat.

He cupped her cheek and stroked his thumb across it. "I understand and respect your decision." He gave a large sigh. "I don't like it, but I will respect it."

Her heart told her not to turn him away, but her head prevailed. Still, she bit her lower lip to keep from giving in.

He leaned down and kissed her forehead. "Sleep well."

As soon as he stepped back from her, she grabbed her pillow and quilt from the floor and left, closing the door hard behind her. She walked along the hallway to the parlor and glanced at the clock. 10:17. It only took her seventeen minutes to come to her senses, and in less than two hours Braeden would come to his.

She stripped down to her shift and crawled onto the settee, pulling her quilt to her chin, her stomach still in knots and her eyes still moist with unshed tears. Tomorrow she would face a lot of questions from her fellow villagers and another week preparing for the festival. Braeden would face another year. But deep in her heart, an ember of hope refused to go out.

Cold. Braeden rolled onto his back. Something itched his butt. He scratched at it, but the dominant feeling was cold. Blindly, he reached for the quilt he'd crawled under when Kat left him and grasped nothing.

It must have fallen off the bed. Damn. Opening his eyes

reluctantly, he stared up at the night sky, the stars twinkling in the crisp autumn air. "What the fuck?"

He sat up and stared. His ass itched because he lay on grass. Grass? Where the hell was he? Had he been kidnapped while he slept? He rose, surveying the area for any threat, but all he could make out in the darkness were trees and bushes, the crickets loud enough to give a person a headache.

"Shit." No wonder he was cold. There was frost on the ground and he'd been lying there buck-naked. Seeing his pants nearby, he quickly put them on along with damp socks and his boots. Where the hell was his shirt?

Since it was black, he might never find it, but his bag stood out like a lone rock in a flat meadow. Burrowing into it, he pulled out another t-shirt and his suede jacket. Once clothed, he grabbed his car keys and pushed the small flashlight on the ring. Sweeping it around, he found his cell phone and Rolex. It was only 12:32 a.m. He hadn't even been asleep two hours.

"What the hell is going on?"

No one answered him, but the crickets kept chirping. The sound of an owl in the distance added to the night, but other than that, he didn't sense a single human in the area. Not that he'd ever been a Boy Scout or expert camper, but he'd camped out a few times when rock climbing before he gave it up.

He tried the cell phone light because it was brighter, but the phone was dead. He hadn't been able to charge it all weekend because Kat's inn had no plugs. Kat's inn?

He examined the area as best he could with the keychain light. It was little help until it flashed off the metal of a car. His car? He hefted his bag over his shoulder and headed for the vehicle. Relief calmed him as he recognized his Infiniti. Unlocking the door, he threw his possessions inside. The smart thing to do would be to drive home. Wait, did that mean his car was where he left it at the festival?

Digging into his trunk, he found his emergency kit and his big flashlight. It was stupid to do this in the dark. He should wait until morning, but he wouldn't. He had to discover what happened.

Determinedly, he walked back to where he woke. Sweeping the flashlight across his path, he recognized the dirt road that ran through the festival village, but there wasn't any village. There wasn't even any litter. There was no chance Kat's inn and the pub could possibly be mobile. He examined the dirt and grass carefully. There wasn't even an indent from where the buildings had been.

"This is so screwed." Striding to where the booths had been, he found no indentations in the ground there either. He searched for the scorched earth from the bonfire the night he rode Daredevil, but the grass was not burned. Maybe he was in the wrong spot.

He walked back to his car and pulled an old army blanket his father had given him from the trunk. Getting into the passenger seat, he leaned it all the way back, covered himself and waited for dawn. He was not leaving until he had some answers.

## *Oldtime—Monday*

Kat yawned as she uncurled herself from the settee. Good thing she was short or it could have been a difficult night sleeping. Braeden could never have fit—Braeden. Was he still here? She sat up and re-braided her hair. Her heart pounded at the possibility he might be in her bed.

Oldtime and Newtime only intersected from Thursday midnight until Sunday midnight. It was now Monday. Her fingers fumbled as she knotted the leather tie. What if he was now in Oldtime? What would the village say? What would he say? Her stomach contracted. There was no way back to Newtime until next weekend, but that would be a year later for him.

Finally, she finished her hair and stood. He couldn't still be in the inn. He was a Newtimer, but any objects not owned by Newtimers always stayed with the village. Even items stolen from Oldtime stayed with the Newtimer thief, as a few villagers had discovered. But Braeden wasn't an object and he wasn't owned by anyone. They never had a Newtimer stay in the village past midnight on Sunday.

She walked down the hall to her bedroom with feet of granite. Stopping in front of her door, she tried to control her trembling. She wanted him to be inside, but that was wrong. He didn't belong in her time.

She reached for the door handle and snatched her hand back to wipe the sweat from her palm. Oh Lord, she had to find out sometime.

Torn between wanting him to still be in her bed and wanting him gone, she squeezed her eyes shut and opened the door.

The scent of him greeted her and her heart soared. Opening one eye, she looked at the bed. He was gone. Nothing but sunlight filled the room.

The ache in her heart caused her eyes to water and she rubbed them with the back of her hand. What was she doing, mooning over a man she'd only known a full day? But was it Braeden she missed or his similarity to Brom? She would give anything to have Brom back, to have everything the way it had been. She breathed in the bayberry aroma that was specifically Braeden, a man of whom she knew almost nothing. She had too much to do to worry about a man she'd never see again.

Striding forward, she noticed the lantern on the table had burned out. What a waste of good oil. She had a lot to do today, and the morning's town meeting was bound to be long with one particular subject on everyone's mind—Braeden.

After picking up the pieces of the pitcher she'd broken the night before, she moved to her armoire, chose a clean dress and changed. What had happened to Braeden? Where did he find himself when he woke this morning? How did their village appear in Newtime? Maybe he slept soundly on a modern bed in a fancy new inn.

"Hmph." Her inn was just fine with her, as was her large bed. Bending to pull off the sheets, she stilled. Braeden's warm, wooded scent was so strong it filled her lungs. Evergreens. She breathed deeply, her mind filling with images of the two of them deep in the forest.

"By the saints! What am I thinking?" She dropped the quilt as if it were a rattlesnake and stepped away from the bed. "I can do that later. Max will be here soon. He'll be hungry."

She spun on her heel and headed for the kitchen. The grandmother clock on the wall chimed it was half past seven, and as Kat entered the kitchen from the reception area, Max entered through the back door. He glanced at the stove before greeting her.

She shook her head. "Don't worry, I'm making breakfast now. Grab some wood while I get started."

"Right!" He ran back outside with a big smile, which helped her focus on what was important. Though Max worked for her during the week, he gave every penny to Dame Vandend, his grandmama. They didn't have much, and Kat provided him with breakfast to help them without it looking like charity.

After preparing a meal of eggs, cheese and ham, she pushed the last piece of bread at Max. "Here. Take this with you. I need you to dig out the potatoes before we go to the meeting."

"Do you want them in the basket or a box?"

"Use one of the boxes from the root cellar."

"You wouldn't believe the machine they have to keep food cold in Newtime." Max's eyes lit with excitement.

"I'd love to hear about it, but it will have to wait until after the meeting. Why don't you explain it to me when we get back?"

Max tipped his chair getting out of it, his long, lanky limbs still not completely grown into. "You bet!"

"Huh?" she asked, but he was already out the door. Just as well. Max liked to adopt Newtime phrases and some took a while to understand. It was good for the village that Max kept them updated on what life was like in Newtime. She just didn't want any of their inventions in Oldtime. Life was good as it was without all the machines and information that made Newtime move so fast. In fact, Oldtime would have been perfect if Brom hadn't disappeared.

Disturbed by his constant presence in her mind lately, she shook her thoughts away. She needed to strip the beds to let them air with the windows open.

She used the water Max had brought in to wash the dishes. She was almost finished when the back door opened. Without looking, she spoke over her shoulder. "If you've finished digging out the potatoes already, you missed at least half."

"I'm not here about potatoes."

She spun at the sound of Jurgen's voice. "What do you want now, Jurgen? I don't have time for idle gossip."

The man stood between her and the large sturdy table in her kitchen, effectively blocking a polite retreat. "I came to warn you. The village is abuzz about the man who looks like Brom. Where is he?"

Though her stomach tensed, she refused to let him see her

nervousness at the thought of facing everyone, so she rolled her eyes. "He's not here, if that's what you wanted to know. He's a Newtimer, which means he's in Newtime. Now move, I have to go upstairs."

Jurgen's muscular arm shot out and blocked her in. "Katrina, this is serious. I'm concerned about you."

She raised her brow at that. "That's very nice of you, but I can take care of myself just fine."

His stance relaxed and the normal, friendly Jurgen revealed himself. "I know you can, but you shouldn't have to. You should have a husband to care for you and for you to care for him, not an old inn."

Kat lowered her gaze. She refused to allow Jurgen to see how much his words stung. That dream was exactly what she and Brom had planned to fulfill before he vanished. She shook her head and wiped her hands on her apron to avoid Jurgen's gaze. "I'm perfectly happy running my grandmama's inn." She lifted her head. "Which means I need to get my chores done if I am to make the meeting in time."

"Of course." He moved his arm away and bent it behind his back. "I just wanted to let you know people are going to have a lot of questions. I want to help you if I can. You can always depend on me."

She smiled sadly. Jurgen was considered a great catch and had been one of the four men who followed Brom no matter what he led them into. Maybe if Brom had never existed, Jurgen and she could have found love, but that was not to be. If only he would accept that. She put her hand on his biceps. "I know I can. I appreciate that."

He opened his mouth to say more, but closed it and nodded once before walking to the door. He stopped and looked back at her. "I'll see you at the meeting."

"You will." He was concerned for her. What were they all saying? Braeden had been the Headless Horseman, stayed in her inn, and walked the festival with her. What was wrong with that? "Everything."

With slumping shoulders, she dragged herself up to the third floor and began opening windows while her mind worked furiously to figure out what to say.

## *Newtime—November*

Braeden paced Stephen's room. It agitated the hell out of him to see his older brother so weak. Stephen was always thin, but he appeared downright scrawny and his dark hair had grown past his ears. That wasn't the Stephen he knew. He wanted to do something to help, but he was useless.

"Please, Braeden, sit down. You're making me dizzy."

He stopped and stalked to the armchair near the bed. "Isn't there something I can do? Pay a babysitter to take the children off Marilyn's hands for a while so you two can spend time together? How about a maid? That would help, wouldn't it?"

Stephen chuckled. "Listen, little brother, the only thing that's going to make me better now is time. You can't buy that. Now get off the 'poor Stephen' shit and tell me why you really came here."

"What? I can't come see how my brother is recuperating?"

Stephen shook his head. "Come on. I know you better than that. You only leave your penthouse for Christmas and family birthdays and since it isn't either, it must be something else and it must be pretty important."

"You don't believe I'm here to see how you're doing?"

"No."

"Shit." Braeden stood again. His brother knew him too well. He would have sent flowers, emailed, texted and phoned, but coming to see Stephen was all for selfish reasons. Reasons he couldn't even articulate. He stopped and stared at his brother. "You know I do care about you."

Stephen took a sip of juice his wife had left on the nightstand. "Uh-huh, yeah. I know that. I have it in a trillion emails from you. When are you going to stop hiding behind your computers and join the living to prove it?"

Braeden resumed his pacing. "I do less damage behind computers. No one gets hurt."

"Dammit, Braeden. You can't still be hiding from the world because of Reed. You didn't know that woman was the one he'd fallen for. If she felt half as much as he did, she would have never climbed into your bed."

He closed his eyes as the hurt spread from his chest to every extremity of his body. His best friend was permanently brain injured because of him. He didn't want anyone else to be hurt by his presence. "I'm not here to talk about that."

"All right. Then what are you here to talk about?"

"I want to know about Sleepy Hollow."

"Well, I'll be a—"

Braeden spun around and held up his hand. "Please. Spare me the shock. Can you just tell me what you know about the festival, the town and the people?"

Stephen studied his face and it was all Braeden could do not to look away. "Sure. What do you want to know?"

"How long have you been the Headless Horseman?"

"That's easy. Except for this year, it's been fourteen years. I was twenty when I took over for Uncle Richard."

"Uncle Richard used to ride?" Braeden moved back to the chair and sat. "How did he get involved?"

Stephen grinned. "Grandpa Van Brunt passed it on to him. Hell, it's been in the family since the very first Washington Irving Festival. Actually, even earlier. I believe it goes back to an old Halloween celebration the Van Brunts joined."

"This is news to me."

"Of course it is. You can't find everything on the internet. Sometimes hanging out with the relatives is very informative."

Braeden looked away. He had no argument to counter Stephen's point, so he kept silent.

"Only one person needs to ride every year and we all love the rush, so we certainly aren't going to share the pleasure." Stephen coughed and reached for the juice again. Taking a sip, he pointed at Braeden. "Don't get me started or I'll get excited all over again. Why? Did you enjoy it?"

Did he? Hell, yeah. If he'd known what a blast it was to be the Headless Horseman, he would have wrestled Stephen for the honor years ago. "Yeah, I did. It's been a long time since I've ridden a horse like Daredevil."

"You rode Daredevil?" Stephen's eyes widened, making his pale face look ghoulish.

Braeden shrugged. "Yeah. I needed a big enough horse."

"I should have known."

"So the Van Brunts have been playing the Headless Horseman for generations. What about the re-enacters? All those people in that village. They are very focused on being authentic. Did you know in addition to having no electricity, there's no cell phone service either?"

"Really? How about that. You must have been lost. Good

thing you only had to be there a couple hours." Stephen's crooked grin proved he thought Braeden incapable of functioning without technology.

How wrong he was. Braeden straightened. "As a matter of fact, I spent two nights at the Sleepy Hollow Inn."

"How the hell did you pull that off?"

Braeden stood again. "I begged."

"What?"

He faced his brother and grinned sheepishly. "I begged. I never made a reservation and I didn't get in until almost nine. Katrina Van Tassel took pity on me."

"Funny, she never took pity on me. Then again, I never rolled into the village the night of the ride without a room."

Braeden ignored his brother's admonishment and started to pace. "But something strange happened. Actually, many strange events occurred, but the one that bothers me the most is the fact the entire village disappeared Sunday night."

Stephen's brows drew down. "What do you mean, disappeared? You mean they packed up their stalls and went home? That sounds pretty normal for a fair."

"No, I mean the buildings, the people, even the litter disappeared. I slept in that inn. It was a solid building. In fact, I was asleep in one of its beds when it disappeared and I woke in the field. Can you explain that?"

"No, but it could have been a prank. Maybe they moved you to another field."

"But my car was right where I left it, and there's no way anyone can get into that baby without setting off enough alarms for the police to hear it all the way into town. No, the entire village vanished." He'd found no trace of anything the next morning despite searching the area all day. He'd finally given up and driven home. He'd even charged his phone off his car and took photos.

Stephen remained silent.

Braeden stopped pacing. "Well, what do you think?"

His brother started as if he'd been in deep thought. "I think that Sleepy Hollow has always had strange things happen there. I guess this is just another. As long as the village 'reappears' next year, that's all that matters."

Braeden studied his older brother, positive he knew more than he was telling, and that bothered him. They'd always shared secrets, triumphs and failures. Only Stephen knew how devastating the fiasco with Reed had been to him. And only he knew when Stephen married Marilyn, they were both virgins. Yet now Stephen held back. Why?

Stephen looked so frail, Braeden squashed his need to shake the information out of him. Guilt shot through him just for having the thought. Maybe he could take a different tack. "I also met a woman there who told me 'no'."

Stephen's gaze returned to his. "What? Really?" He glanced toward the door. "Who is she? Where is she? I want to meet her. You did bring her with you, right?"

"Didn't you just hear me?" Braeden shook his head. "She turned me down. So no, she is not here."

Stephen's shoulders fell and he coughed again. "I'm sorry, Braeden. I just assumed if she turned you down, you charmed her into changing her mind. See what happens when you leave your little world? You might actually meet someone who isn't just interested in your strength. You need a wife."

Braeden plopped himself into the chair again. "Please. You've had enough children for the both of us. It was bad enough when Kat and I walked—"

"Kat? Did you say Kat?"

"Yeah." He grinned. "I got Kat to explain the 1790s to me by taking me through the festival."

"Sweet, hardworking, never-leaves-her-inn Katrina Van Tassel?" Stephen's disbelief bothered Braeden.

"I don't know about sweet and not leaving the inn because it was obvious I irritated the hell out of her, and I had to bargain with her and do chores just to get her to go with me."

Stephen shook his head. "Now that's far stranger than the village disappearing. Is she the one who turned you down?"

"Yeah." He expected his brother to laugh, but when he didn't, he looked up. Stephen's disappointment was obvious. "What is it?"

"Nothing. Just thought maybe you'd find someone. Any chance you could ride for me again next year? I'm thinking I want to spend as much time with Marilyn and the kids as I can. The doctors gave me a second chance, and I'm not going to blow it."

Braeden tensed. It wasn't money that made Stephen work too much. It was his need to do well. If he couldn't do something well, he worked at it until he could. "Let me think about it. Okay?"

Stephen nodded, his eyelids drooping.

Braeden stood and placed his hand on his brother's arm. "Thanks for the information. I'm sorry I tired you out."

Stephen opened his mouth as his head started to shake.

"No. Don't say it. I did. Just rest and get better. Those four kids need their dad as soon as possible."

At Stephen's halfhearted grin, Braeden squeezed his arm. "Love you, bro." He walked to the door, the feeling of having messed up again sitting as solid as a fifty-pound weight in his stomach. He looked back at Stephen to find him already sleeping. Yeah, he'd tired out his brother for his own selfish reasons. He should have stayed home.

Striding through the living room, he paused to watch two of the boys hanging blankets over a clothesline strung around three trees. He grinned. It was good to see some things didn't change. He opened the front door.

"Braeden. Aren't you going to stay for supper?"

He turned toward Marilyn as she dried her hands with a dishcloth. She and Stephen were as in love today as they had been the night they met, the best night of her life, as she always said. Stephen was in good hands. "No, I have to go, but thank you anyway."

"He loves having you visit. He talks about it for days afterward. Could you at least say hello to the boys? With Stephen recovering, they aren't getting much male attention."

"Sure." He nodded once and exited the house. Making his way across the front lawn, he smiled at the misshaped tent being built. He and Stephen had made some pretty strange forts in their day. "Hey, guys, what are you doing here?"

Two heads popped out of an opening. "Uncle Braeden!" In no time Michael and his brother Julian had scrambled out and were pulling him toward their pride and joy.

"You have to come inside, Uncle Braeden. Julian made shelves out of rocks."

"Really? Now that is creative. Have you set up a table yet? An upside-down box works pretty well."

Michael rolled his eyes. "That won't last if it rains. I'm going to use the old rabbit cage and put a piece of wood on it."

Braeden didn't have the heart to tell the boy that if it rained, the entire fort would be obliterated. That was the joy of innocence.

"Can you help us get this last rope tied up on that tree?"

Braeden smiled. "Sure." He stepped around the back of the tent and took the rope Michael handed him. It was so light it felt as if it would break at any moment. Carefully, he lifted it toward the tree. "Is this where you want it?"

Michael pointed. "No, a little higher."

He really didn't want to ruin the boys' fort, but the rope felt as if it would snap. He moved it up just a few inches and gingerly tied it around the tree. When he stepped back, the rope remained and he wiped the sweat from his brow. It was hard holding back his strength.

He crouched down to the boys' level. "Listen, you two. You be good for Mom while Daddy is recovering and next time I come, we'll play checkers, okay?"

Dual squeals of "yes" and high-fives put the boys back to working on their tent and Braeden rose. He wished he could spend more time with his nephews, but even giving a high-five that wouldn't knock them over was a strain. Maybe when they were older, bigger, he could visit more often. Maybe, but in his heart, he doubted it.

# Chapter Five

They had all gone mad. That was the only explanation Kat could conjure for the wild accusations flying about the town square, though to be fair it was more of a circle. Maybe she was joining them in their insanity if she could stand at the center of the circle and calmly allow them all to talk to her at once.

Except they weren't actually talking to her. Janna and Ria were arguing with each other about Braeden, and she blushed as she focused on their conversation, his prowess in bed being the current topic. Jurgen gestured and spoke loudly about their way of life to the other three men who used to ride with Brom. Ludo had the three Aldershoe sisters enthralled with his description of Braeden. The elderly ladies were too frail to participate in festival and so missed seeing him. Max talked excitedly to Liesbeth and from his gestures, she doubted it had anything to do with Brom's descendant. Even her own parents were talking with another family since they didn't come to festival as usual, the farm taking all her papa's time. The only one who wasn't vocal was Dame Vandend, Max's grandmama, who sat comfortably on a bale of hay in her usual black dress.

Kat caught the old woman's gaze. She gave Kat a toothless smile. Why wasn't she as excited as everyone else?

It appeared Kat could stand at the center, the place of speaking, all day and let her neighbors exhaust themselves, but that wouldn't be healthy for the Aldershoe sisters and she still had a lot of chores to do.

Taking a deep breath, she yelled with everything she had. "Silence!"

The talking ceased. "That's better. Now I suggest you listen to what I have to say because I will only say this once and then I am going home."

She glanced around the circle of forty-six people. They all remained quiet. "Good. There's no reason for concern. First, the man you saw who resembles Brom is a descendant of Brom's. His name is Braeden Van Brunt and he is Stephen's brother." She paused as people relaxed at the mention of Stephen. Good.

"Second, he came to the Sleepy Hollow Inn for a room at which point I refused, but when I learned he had no place to stay and was here to ride as the Headless Horseman, I allowed him a room for the night."

She ignored the twittering her comment stirred. "As for me walking the festival with him, it was because he asked and promised to do chores afterward that I agreed."

"Does that mean he'll be back next year?" Ludo spoke from behind her, so she turned to face him.

"I don't think so. He was reluctant to play the Headless Horseman, and we all know how much Stephen loves to ride, so I'm sure he'll insist on returning. From what I understand, Stephen was not well, but he is expected to be better in time for the next festival."

"Won't this Braeden come back to see you?"

Kat glared at Jurgen for asking such a question. "I very much doubt that. I turned him down." The gasp in the crowd issued from all the women except the Aldershoe sisters. "And I think many of you noticed, he can easily find someone else." Kat swallowed hard at the sting in her chest at that fact.

"He's welcome to have me!" Janna yelled.

"No, he can have me." Ria sashayed forward, her hands on her hips.

Jurgen couldn't let their silly remarks pass. "No one can have him. A Newtimer and an Oldtimer cannot join. It will bring bad luck. It may even raise the Hessian from his grave again. No one is allowed to join with a Newtimer."

Nora Addens, a widow with two almost grown girls pointed her finger at Jurgen. "There is no rule about that."

"There should be."

Arguing broke out amongst the villagers and chaos ensued once more. Kat threw her hands up and walked to the edge of the circle. Dame Vandend grabbed her arm as she passed.

Kat looked down at the old woman, who shook her head. "This portends change, *meisje*."

"Good or bad?"

The woman shrugged.

Kat nodded to show she understood and Dame Vandend let her go. She was halfway to her inn when she turned back to look at the old woman. She'd called her *meisje*, maiden. Why? She wasn't exactly a maiden anymore, but then again no one knew that.

The arguing continued in the town circle. Did she want to face that melee again to find out what the woman meant? No, she had chores to do.

## *Newtime—May*

Braeden cut the skirt at the waist, too impatient to undress

Kat. She stood next to the bed as he knelt on the floor and worked around her with the scissors, careful not to cut too close to her skin. When he was done, he ran his hands up her thighs, the soft flesh quivering at his touch.

He wanted her so bad he could taste it. Ah, taste. He nudged her legs apart. "Hold on to the post."

With her back to him, he cupped her perfectly rounded ass cheeks and kneaded them. So full, perfect for his large hands. Gently, he moved his fingers closer to her pussy. Touching her labia, he spread her. She was pink and blurry. He tried to focus again. Who needed to see when he could taste? He moved forward and used his tongue to lap at the opening revealed by his fingers, but he tasted nothing.

Surely she was wet for him. She had moaned. He needed to taste her like a bear needed honey. Lapping again with his tongue, he pushed it into her, forcing her to open for him. He mimicked what he would do with his cock.

She moaned again. *Yes, Kat. I want you to come for me. Just for me.* His tongue worked hard. There was no taste to her. He needed to make her come like she had for him before. He left her opening and moved between her and the bed, facing her mons, her hands still grasping the post.

Reaching between her legs, he slid two fingers in as far as they would go.

She undulated her hips to fit his digits to her body. Keeping his hand still, he licked his way to her pretty pink clit and gave it a slow lap. Her small body shuddered and she tightened around his fingers. "Do you like that?"

He spoke against her clit and her response was no more than a whimper. "I'll take that as a 'yes'." He lapped up her clit again and then down it. Her legs trembled. He wrapped his arm around to her ass and held her steady as he circled her clit again. It was so hard. He flicked his tongue at it and he was rewarded with another moan as his fingers were sucked harder.

She was so close. Soon he could taste her. With a new pace, he flicked her clit and moved his fingers out and in deeply. Her tightening walls told him all he needed to know. Continuing the steady rhythm, he sucked her clit into his mouth while his tongue pressed against it.

"Braeden!"

Her yell was punctuated by a jerk of her hips as she came. He held on to her nub as his fingers pushed in and out again, until he found himself holding her upright. With anticipation, he removed his fingers and put them in his mouth.

Nothing.

Braeden woke, his cock hard, his frustration mounting. "What the hell?" He glanced at the clock. It was midnight *again*. Always at midnight. It was time to start staying up later. He couldn't take much more of the sex dreams.

He threw the crumpled sheet to the side and rose. He was tired of the hand jobs, the frustration and the titillating dreams. He wanted Kat and he wanted her now. Every night another dream, sometimes a different one, sometimes a repeat, but always the same. He couldn't taste her, smell her or even see her clearly. All he could do was touch and be touched. He had to find her.

Striding to the bathroom, he turned on the shower. Enough was enough. He'd tried to ignore the need to see her, the strange sensation that he missed her. It couldn't be. They'd only known each other a day.

Stepping into the warm water, he reached for the hot knob to turn it down. Maybe a cold shower would help. He'd rather Kat was in the shower with him. Ignoring the cold water idea, he grabbed the body wash instead. Would she want to be washed or wash him?

While his past sexual experience with the women he fucked was vast, his relationship experience was minimal. Ever since he'd discovered his first high school girlfriend, Elaina Frederickson, had only wanted his body, he'd closed himself off to real relationships and taken what was offered. Offered being the key.

Soaping his hand, Braeden stroked his cock. But Kat hadn't offered. Was he just preoccupied with Kat because she'd refused him, even pushed him away multiple times? Was it that he was instinctually careful with her? For some reason, he didn't have to think about being gentle, it just happened, which made it so easy to be with her. Or was it simply the thrill of the hunt?

He swallowed as his hand increased its pace. The warm water relaxed the muscles in his back, even as his balls tightened. He was a damn virgin at hunting and he'd obviously screwed up because he'd come home with nothing, nothing but a craving that wouldn't be quenched.

When he remembered the look on Kat's face as she sucked him into her mouth his heart raced and his blood pounded in his ears. He cupped his balls with his other hand, unable to stop stroking himself. Having Kat do the same made him want her even more. He wanted to pleasure her like she'd never been pleasured. He must have some experience that she didn't, especially after all the women he'd slept with. Had she done it in a shower like now?

He caught his breath as his eyes closed and he imagined her with him. Her soapy breasts pressed on either side of his cock as he slid up and down. Her, holding them against him, making the suction tighter while she bit on her lower lip, anxious to feel him inside her.

He pumped his hand faster even as he saw himself pulling from her and turning her against the glass wall of his shower, pressing her small body to it as he entered her from behind. Moving his hand around her to play with her clit even as he slid in and out of her sheath. Her breasts pressed against the glass, moving as he rocked her, clear in the mirror across from the shower.

"Arrr." Braeden tensed as his climax sprinted through him and he pumped his come onto the shower walls. Instead of relief, he felt empty. Though he'd toyed with finding a quick fuck, he didn't. It wouldn't satisfy him any more than a shower and a hand job.

Washing the rest of his body, he quickly rinsed off and stepped out. He only had one choice. He had to find Kat.

Throwing the towel over the shower door and grabbing a clean one from the towel warmer, he grabbed the comb he'd taken from Kat's room and strode into his home office. "Low lights." As the room's lighting glowed, he passed his work desk with its multiple monitors and moved to a smaller wooden desk where he flicked on his personal laptop and set the towel on his chair.

It was time to let technology do its magic. He sat and opened his email as he fingered Kat's comb. Everything about it was practical like her—simple, functional and beautiful. He should never have taken it. He'd regretted his impulse, but tonight it soothed him. It made her feel closer, within reach.

Stephen's message stood out from the other family member emails by its subject line "Headless Horseman?" The message was sent at 11:53 p.m. What the hell was Stephen doing up so late? He was usually asleep by nine. Braeden glanced at the electronic calendar on his desk. Friday night. Stephen and Marilyn had instituted date night after his heart surgery. He smiled. Stephen sounded a lot better these days. He'd recovered well and was more relaxed about life. As for the Headless Horseman, that could wait. It was only the middle of May. He didn't want to disappoint his brother so early by declining the offer.

Now to find Kat. He clicked his browser open. How many Katrina Van Tassels could there be in the United States? It shouldn't take long to narrow it down. Setting the comb next to the computer, he typed in the name and waited.

Over 120,000 sites? This could be harder than he expected. Reading the summary of the first site, he quickly dismissed it. He wasn't looking for a fictional character from a Washington Irving story. Skimming the rest on the list, he found them all to be the same. Katrina Van Tassel was a character in *The Legend of Sleepy Hollow*, in which there was a headless horseman.

"Damn!" Braeden slammed his hand down on his desk. He should have known. She insisted on authenticity. The question was, how far did she go? Did she simply call herself Katrina Van Tassel or did she legally change her name? On one hand, he hoped she used a fake name, as that would make her much more psychologically appealing, but unfortunately also impossible to find.

Not willing to give up, he searched the white pages and found three Katrina Vantassels. He would call all of them in the morning, or rather later in the morning. And if none of them were his Kat?

He returned his focus to the internet. Then he would find a private investigator.

## *Oldtime—Wednesday*

Katrina carried the ham bone in a cloth as she made her way back toward the village center. She would drop it off at Ludo's. His father, Hans, had an old dog who was partial to bones. Thankfully,

Janna had told her how poorly Dame Van Brunt was feeling and she'd brought the rest of her ham to the poor woman.

Though darkness edged the road, the next farm was Ludo's. The bone was a bit dried now, but she doubted the dog would care. She was glad she'd rushed to Dame Van Brunt's. The older woman was too weak to make herself dinner. The ham Kat brought would keep her for a few days, but she would visit again tomorrow with fresh eggs as well. It looked as if she'd have to ask her mom for help with the inn. She hated to take her away from the farm but—

Someone watched her. She stopped and looked around. There was no one and nothing she could see. Shrugging, she started forward, but caught movement to her right, in the woods. Not sure if it was human, animal or supernatural, she increased her pace to Ludo's. Just as she heard the dog bark, a figure in black raced by her on horseback, knocking her to the ground.

By the time she looked up, the horse had disappeared into the wood across the lane. She shivered. The Headless Horseman was an old story Brom had used to scare Ichabod out of Sleepy Hollow, but the decapitated figure had never actually existed. So what was that?

Braeden? His name came to her mind against her wishes. Despite her attempts to forget him, he kept confusing her heart, whether she did chores or walked through the village square. Was it her fate to be tortured by a descendant of the man she loved? She sat up and brushed the dirt from her hands. It wasn't that she loved Braeden. It was that she had loved Brom.

Ludo's dog trotted over to her and tried to lick her face. "No, boy. There's a bone around here somewhere for you." She searched for it in the fading light, but it might have become buried by the leaves on the ground when she fell. Standing up, she pointed the dog in the direction she dropped it. In no time the dog had it in his mouth, his tail held high as he trotted back home. She waved at Hans Van Ripper, who stood in his doorway, and the old man nodded before turning back inside.

Not dallying to brush off her skirts, she strode past the farm and into the village center. The lanterns in the pub next to her inn guided her footsteps. Everyone was already inside for dinner. She'd eaten with Dame Van Brunt at her insistence, which meant she might have time to make bread before heading to bed.

The cloaked figure that knocked her down bothered her more than she cared to admit. It had to be one of the villagers, which meant someone had been very rude. She had a suspicion it was one of the—

"Katrina, what are you doing out here so late?"

She jumped at the sound of Jurgen's voice so close to her. "Oh my heart, Jurgen, you fairly scared the life from me."

"I'm sorry. I called you when you walked by my shop, but you didn't respond."

"Oh, I guess I owe you an apology. I was thinking." She shrugged, surprised she hadn't heard him.

"About him?"

Did Jurgen know who the horseman was that ran her down? "Who?"

"That man who looks like Brom."

She couldn't see Jurgen's face clearly, but his tone made it clear he wasn't happy. "No, as a matter of fact, I wasn't thinking about him. And he doesn't look like Brom. He just has the same build. Or I should say *had* the same build. He won't be back here."

Jurgen put his hand on her arm. "He's not Brom. He doesn't love you. You can't make him into Brom."

"What? I'm not doing that. He is Braeden and Brom was Brom.

They aren't alike in looks or personality, so don't worry about me. Besides, as I told you, he won't be returning."

"Are you sure?"

She pulled her arm from his grasp and put her hands on her hips, her patience waning. "Jurgen, I think I know my own mind and my own heart. My heart is with Brom and my mind is bent on making bread before bed. A pleasant night to you."

She stalked the rest of the way to her inn, too irritated with Jurgen for suggesting she couldn't keep the two men separate. Of course she could tell the difference between Brom, the man she loved, the man she was supposed to wed, and Braeden, a Newtimer who made her feel alive, and made her yearn for what she used to have even more.

She opened the door to the inn and lit a lantern, placing it on the registry counter. Yes, at first she thought Braeden was Brom from the back, but one look into his warm brown eyes and she'd seen a difference, not just in color, but in soul.

Brom was wild, full of life, the center of every crowd. People were drawn to him. Braeden was reserved, quiet, uncomfortable around others.

She walked into the kitchen and lit another lantern. She gathered the flour and yeast, mixing them with water until she had a nice dough. Brom made love like he lived life, wildly, fast, overpowering, but satisfying. It was who he was, and he wouldn't have changed simply because he had a family. She used to wonder what his wife had been like, but she didn't anymore.

Braeden made love slowly, teasingly. He loved how she had licked him. She'd been so pleased she could give him pleasure, but he was gone now. She sighed as she set the dough to rise. Braeden had probably found another woman to satisfy him by now.

Her hand gripped the counter edge. She didn't want to give him up. It was wrong, but she didn't want him to be happy in Newtime. She wanted him with her. Her stomach clenched, a painful yearning far beyond her ability to satisfy. She should remember Brom and their love. That was what had sustained her since he'd disappeared. She'd given him her heart.

And he'd married, had children and lived a full life while she existed in Oldtime, heartbroken with their unfulfilled dreams.

*But his dreams were fulfilled.*

She didn't have a choice. She could only choose among the villagers and she didn't love any of them that way. She loved Brae—Brom. She loved Brom.

She sat down heavily in one of the chairs. Was that what Jurgen meant? Was she mixing her feelings for Brom with Braeden?

She shook her head, but her heart wasn't so sure.

## *Newtime—October/Oldtime—Friday*

Braeden was glad he'd brought the truck this time. The dirt road to the Sleepy Hollow Village was covered in ruts and his suspension handled it well. The sun hadn't even risen yet, but he was determined to discover how the village could set up so quickly. He'd driven into the area yesterday evening and there was nothing, so he stayed in Tarrytown, lucky to get a room for one night before the festival started.

Coming around the wooded corner, he slowed the car.

It couldn't be.

The stable came into view and then the rest of the village. He parked across the road from the stable and exited his vehicle. "What the fuck?" He slammed the door hard.

He'd searched half a year for his supposed Katrina Van Tassel, hired the best private investigators and driven to Sleepy Hollow multiple times to try to find clues. His before and after pictures in his cell phone were the only evidence that kept the detectives from having him committed, but even they decided that he must have mixed up the towns and quit.

Yet here it was in all its glory. Sure, people were hanging signs and displaying product, but the entire village was suddenly present. And if it was here, that meant Kat was here.

With a purpose bolstered by many frustrated nights, Braeden stalked toward the Sleepy Hollow Inn. Windows upstairs were open, but the front door remained closed. He opened the door with more force than needed, announcing his presence as it banged against the wall. No one was within sight, so he pummeled the bell.

"I'm coming, I'm coming." Kat's voice sounded from upstairs. He strode down the hall to where the stairs ended just as she stepped off the last step.

"Braeden!"

He took in her breathless greeting, shining blue eyes, and all-over-disheveled appearance and pulled her into his arms. He stared for one second before he kissed her.

She melted against him as he plundered her mouth, the teasing scent of chocolate floating into his brain while her breasts pressed against his chest, awakening his aching cock.

It took him a good few seconds to notice she had started to break away. He let her go.

She stepped back and up one step, her hands finding her hips. "What are you doing here?"

His frustration flooded back and he scowled. "What am I doing here? I'm looking for you. Just like I've been doing for the last six months!" At his raised voice, her eyes widened and he gripped his hands into fists to control his anger. "I wanted to see you again. Do you have any idea how it felt to have you disappear and then to find you here as if you hadn't been in hiding all this time?"

Kat's mouth opened and formed a small O before she crossed her arms over her stomach.

"I couldn't find Katrina Van Tassel anywhere." He ran his hand through his hair at her silence. "I assume that's a fake name for this festival. I want to know your real name."

She looked at him like a cat eyed a bowl of cream just out of reach. Wanting and calculation flitted across her features. "You said you wouldn't be coming back."

Her softly spoken words stopped his anger in its tracks. Had he said that? He racked his brain for the conversation. Having played over every discussion they had had, it didn't take long to remember. "No, you said I wouldn't be back because Stephen would be the Headless Horseman. I only said I hoped he would be because that meant he had regained his health."

Kat's face fell. "Does this mean Stephen is still not well or…"

At the tears forming in her eyes, he cursed himself. "No. Not at all. Stephen is as healthy as a horse. He decided he wanted to stay with his family this year and give me another chance to play the Headless Horseman since I didn't do such a great job last time." He gave her a crooked smile, hoping to distract her.

"You were a wonderful Headless Horseman. Everyone said so."

"No, I lost my pumpkin head that night. Did anyone find it?"

Her brows furrowed, but her arms had at last relaxed and fallen to her sides. "No one said they found it. I didn't even know you lost it."

She bit at her lower lip and Braeden wanted to kiss her all over again. He missed her. What was it about this small feisty woman that made him feel alive…normal? Whatever it was, he wanted to find out, along with some other mysteries associated with the little village.

"So you don't have your pumpkin head? We will have to make one because it is important you have it, otherwise the villagers will get nervous." She shivered with her statement.

Braeden stepped closer to her. She was a bit taller standing on the step, but still shorter than him. He cupped her cheek. "I want you."

Her intake of breath made him grin. He leaned in and gave her a chaste kiss on the lips.

"Katrina! Katrina, where are you?"

"Oh no. That's Mama."

Braeden dropped his hand. "Your mother?"

She rolled her eyes. "Yes, my mother. Don't you have a mother?" She pushed her way by him. "I'm back here, Mama."

Her mother? Of course she had one, but meeting a parent wasn't something he'd expected. He looked down the hall toward Kat's room. Was there another exit?

Kat's chuckle interrupted his escape plan. "Are you afraid to meet my mother?"

He turned back to face her and found her smirking. "Is that a challenge?"

She shrugged, turned her back on him and sashayed up the hall.

Her mother. His back stiffened. He'd never met a woman's mother. Of course, meeting Kat's mom could provide him the opportunity to discover more about Kat, such as where she lived when not at the festival. Maybe he could charm Mrs. Van Tassel into revealing a fact or two. He strode down the hall, the anticipation of success speeding him along.

~~*~~

"Katrina, I brought some blueberry muffins I made this morning. I thought that would help you for tomorrow's breakfast."

"Mama, that's a wonderful idea. Thank you." She took the plate and put it in an upper cupboard where Max wouldn't think to look. She glanced at the kitchen door. Would Braeden dare meet her mama or would he hide? Brom had been full of charm and energy the first time he'd met her mother.

"Dame Van Brunt is finished with the ham you brought, so I started a chicken stew. Maybe you could send Max by to bring it to her."

Kat refocused on her mother, listening for the creak of a floorboard in the next room. "I will."

"So how can I help?" Her mama took an apron from the pegs by the back door. "I have to say it is nice to come to town during festival for a change. Sometimes I think your papa loves that farm more than me."

The twinkle in her mother's eyes belied her words and Kat smiled. "I doubt that, but won't he be pleased with whatever you decide to buy?" She winked to support her mother's brief holiday from the farm.

"Don't encourage me, young lady. Now, tell me where you want me to start."

"I still need—"

The creak in the floor warned her just before the kitchen door swung open.

"Good morning, ladies."

She tried to look at Braeden as her mother would and saw a tall, dark-haired, handsome man in a short-sleeved shirt with bulging muscles, a narrow waist and dark blue jeans, but when she glanced at her mother, the woman was in pure shock.

"Braeden, I'd like you to meet my mother, Dame Van Tassel."

Braeden bowed and reached out his hand.

Her mama hesitated before putting hers in his. He brought it to his lips in true European style. Now where did he learn that?

"It's a pleasure to meet you. I'm not surprised by your beauty as it shines also in your daughter."

Her mama's full cheeks turned as pink as wild roses even as she lowered her lashes. Her blonde hair, now sprinkled with white, made the change in her pale face more striking.

Kat could suddenly imagine what her papa had seen when he'd met her mother. She'd never thought about it before, but her mama was a beautiful woman with a beautiful heart.

Braeden dropped her mother's hand and grinned. A little too pleased with himself for Kat's comfort.

Her mama lifted her gaze again and looked at Kat. "He looks like—"

"Like he wants to help me prepare for the festival. I agree." She looped her arm around Braeden's and turned him toward the exit. "I have a pile of logs that need to be split so I can use the wood for cooking. You'll find the axe in the shed."

Braeden resisted her pull at the door. He turned to look back at her mother. "It was nice to meet you." He gave her a studying look before he took himself outside.

As soon as the door closed, her mama grabbed her arm.

"Katrina. He looks like Brom. What are you doing? What is he doing?" Her mother pulled her to the table and made her sit. "This is the man the village was upset about last weekend, no?"

Kat nodded. What could she say? Her heart was filled with joy at his arrival, but fear for what it could mean.

"You think you like him, yah?"

She remained silent.

"Katrina, he is not Brom."

She pushed her chair back and walked to the counter. "I know. He is nothing like Brom."

"That I do not know, but his appearance is similar."

"Only in build." She pulled a plate from the cupboard. "His hair is darker. His eyes are warmer."

Her mama cocked her head. "He's as tall and as broad and has Brom's muscles, but he is a Newtimer."

"Yes, he is, and that is the crux of the situation. What does it matter if I like him? For every week of my life, he lives a year. There can be no happiness in that."

Her mama rose and grasped her shoulders. "My poor Katrina. Down this road is trouble. Yah?"

"Yes."

She was pulled into a sturdy embrace. "I think you yearn for Brom too much, little one." He mother gave her back a pat and released her. "Now, if Braeden is working as you told him to, it is best we do as well."

Kat nodded before walking over to the window in the kitchen to see if Braeden even knew how to split logs. The sight that greeted her had her body flushing with need. He'd taken off his shirt, his chest glistening with sweat as he confidently swung the axe over his shoulder and down through the log. He bent to pick up a half and set it in place before his abs rippled as he swung the axe up again and brought it down, his aim true.

"Katrina, what is it?" Her mama bustled over before she could get a word past her tight throat. "Oh my."

She had no idea how long they stood there, but when Braeden wiped his brow with the back of his hand, it brought her to her senses. "He probably needs water. Could you fill the pitchers in the rooms while I get him some?"

Her mother nodded, fanning herself with her hand. "Of course." She stopped Kat as Kat headed outside with a pitcher and cup. "Anything is possible, yah?"

# Chapter Six

Kat slipped outside and strode to the water pump without looking at Braeden. If she caught sight of him, she'd forget what she needed to do. Viewing his naked torso in the sunlight as he worked was a very different experience from seeing him by lantern light.

After filling her pitcher, she turned to find him watching her. Men in her village didn't take their shirts off to work or for any reason except bathing and sometimes bed. She'd seen Newtimers without shirts on occasion when Indian summer graced the village during festival, but that wasn't often.

As she walked toward Braeden, she couldn't take her gaze from his chest.

"Is that for me?"

At the sound of his deep voice, she looked up to find his lips twitching. The man thought too much of himself. She handed him the pitcher and cup. "Here. I thought you might be thirsty."

He nodded solemnly. "I am. Thank you."

As he filled the glass and gulped the water, she couldn't tear her gaze away from his corded neck and the Adam's apple that moved as he swallowed. Some of the water dribbled past the side of the glass and trailed down his jaw to drop in the dark hair of his chest.

She wanted to lick the spot and bit her lower lip at the imagined taste and texture.

"Kat?"

"Yes."

"Did you want something?"

She looked up into his serious face. He gazed at her as if he wanted to eat her. Was that how she stared at him? "No."

He tilted his head. "Are you sure? You look as if you need a kiss from me."

"Huh? Oh no." She stepped back. "No, I just wanted to thank you for helping me."

He grinned. "No need to thank me. I'm just working for my room tonight. I'd like the same one I had last time."

"My room?"

"Yes." He lost his smile. The desire in his eyes stopped her breath. "But I want you in it this time."

She gasped and spun on her heel, retreating into the inn. After closing the kitchen door, she leaned against it. She couldn't resist him. He was too much male to resist. What was she going to do?

Her mother's footsteps on the stairs brought her back to her preparations. She left the kitchen and ducked behind the registry to grab her stool for dusting.

"Katrina, you seem to be missing a pitcher."

She'd forgotten she'd taken one from a guest room for herself. "I broke one last weekend. Did you want to go to the square and fetch me another?"

Her mother's face brightened. "I'd be pleased to."

"Let me get you the coin." She ran to her room at the back of the inn and pulled out a few bills and some half dimes. When she returned her pouch to the armoire, she couldn't resist opening the other door to check her appearance. Her hair was everywhere but in her braid, and her apron had blackberry stains from the jam she made the day before.

Discouraged, she closed the armoire and ran back to the kitchen. "Here you are, Mama. Also, if you see a nice comb, could you get it? I can't find the one Grandmama gave me. I'm sure it will turn up, but until then I need something for Sundays. And if you see anything else you think I might like, please buy it." She winked.

"You're the best daughter, Katrina." Her mother enveloped her in another warm hug before practically skipping out the front door.

It was the smallest things that made her mother happy and shopping was one of them. She rarely remembered her mother being unhappy. The last sad day her mother experienced was the day of Kat's wedding when Brom never made it to the church. At first people had thought he'd changed his mind, but when he never reappeared, the village realized something greater was at work.

Shaking off her thoughts, Kat went into the kitchen to find a rag for dusting. She couldn't help stopping at the window to view Braeden. She was sorry she did. He was at the water pump filling the pitcher. She stared, mesmerized by his biceps as he easily worked the pump to fill the pitcher with one hand, a chore that took her two hands to accomplish.

He lifted the pitcher high and poured it over his head. She gasped. The water streamed over his hair and dropped down onto his shoulders before running over his chest. She watched as water droplets caught in the curly hairs there before flattening them down. He bent and filled the pitcher again and repeated the process. After wiping the water from his eyes with his hand, he grabbed his shirt and headed for the door.

Startled from her trance by his approach, she moved away from the window, crouched down to open a lower cupboard and retrieved a rag. When she stood, he was there, studying her.

"I would love to see that ass with all those clothes off you."

Her hand flew to her chest at his comment in a useless effort to stop her heart from fluttering. "Do you mean my arse? If that's how you talk to the women you meet, it's no wonder they throw themselves at you."

His smirk returned. "No, I rarely have a chance to say much."

"Why?"

"Because they aren't interested in my conversational skills. In fact, they couldn't care less if I have a brain. All they care about is this." He flicked his hand at his muscled chest like he'd bat away a fly.

Though her gaze had moved to where his hand indicated, her own anger at his comment caused her to look into his eyes. There was pain there and she found herself wanting to strike out at those who caused it. "Then they are slets." She colored at the word, but it was true.

His smile reappeared. "Do you mean sluts?"

"I mean women who have sex with many men. Is that what you call them?"

"You have some strange words in your vocabulary, and I noticed the same with those in your village as well."

"We are of Dutch descent and many of the elders cling to old words and old ways."

He nodded. "That explains it. So what would you call a nice ass?"

Oh Lord, was he back to that? "A nice arse. Now I need to get the dusting done before my guests arrive." She started forward, but he blocked her way.

"I didn't search for you for half a year to be brushed off because your mother is here."

"She's not…" Oh no.

"She's not here, is she? Where did she go?" He moved closer and she took a step back, wringing the cloth in her hands.

"She went to the village square for a new pitcher. Remember, I broke one."

"So she will be a while and we have time to talk."

She swallowed. "I thought you wanted to see my ar—ass."

He laughed, the sound so beautiful she wanted to hear it again and again. She wanted to go to sleep at night and dream about it.

"So you would rather strip than talk. You're hiding things from me, Katrina Van Tassel, and by the end of this weekend, I will discover everything there is to know about you, from the secrets you keep in that sharp brain of yours to the smallest mole on your pussy."

She gasped as warmth flooded her body. They were alone and if her mother enjoyed herself, they would be so for hours. She backed into the table and her heart pounded as he took the step that brought him to her. She stubbornly stared at his chest, but the water droplets there didn't help her breathing.

He grasped her wrist and placed her hand with the rag against his well-developed pectoral muscles. "I believe I'm dripping all over your kitchen floor."

She glanced up at him and found his eyebrow raised.

"Would you dry me off?"

Oh Lord. He read her mind. Slowly, she circled one large nipple, stroking in ever-widening arcs with the clean rag. When she finished that side, she couldn't resist any longer and flicked her tongue across the wet tip of the other.

Braeden sucked in air. "Your tongue is much more enjoyable." He pulled the rag from her hand and tossed it aside.

With no choice in the matter, she licked each water droplet she could find. She traced the line of hair that disappeared into his jeans, fascinated by the movement of the muscles in his abdomen as she licked her way down. She noticed the large bulge beneath the waistband, but once she'd licked every droplet, she stopped and stood straight. His eyes were closed, his jaw rigid. She allowed a slow smile to spread across her face. "You're dry now, so you can put your shirt back on."

His eyes flew open and his look turned predatory, which sent a shiver of excitement racing up her spine. "Oh no. The last thing I'm doing is putting clothes *on*." He reached down and opened his jeans.

"Braeden! You can't do that. It's not even noon. We are in the *kitchen*."

His brows lowered. "You're serious. Are you telling me you have never had sex during the day or in the kitchen?"

"Of course not. It's just not done."

His gaze softened, but she wasn't sure what that meant. What she was sure of was he needed to get dressed.

He placed his hands on her shoulders. "Kat, I'm going to make love to you right here and right now."

Moisture pooled at the juncture of her legs and her knees buckled.

Braeden caught her and sat her on the table. His hands left her waist to cup her breasts beneath her stays. He grumbled. "One of these days I'm going to figure out how to get you out of these, but right now I'm too impatient. I want you now. I've been needing you for months."

Her need was just as strong. Despite her brain telling her they couldn't do this for so many reasons, she reached down and stroked his cock. Its steely hardness testified to the truth of his words.

Braeden slipped his hand inside her neckline and coaxed each breast out above it. The stays were rough underneath them, but Braeden's look made her nipples turn hard.

"Have I told you how much I like your breasts? They are so full, so perfectly shaped." He traced his fingers around each nipple and she watched to see her skin pucker around it as it grew harder, just as his had done.

He took each nipple between his thumb and forefinger and squeezed gently. Tingles of excitement raced from his fingers to her groin, producing more moisture between her legs.

He made her feel beautiful.

Braeden pulled her nipples toward him, forcing her to lean forward. He licked at her lips and she opened her mouth, but he didn't accept the invitation. Instead, he held her nipples as he nipped at her lips and her head fell back in surrender. He traced his tongue along her chin to the base of her ear, his grip gentle yet firm. When he released her breasts she whimpered, but he grasped her against his chest and tilted her head back with his hand. Finally, he met her mouth with his and slipped his tongue inside.

She moaned as she grasped his back, instinctually spreading her skirt-covered legs and moving her hips forward.

He pulled back from the kiss. "I'm going to come all over your dress if we don't get it out of the way." Before she knew what he was about, he'd taken the hem and rolled it up until it was at her waist, exposing her to the light. That he could see her in the sunlight made her shy, and she placed a hand over her mons.

"Lift your hips."

She did as he told her and he tucked the material under her butt. It was a strange position and not very comfortable.

"Kat."

She glanced at him.

"Give me your hands."

"But it's so bright."

"Exactly. I want to see how beautiful you are. I have dreamed of your pussy lips. I need to see if my dreams were correct."

Pussy lips? He had to mean her quim. He dreamed of what she looked like down there? *She* didn't even know what she looked like.

"Kat, please."

Did she dare? She gazed into his pleading eyes and couldn't deny him. Feeling adventurous, she gave him her hands, revealing her desire for him in her moist folds.

Gently, he laid her back on the table, her breasts no longer heavy on her stays, but her bunched skirt tilted her hips upward, spreading her legs farther, opening her to his view. Her heart pounded as he held her thighs apart.

"Beautiful. You are so pink and so wet for me. Do you have any idea how that makes me feel?"

She shook her head but he didn't see. His gaze was focused between her legs and her breathing increased. Need spiraled down to her core.

Reverently, he brushed through her blonde curls before he moved his hands to her folds and spread them, revealing her opening, her womanhood.

She clenched her vaginal muscles as her wanting became overbearing.

One of his large fingers pushed through her tightness and delved deep inside her. She lifted her hips to meet his hand. "Braeden, please. I need you."

He retracted his finger and brought it to his mouth. "I've wanted to taste you again for so long."

She watched, captivated as he sucked on his finger, his eyes closing in obvious pleasure. Her cheeks heated. Only he had ever tasted her. When he removed his finger from his mouth, he opened his eyes and grinned. "Better than I remembered. You blow away all my expectations. You're a gem."

Her heart warmed at his comment, but her quim was bereft. "What I am…is in need."

"I think I may be able to help you with that."

She expected him to lift her up so they could go to her bedroom, but instead, he brushed the tip of his cock against her opening. Oh Lord, he planned to enter her on her kitchen table. The unexpected thrill had her moaning.

"Don't worry. I'm right here." Slowly, he pushed his wide cock head into her.

"More."

"Demanding little woman, aren't you?"

"Yessss." Her word sounded like a hiss to her, but he understood.

"I need to go slowly. I don't want to hurt you. You're so small and it feels too good."

She pushed her hips up, forcing another inch of him to slide in. Her sheath stretched to accommodate him, though it had been so long, and he was so large.

He groaned even as he grasped her hips and forced her to be still, but at least he wasn't. He continued the long, slow glide into her. When his balls touched her butt, she sighed. Finally. Finally she felt full, complete.

She gazed at her huge, gentle lover. Perspiration beaded his upper lip and the tendons in his neck stood rigid.

"Braeden." Her whisper brought his gaze to her.

"Are you okay?" His concern touched her.

"I'm fine." She raised her brows. "Can you couple with me now? I need you."

His head dropped, so she missed his expression. He pulled his hips back and her vaginal walls sucked at him as if she didn't want him to go. She didn't, but the friction of his cock spearing her again sent pleasure zigzagging through her.

His hands left her hips and settled on the table as he pulled his pelvis back and then sank into her quickly. Shocks of delight flew through her body. "Yes."

He pumped into her again and she gripped the edge of the table to push herself toward him as his balls slapped against her. The pleasure intensified and she craved his next entrance.

"I can't stop." Braeden's thrusts became faster. She held on to the table, pushing against him each time he slid to the hilt, her own body greedy for the satisfaction just out of reach but coming closer and closer.

Sweat beaded on his face now, but she needed more.

Her excitement escalated and her body grew tighter. "Let go. Please."

Braeden did. With unleashed power, he pumped his cock, rushing into her, his hardness filling her. Her world started to splinter. "Yes!"

He rammed into her again and again and her orgasm struck, pulling at his cock, grasping at the sensations of fire that filled her soul.

"Argh!" Braeden pushed into her and held himself deep inside, his warm seed flowing into her core, prolonging her own pleasure.

*Whole.* The word flew through her mind and sprayed throughout her body like a fading firework.

Braeden pulled her close with one arm as he bent over the table, his other arm holding himself above her to keep from crushing her.

She looped her arms around his neck and kissed his shoulder. "That was beautiful."

He carefully laid her back on the table and looked down at her. "It was?"

His concern for her placed him closer to her heart. She nodded. "Mm-hmm. I saw stars."

"If you saw stars in the kitchen, I wonder what you'll see when we have sex outside."

Oh, the man was far too full of himself. "Actually, I've done things outside before."

"Things?" His eyebrow rose. "What kind of things?"

The image of her kneeling, bringing Brom pleasure as he stood against a tree one evening clouded her mind and she gently pushed it away. "Never you mind. It was long ago. I'm sure there's much you have done."

Braeden's face fell as he mentally withdrew from her. "We should clear out of the kitchen before your mother returns."

By the saints! She'd forgotten her mother, the festival, everything. "The dusting, the lanterns. I have so much to do."

"Hey." His hand on her face calmed her panic. "I'll help. I'm sorry but I just couldn't wait. Six months is a long time to want a woman and not have her."

"Did you really not… I mean you waited until…"

His grin returned. "I only wanted you, Kat, so I had no choice but to wait. Now come here." He lifted her into a sitting position, his cock still inside her. "I don't want to leave your warm pussy." He ground his hips for emphasis.

She grabbed his neck and pulled his face down to hers. "You

better stop that this instant or I will expect you to pleasure me again, right now."

His hips continued to grind.

"Oh." She pushed him away, but he let her. As he slipped from inside her, she wanted him back, but kept her moan silent.

Braeden helped her to her feet. "One of these days, I'm going to get to see that whole delicious body of yours at once. I'm looking forward to that."

As she squeezed her breasts back into place beneath her stays, she couldn't help but think he'd seen far more of her than she had.

Braeden strolled through the square, more at ease in public than he'd been since high school. With Mrs. Van Tassel on his left arm and Kat on his right, he found himself enjoying the day. Stealing Kat away from her "chores" had taken the usual bargaining, and shit, could the woman bargain! But so far the day was well worth the composting he would be forced to do tomorrow.

Kat's mom halted their progress. "Katrina, we must stop in Jurgen's furniture shop. I've been meaning to talk to him about building a table for that corner in the entryway."

"Do you think now is a good time? Wouldn't it be better if you waited until after the festival?"

"But we are here now and no one else is about."

Braeden heard the wanting in Mrs. Van Tassel's voice and couldn't deny her. She was such a happy soul. It was clear Kat's sunny side came from her. Her feistiness, however, was another story. "I'd like to see the shop as well. I've never thought about how furniture was made in the 1790s."

"Fine." Kat shrugged and the three of them moved into the

shade of the building, its wide barn-like doors open to entice people to enter and look around.

Mrs. Van Tassel went in search of the owner while he kept tight hold of Kat's arm. "Is everything made to order or are these pieces for sale?"

She ran her hand along a pine chest. "For those of us who participate in the festival, Jurgen makes us what we need. These pieces are for those who attend."

"Does he deliver the custom-made pieces to you as well?"

"Sometimes."

Braeden studied Kat. "So it's not far to where you live."

She shook her head. "No. You know…wait. What do you mean?"

"I mean, he couldn't deliver them to the inn because the inn isn't here after Sunday night."

Kat tried to pull away, but he wouldn't let go, the frustration of his search returning with a vengeance.

"Where did you go, Kat? Why couldn't I find you?"

She stopped trying to pull away and faced him. "You wouldn't believe me if I told you."

"Try me."

Her eyes never left his face, revealing her inner turmoil. What was she hiding?

"Not here. *If* I'm going to tell you the truth, it must be in private."

He glanced over her head to see her mother coming with the blond man he'd seen holding Kat in her kitchen at the last festival.

Her mother glowed with excitement. "Katrina, Jurgen has a wonderful idea for the entry table." Kat's arm tensed as she turned to face her mother and the man called Jurgen. The man's brows were lowered, his mouth tight.

Mrs. Van Tassel didn't notice any of it. "Oh Jurgen, you must meet our escort for today. This is Braeden Van Brunt."

Jurgen nodded stiffly.

Braeden refused to let the man stew silently. "We've met already. I believe you were trying to keep Kat from doing something. Now what was that?"

The man's large biceps stiffened but Braeden wasn't impressed. "I was trying to talk some sense into her, but since you're here, I obviously failed."

Braeden raised his brow before moving his gaze to Kat. "So he didn't want you to see me?"

"No, he didn't." She addressed Jurgen. "But I make my own choices."

Braeden smiled inside at Kat's attitude. Jurgen squirmed at her rebuke but still looked pissed.

"Oh my, Jurgen. Why ever not?" Mrs. Van Tassel placed her hand on Jurgen's shoulder. "Braeden is an absolute gentleman. Surely you aren't still holding a flame for Katrina."

"No, I was concerned about the village and what effect Kat's passing interest might have on all of us."

"Oh." Mrs. Van Tassel removed her hand.

Katrina advanced a step and Braeden moved with her. "I'm not stupid, Jurgen Zeeger, and I resent your assumption that I am. I'm well aware of our village and how each of us is linked to it. Now, if you will excuse us, we would like to *enjoy* the rest of our day."

Braeden escorted Kat outside, his pride in her ability to handle herself completely unearned. Mrs. Van Tassel remained behind, probably to make arrangements for the new table she'd ordered.

Kat's stride was quick.

He understood her need to walk off her anger, so he steered

them toward the path he'd taken as the Headless Horseman. Eventually, they were surrounded by trees instead of people and he sensed her beginning to relax.

"Did you want me to leave?"

Kat's arm jerked within his. "No. Why would you ask that?"

"I don't want to make things difficult for you with your friends." Inwardly, he kicked himself for giving her a choice, but he needed to know she wanted him to stay.

"Jurgen? A friend? Ha. He lied. He does want me. He's even asked me to marry him multiple times. I've turned him down but he keeps coming back. It's very frustrating and awkward."

"Do you want me to break his legs for you?"

She stopped, causing him to do so as well. "No, I don't." She studied his arms. "Though I don't doubt you could. But fighting won't change anything. The fact is, I don't love him. I don't know if I can ever love again." She sighed. "But he won't accept it. I keep hoping someone else will catch his attention."

Braeden looped his other arm around her waist and pulled her closer. Her comment about loving again bothered him. "So you do want me to stay?" Though careful to keep his touch light, his body tensed, her reply meaning more to him than he wanted it to.

She didn't look at him. Instead, she stared at his chest. "I shouldn't, but I do."

Not exactly the resounding "yes" he'd hoped for, but he'd take it. He tilted her chin up so he could see her eyes. "Do you know what I thought about your eyes the first time I met you?"

"That they were too big?"

He smiled. "No. I thought that the blue of your eyes was the exact color of the blue in a frozen ice stream."

"Did you?"

"I did. And looking into them now, I'm positive they are. Now, if I could just make a frozen ice stream appear so I could prove it to you."

She chuckled.

The sound spread warmth through his chest. He had to know more about her. "So how did you end up running your own inn?"

Her lashes covered the blue he enjoyed and her brow furrowed. "It was my grandmama's. I used to help her on occasion when I was young, but my father planned for me to inherit the farm. It wasn't until…until our plans were disrupted that I began to help her in earnest. She was getting older and couldn't handle it on her own. When she died, I took it over."

"What about the farm?"

She titled her head to look at him again. "Papa still runs it with Mama and some hired help. It is just as well, as I could never truly take it over while he's alive. He loves that farm and—"

"Katrina! Hey, Katrina." The thin, awkward man known as Irwin strode along the path they had come. "I've been looking everywhere for you."

# Chapter Seven

Irwin reminded Braeden of a cartoon character. His arms and legs seemed too long for his body and his elongated face did have a dog-like appearance. His eyes were big and his thin black hair pulled back in a ponytail didn't help his looks.

Kat turned at Irwin's yell. Braeden stepped next to her and put his hand around her waist. The move wasn't lost on Irwin, though the man pretended not to see. *Interesting.*

Irwin stopped not three feet in front of them. "What are you doing way out here? Who is taking care of the inn? Don't you have things to do?"

Braeden fought the urge to smile as Kat's hands found her hips. "Irwin Crane. I think I know a bit more about the work I need to do than you do. How dare you come out here to tell me I need to get to work?"

To give the man credit, he did blush, but he didn't let it go. "I was just worried because I know the inn is very important to you and I saw your mother heading that way. I thought you might want to know."

"My mother was going to the inn because she is helping me this weekend. Now is there anything else you need?"

Irwin's gaze lifted to Braeden before it moved back to Kat. "What are you doing out here?"

Braeden could have sworn he heard Kat growl, but it was so low in her throat he wasn't sure.

"I'm giving Braeden a tour, what else would I be doing?"

"A tour? Oh, you mean of the old Dutch church. The whole story really is fascinating. Maybe someone should lead regular tours through here. Do you think the organizers would like that idea?"

Irwin walked past them in the direction they were headed, clueless about how unwanted his presence was. "Aren't you coming? You really want to see the graveyard during the day when you can read the headstones. At night it is haunted and not a safe place to be."

Kat turned from Irwin as he strode by and looked at Braeden. "I'm sorry. We can go back to the festival if you like."

He wanted to be alone with Kat and the festival would not allow for that. More sure he could rid them of Irwin, he declined. "No, I want to see this church in the daylight. I've only seen it at night and it raised a lot of questions for me."

She hooked her arm with his and placed her other hand on his biceps. "It did? Then I guess we better follow Irwin and get the full tour."

Braeden gazed into her smiling eyes. "I hope to take my own tour of a very interesting landmark later."

"Really?"

He let his gaze slip to her cleavage before returning to her face. "Most definitely."

"Braeden." Though she used his name as a reprimand, her cheeks flushed.

He grinned as he turned them to follow Irwin. It wasn't a long stroll since they had walked most of the forest path already. As they came upon the clearing where the old church sat, they could see Irwin already among the gravestones to the right of the small building. "Is this church still used?"

"Oh yes. It may not look like much on the outside, but it is well cared for." Kat let go of his arm and picked up her skirt to walk across the grass. "There are graves here that date back to the 1600s."

Irwin waved them over. "Come check this out. It's Doffue Martling, the blue-bearded Dutchman. Have you heard the story of how he almost sank an English ship singlehandedly?"

Braeden shook his head. "Why didn't he actually sink it?"

Irwin shrugged. "His cannon burst on the sixth charge."

Braeden grimaced and looked at Kat in question.

"Irwin is an historian. He specializes in the Revolutionary War and New York's part in it."

They reached the tombstone Irwin pointed to. Braeden stared long and hard. The spelling of many of the words was odd. Then again, the late 1700s was a long time ago.

Kat continued to stroll along the headstones. She stopped at one and laid her hand on it. "This is old Van Bueren's grave. He was quite the drunk, but he never hurt anyone. I always feel sad when I see this one. He didn't deserve the end he got."

Braeden stood solemnly next to her. It was as if she had known the man but he died in 1791. "What happened?"

"We aren't sure. All they found was his skeleton with pieces of his clothes still on it."

She shivered and he pulled her up against his side. He liked having her full curves pressed against him.

"Hey, you two. Do you want to see one of the most interesting graves?" Irwin stood next to a tombstone a couple rows back and near the end of a row.

Kat pulled from Braeden's embrace but took his hand. "Come. You better look and placate him, otherwise he'll talk about it for the next two days."

He walked with her across the healthy grass. It didn't appear many people came to visit the graves, but that made sense as they were so old. Wandering through cemeteries wasn't his usual pastime, but Katrina's hand felt so natural in his, he didn't mind at all.

They maneuvered around the headstones until they stood next to Irwin. He pointed. "This is the galloping Hessian. You must know about him."

Irwin looked at him as if they shared some kind of secret, but he had no idea what it might be. "Can't say that I do."

Irritation flitted across the man's face. "You should. This is the grave of the original headless horseman."

Braeden glanced at Kat for confirmation. At her nod, he examined the marker closely. It was easy to read its death date, 1776. Also easy to read were the words Hessian Soldier, but no name could be seen. Had it weathered somehow or was it never there to begin with? Maybe the man really had died with no head and so they hadn't known his identity. "How did people during this time know this was a Hessian?"

Irwin rolled his eyes. "Because he was wearing his German uniform." He glanced at Kat as if looking for patience with a child. "The man was headless, so they could only identify him as a Hessian."

That made sense. "How did he lose his head? Bayonet?"

"Cannonball."

"Ouch."

Irwin's eyes grew bright. "I know. But they say every night when there's a moon, he rides back to the scene of the battle looking for his head, but he must race back here before dawn breaks. That's why he rides so fast."

Braeden watched the scrawny man become animated with his story. There was more behind his interest in this particular grave than simply history. "How long have you been attending these festivals, Irwin?"

The man started as if his mind had been far away. "Ever since I was five, at least, that is the earliest I remember."

"And you have never missed one?"

Irwin shook his head. "Of course not. Come down by the bridge. There's more to this story." The man strode off in the direction of the small stream that ran along the other side of the church.

Braeden looked at Kat. "Is he okay?"

"I don't know. I think he's just a bit too caught up in the legends of the area."

Something in his gut told him there was more to it, but he let it go. It wouldn't hurt to do some internet investigation on Irwin Crane when he returned home.

They meandered their way between the stones when a clear name caught his eye. He froze.

Van Brunt. 1722–1781.

Kat turned back. "What is it?"

"It's my name." A coolness settled into his body as if a ghost passed through him, but it was daylight, and there were no such things as ghosts.

"I know." Kat took his hand. "There are a few stones with your name here as there are with mine. That is why our families are part of the festival."

He tore his gaze from the grave and found her sympathetic eyes warming. Of course. It was an ancestor. That made sense as he was of Dutch descent on his father's side and this area was known for being settled by those from Holland. Still, he couldn't shake the discomfort. Instead, he focused on Kat's warm hand within his.

As they drew closer to the church, he tugged her toward it and put a finger to his lips.

She glanced over her shoulder to where Irwin had trotted off and nodded.

Quickly, they both ran around the corner of the building like high-school students looking for a place to make out. Braeden sobered.

"Braeden, is something wrong?"

He gazed down at her. She was nothing like the girls in high school, or any of the women afterward. He cupped her cheek. "Sorry, just bad memories of my younger days. All best forgotten."

She laid her hand over his. "Mama says the best way to bury old memories is to replace them with new ones."

"Your mother is a wise woman." He smirked, more than willing to kiss away his past.

"So first you must tell me your bad memory."

"Huh?"

Kat pulled his hand away from her face and took his other hand. "First, you must tell me your bad memory."

Not exactly what he'd planned, nor something he wished to do. "I'd rather not."

"Uh-huh. You have to now. It stepped up and interrupted us, so you have to let it out. What was the memory?"

"Damn, but you're stubborn."

"Yes, I am. I'm also persistent, patient and headstrong, according to my papa, but you still have to tell me your memory."

"All right, all right." He pulled away from her and leaned back against the variegated brick wall of the church. "The way we are hiding from Irwin reminded me of something we would do in high school. You know, how as teenage couples we would hide from teachers, parents, basically any adult so we could make out."

"And…"

He ran his hand through his hair. Her father was right. She was persistent. "I did it with my last high-school girlfriend." He paused and studied her. She stood with her hands on her hips and no expression at all on her face.

The only person he'd ever told was his best friend Reed, but not even he would remember now. Shit. He moved his gaze to the gravestones. He didn't want to admit he'd lost control of his strength or that he would need more lessons on control before he got it through his thick skull.

"I went too far, got too excited." He couldn't look at Kat. "I left bruises on her arms from holding her too tight. I didn't mean to, but my damn strength. I didn't know how to hold it back. The next day she broke up with me and told everyone about it. I never had another date in school. The girls were afraid of me." He ran his hand through his hair, irritated that he had to relive his first embarrassment. "After that I didn't have time for dating anyway. I was too busy fighting all the guys who thought they had to prove themselves against me. The more I defended myself, the more black eyes and broken bones showed up at school."

He laughed, the sound coming out anguished even to his own ears. "I tried not working out, but my muscles would burn until I couldn't take the pain."

That was when his frustration had turned real because he'd needed a job just so he could pay for a gym membership. Working out in the school gym had become too uncomfortable.

He couldn't even imagine what Kat must think of his lack of control in high school.

"Braeden, look at me." Her voice was soft, cajoling.

He squeezed his fists again and forced himself to meet her gaze. Her honest eyes held sympathy and…anger?

"You were young." She stepped closer to him. "Your classmates couldn't see what you would become, what I saw when I first met you. That you're a gentle, caring, dedicated man who would never hurt those he cared about and who would do anything for his family no matter how much he didn't want to."

He smirked at his original disinterest in playing the Headless Horseman.

"I also quickly learned you're charming, helpful and kind." She laid her hand over his heart.

He took a deep breath as the warmth of her palm relaxed him. "I think you may be romanticizing me a bit."

"Oh no, I also discovered you're impatient, too attached to your technology and pushy."

"Pushy? Me?"

At her nod, he grabbed her shoulders and spun her around, setting her against the church wall carefully.

"Braeden." Despite her surprise, the huskiness of her voice gave her excitement away.

He grinned. "What about how strong and handsome I am? And don't forget I'm an amazing lover."

She rolled her eyes. "Are you? Hmm, I think I did forget that."

"Then let me help you remember."

Kat gasped as Braeden pulled her hands above her head and pushed his hardened cock against her stomach. Before she could close her mouth, his claimed hers. His tongue explored as he nudged her legs apart.

Tight circles of excitement buzzed deep inside her, causing her to melt against him. She wanted to erase his bad memory, but he'd taken over. She couldn't even touch him. She moaned in frustration.

He abandoned her mouth to spread kisses along her jaw. "Do you want me, Kat?"

"Yes." She tried to wriggle her hands free, but he held them tight.

"Why?" He spoke against the side of her neck. "Why do you want me to suck upon your nipples until they are hard and erect? Why do you want to feel me slide in and out of your tight pussy? Why do you want me to circle your clit with my fingers until you scream in ecstasy?"

Her brain tried to function, but his attention to her bare skin just above her neckline had her body demanding her thoughts. There was only one answer that came to her. "Because I trust you with my body."

Braeden stilled. He lifted his head and stared into her eyes. The uncertainty in his gaze had her heart breaking for him.

"I trust you, Braeden Van Brunt, more than I have trusted anyone in over four years."

His gaze shifted away, but not before she caught a glimpse of stark loneliness. She wanted to touch him, reassure him. Her excitement calmed beneath the sorrow of his life.

He took a deep breath and finally returned his gaze to her. He opened his mouth, but closed it again. Releasing her hands, he let his head drop.

She cupped his face. "You're very special to me. I like holding your hand, talking to you, listening to your laugh. I also like arguing with you and pushing you to do what I want."

He studied her.

She let her hands fall to his sides and linked them with his. "If you're looking for a sign that I lie, you will not find it. I tell the truth, even if it's not comfortable. In this case, it isn't comfortable. That I like you is a problem."

His interest was finally caught and one eyebrow rose. "It's a problem that you like me?"

She nodded. If he only knew. "But I can't help it."

"I think I like being a problem for you."

"Of course you do. Heaven forbid you should be easy. No, you have to waltz into my life when I least expect it. When I have so much—"

His mouth stopped her tirade as he pulled her tight against him.

She sensed the change in him. The kiss was gentle and the pressure of his hand upon her back was to hold her close, not to grind into her. She kissed him back, letting her new feelings for him show, pushing away the certainty that she was bound for heartbreak again. She might trust him with her body, but not with her heart.

Braeden broke their kiss and stroked the errant strands of hair from her face. "You're one of a kind, Katrina Van Tassel."

She smirked. "That's what my papa says."

"Hmm, I think I would like to meet your father. Does he live nearby?"

A cloud flitted over the sun at that moment and she shivered at the change in temperature, ignoring his question. "It's getting late. We have to get back to the inn."

He stared hard at her. "Why won't you tell me where you live?

You said you would when we were alone." He paused and looked around. "From what I can see, we are…no, maybe we aren't."

Kat looked toward the path. She'd know that stride anywhere. "Jurgen."

"That man is like a dog with a bone." Braeden pulled her back into his embrace. "Kiss me."

"But Jurgen."

He grinned. "Exactly."

Maybe she could finally show Jurgen she had no feelings for him. Looping her arms around Braeden's neck, she pulled his head down for a kiss. Gently, she nudged his lips open so she could taste him. He tasted of the sweets they had in town. He let her lead the kiss, wrapping his arms lightly about her.

She played with the silky hair at the nape of his neck while her tongue licked along his teeth. She pulled back a bit to nip at his lips before moving back in to taste him thoroughly.

He growled low in his throat as his arms tightened around her and his tongue moved into her mouth. He bent her backward, cradling her head in his hand as he crushed her breasts against his chest.

"Ow!" He broke their contact, straightening.

She opened her eyes to find Jurgen standing nearby, grinning. "Jurgen! What did you do?"

"Nothing."

She looked at Braeden. "What happened?"

"Something hit me. Hard."

She spun on Jurgen. "What did you hit him with?"

"I didn't hit him with anything. Maybe it was an acorn."

She scowled at him. Jurgen was known for his ability to knock bottles from a log with his aim. She didn't doubt for a minute he'd thrown a rock at Braeden. "Why are you here, besides to bother me?"

"I came to walk you back. Your mother needs help and it *is* your inn." He reached out to grab her arm, but Braeden was faster and caught his wrist.

"I think Kat can walk back to the village without your help."

Jurgen tried to twist away but Braeden's grip was immovable. She watched the power struggle between the two men. It was clear Jurgen didn't stand a chance. That had to be a new experience for him. He had been second in strength only to Brom.

"Kat! You have to see this." Max ran down the path toward them.

Kat looked at Braeden and he released Jurgen before Max came close enough to witness the animosity between them.

She brushed ahead of them. "What is it, Max?"

The young man's eyes glowed. "Look what Stephen gave me. It has books in it. Hundreds of them. It's like those computers I told you about, only smaller."

Braeden turned his back on Jurgen and approached. "Ah, that's an electronic reader. Have you never seen one before?"

Kat raised her brow at Max to remind him he was with a Newtimer. He took on an air of knowing. "Of course I have, but I have never owned one. He actually gave it to me. He said he knew my birthday was coming. I didn't tell him either."

"Did you say Stephen, as in my brother?"

Max nodded.

"My brother is here?"

Worried, Kat laid her hand on his arm. "Isn't he well enough to attend?"

"Yes, but he asked me to ride tomorrow night because he wouldn't be here. Something must be wrong."

"Not necessarily." Kat squeezed. "Stephen often brings his family to the festival."

Jurgen stepped forward. "Perhaps he wants to make sure you are playing the role correctly."

Kat frowned at him. "Well, whatever the reason, we won't find out standing here. We better get back." She turned her attention to Max. The device would be an issue. They prided themselves on keeping the old ways. "Max, why don't you come by later and show me how your reader works."

He glanced at Braeden before answering. "My grandmother wants me to stay home tonight. She says she gets lonely with me gone all weekend. I'll come by tomorrow."

Kat nodded and Max turned, striding down the path back to the village. Suddenly, he stopped and yelled back, "Oh Jurgen, the widow Addens was looking for you. Something about a hope chest."

Jurgen nodded, but then he looked at them pointedly. "Don't forget your mother." He sent a final scowl at Braeden before following Max toward the village.

She faced Braeden. "Are you all right?"

His angry glare at Jurgen turned toward her, then softened. "No, I'm getting a splitting headache. I wonder if that was his intention."

"What do you mean?"

He hooked her arm within his. "Maybe he hoped if I had a headache, I wouldn't want you in my bed."

"Oh."

"But I just plan on having you kiss it and make it all better." He wiggled his brows to punctuate his idea.

Kat laughed.

~~*~~

Braeden silently cursed but returned his gaze to Stephen. "Here comes another one."

"Now you're full of shit." Stephen took a sip of his wine as they sat at the hotel bar in Tarrytown, Marilyn having taken the children upstairs to bed.

A young man in designer jeans and a collared shirt stopped at their table. "Hey, I saw you looking at my date. You keep your eyes to yourself, you understand?"

Braeden sighed. "I do. I apologize."

The man's own eyes widened in surprise. "You apologize?"

"I do."

"Well, good." The twenty-something tried to look intimidating. "You need to be more respectful."

"Thank you, I will."

The man opened his mouth, but smartly turned and went back to the table with his girlfriend. Braeden hadn't even noticed her before.

Stephen frowned. "I'm sorry. I didn't know it had become so obnoxious."

Braeden shrugged. "It's getting worse. I can't even fill my car with gas without someone confronting me or asking me to lift something for them."

"But you can come to our house more often. The kids love seeing you."

"I know. I just don't want to screw anything up. Last time I was outside with them, I felt like I was going to snap the rope that held their fort up. I could so easily break one of their toys or even a limb." He ran his hand through his hair as he voiced one of his worst nightmares. "But it's different around Katrina. I don't even think about being careful with her, it just comes naturally."

Stephen grinned. "I'm thrilled to hear that."

"So why did you really come to the festival, Stephen?"

His brother looked uncomfortable. "I got a call from Reed's doctor today. They tried to call you, but apparently you couldn't be reached."

Every muscle in Braeden's body tightened. "What did he say?"

"He gave Reed the approval to get his own apartment."

"Holy shit. How can that be? Is he that much improved? Has he…remembered anything?"

Stephen took another swallow of wine then stared at his glass. "The doctor didn't mention his memory, but he did say Reed is more than capable of living on his own, can even get a job. Whether he has remembered the accident or what happened before doesn't impede his progress toward living life now."

Joy conflicted with fear in Braeden's gut. For almost ten years, he'd hoped Reed would get better despite the prognosis. He'd paid the specialists to provide the very best care, and now it was happening.

"Reed wants you to help him pick out his apartment."

"What? Why? Why me?"

Stephen shrugged. "I don't know. Maybe because he looks at you like a big brother. You may only visit him twice a year, but your emails must make him feel closer to you than anyone else. Or maybe, unconsciously, he senses the bond you two had, and in his heart he knows you were, you are, his best friend."

Braeden wanted to do nothing more than celebrate his friend's improvement, but in his gut he feared the day Reed remembered how he was injured in the first place. If it hadn't been for Braeden's ridiculous strength and the wrong woman, Reed would have been living a normal life all along. Braeden picked up his beer. "To Reed and a successful transition to independence."

"To Reed."

They clinked wineglass to beer bottle and swallowed. "Thank you for coming to the festival just to let me know."

"Oh, I didn't come here just to let you know that. There was no rush. I just had to see for myself that you and Kat were an item, and my little brother was actually being seen in public."

He grinned. Stephen was full of shit. He knew exactly how important the news was. "Damn. Here comes another one."

Stephen glanced over his shoulder. "This is crazy. Have you asked Dad if he had this problem?"

"Yes. He said he did and it lasted until he married Mom."

"Then you better settle down soon. Here, this is the key to your room."

Braeden put down his empty beer bottle. "What room?"

"I hope you don't mind, but we booked you a room. I figured you probably forgot again."

More like strategically forgot, on purpose. "Great, thanks."

"No problem."

Braeden grabbed the key before the hefty man in leather chaps and jacket could get too close, and headed for the elevators.

"Don't worry, I've got this," Stephen yelled behind him.

He didn't turn around. He just waved and continued on, in no hurry to prove he was stronger than everyone…again. Once in the elevator by himself, he looked at the key number and hit the fourth-floor button. Tonight he should have been enjoying Kat's body. Instead, he was in this sterile hotel with his family. He grinned. Stephen's kids were getting older and at the age where conversation with them could be fun. It was good to see them. Still…

As he inserted the key card into the door, his cell rang. It was strange to have it working so close to Sleepy Hollow.

It was Stephen. "Hey, you know that man in leathers who was walking toward us before you left?"

"Yeah."

"He was wondering if you could give him a hand with his motorcycle. It broke down and he needs to get it lifted into the bed of his friend's truck. Are you game?"

Braeden sighed. "Sure. I'll be right down. I just have to make a quick call first."

"Great. We'll meet you in the lobby."

Stepping into his room, Braeden hung up his cell and picked up the house phone. "Hi. I'll be checking out tomorrow. Please cancel my remaining reservation."

Kat pulled two split logs from the pile Braeden had made and brought them into the kitchen, dropping them in the wood box. She'd need a few more for making the apple pie for Dame Van Brunt. The woman's appetite was returning and soon she would be back on her feet, fending for herself.

Dusting her hands off, Kat opened the kitchen door only to stop. Standing outside were Janna, Ria, Nora and Liesbeth and it appeared they had been about to knock. "Well, it looks like I have visitors."

Janna stepped forward. "You do. We'd like to talk to you."

"Of course. Come in." She stepped back and they filed into the kitchen.

"Please. Have a seat." She gestured to the large table and couldn't help the heat that filled her body at the memory of the last time she used that particular piece of furniture.

After everyone was seated, she sat at the head. Determined to keep the conversation brief, she didn't offer them anything to drink. The visit was so unusual, it couldn't be good.

Ria cleared her throat. "Let me come right to the point. We want to know what your relationship with Stephen's brother is."

"My relationship? I didn't know I had a relationship with Stephen's brother." Kat looked them each in the eye. "I do have a relationship with Stephen. He is a friend. I don't know Braeden yet, and I may never know him. So if that is all?"

"So you wouldn't mind if we pursued him?" Janna's look of triumph would irritate even the most docile heifer.

"Of course I would mind. You heard what Jurgen said at the meeting. An Oldtimer cannot court a Newtimer."

Janna pouted. "Who put him in charge? There are no rules about that. At least, I haven't seen any."

Nora piped in. "Even if there were written rules, it's not as if you could read them."

Janna gasped. "Are you calling me dumb? I'd say you were the dumb one for wanting to pawn off one of your girls on poor Jurgen. He's almost old enough to be their father."

"Ladies. It is not about rules. It's about timing." Kat stood and set her hands on the table. The subject was one she'd contemplated most of last night as she lay in her bed missing Braeden. "You cannot marry a Newtimer because by time the courting was complete and the wedding planned, the Newtimer would be dead!"

The silence that followed made it clear the ladies hadn't given the situation as much thought as she had. "Liesbeth, is this why you came as well?"

The young woman with the mousy-brown hair and large hazel eyes shook her head and looked down at her hands.

"Why did you come to visit me, then?"

She spoke to the table. "I was looking for Max."

Kat's heart constricted. Max didn't realize what was right in front of him because of his consuming fascination with Newtime. As much as she sympathized with him, she hated to see Liesbeth so lost. "He's not here. His grandmama had him stay home last night and he has not arrived yet."

The woman nodded, quietly rose and walked out the door.

Kat wanted to cry. Here she was, wanting a man who wanted her and she couldn't even contemplate such a thing while Max ignored poor Liesbeth's heart. There weren't many people of the same age in the village, and the two of them rubbed along well. Max could love the woman if he would live in his own time. Irritated, she turned back to the three women at the table. "Did you have any other questions?"

Ria spoke up. "Yes. Why are you spending so much time with Braeden if you cannot marry him?"

"As I said at the meeting, he was the Headless Horseman. I always help the new Van Brunt get used to the role. You know that."

"That may be true, but you have never gone to the festival with them. Yet you have done so twice with Braeden."

Kat dropped her head and spoke to the table. "That's because he asked me to." She raised her head again. "Did you want me to tell him I wouldn't?"

Janna pushed her loose blonde hair behind her ears. "I could have shown him around the village."

Ria pounced. "Yah, and into your bed."

"Well, if he wants to see that, I'm certainly not going to stop him."

Kat slammed her palms on the table. "Enough! The man is not a piece of meat. He is a Newtimer who has been kind enough to play the Headless Horseman role for the festival."

"So if he is going to be the new Headless Horseman, why is Stephen here?" Nora's dark eyes showed true curiosity.

It was a question Kat had been asking herself since yesterday. Yes, she had reassured Braeden that Stephen brought his family occasionally, but if Stephen had told Braeden he wanted to spend time with his family instead of riding, then why was he here? "I don't know for sure. Perhaps he just wants to make sure his little brother does it right."

Ria shook her head, causing her dark curls to bounce. "There is nothing 'little' about that man."

Kat sighed at the inane comment but Nora spoke up. "But only we would know if the Headless Horseman rode as he is supposed to. Stephen wasn't here when Brom first rode. Only we were. I think it's something else. Maybe Stephen is here to ride and Braeden is here for Kat."

"What?" Kat stood straight.

Nora looked at the other two women and nodded sagely. "Jurgen says the man won't let any other woman near him and is constantly holding Kat's arm. He's not too happy about that either, Kat."

"Truly. Well then, I guess Jurgen should take a long swim in Cramer's brook. That man just won't take no for an answer. And now he is trying to stir up trouble for Brom—I mean Braeden—by spreading idle gossip?" Kat swallowed hard as all three women shook their heads.

Ria placed her hand on Kat's arm. "I hope your heart isn't mixing him up with Brom."

The sympathetic look the woman gave her almost broke her, but she wasn't a piece of china. "No, I'm not confusing him with Brom. Brom is never far from my thoughts, but Braeden, for all that he is built like Brom, he—"

"And he looks like him too." Janna looked for clarification from the other women and received unanimous nods.

Kat placed her hands on her hips. "No, he doesn't, if you look beyond his muscles. He has amber eyes, not gray ones. He doesn't have a cleft in his chin like Brom did and his nose is straight, while Brom's was crooked."

"Not that you remarked on it." Janna giggled and the other two women smiled knowingly.

"*God in de Hemel,* I'm done with this idle gossip. I have an inn to run and you three ladies have stalls to ready, so I suggest we all get to work."

Ria grumbled under her breath but rose from her chair, and the other two ladies followed suit. As they filed out the door, Nora stopped and faced Kat. "If you truly don't want Jurgen, I will suggest him to my daughters."

"Your daughters? Isn't he a bit old for them?"

Nora's brow furrowed in worry. "Yes, but who else? Except for Max, there is no Oldtimer who is the right age. I want so much for my girls to be happy, but as the years progress for us, I fear that may not be possible for them."

Kat put her hand on Nora's shoulder. "I understand. You have my full blessing to pursue the man."

The halfhearted smile the widow gave Kat had her mind spinning in a direction it had never gone. She'd always been adamant about preserving Oldtime as it had always been, but there were serious problems with such a philosophy that she hadn't thought about.

She gave a quick final wave and walked around the corner to gather more wood from the large pile Braeden had left her. Pulling up her apron, she added two more split logs. It had been nice of him to do the chore for her even though she hadn't exactly asked him. The more she learned about Bro—Braeden… Oh Lord.

# Chapter Eight

Braeden hit the lock button for his car and strode toward the stables. He loved his brother and his family, but being with Kat was more important to him right now. He'd found himself anxious to leave the concrete little city and return to the woods. He breathed deeply as he crossed the threshold into the stables. Something in the smell of hay fired his blood.

A horse nickered toward the back of the barn and Braeden grinned. That had to be Daredevil. He patted the pocket of his wool jacket, making sure the apple he'd taken from the hotel lobby desk was still there as he approached his new favorite horse.

"Did you miss me, boy?" Braeden reached the stall door at the same time as the horse. Daredevil whinnied before pushing his nose against Braeden's chest.

"Hmm. I'm guessing you smell something you want. Smart horse." He reached into his pocket for the apple.

"A lot smarter than the man who rides him."

Braeden spun to find Jurgen leaning on a pitchfork behind him. "What's your problem now?"

"My problem is you."

Braeden grinned. "It wouldn't be the first time."

"Huh?"

He shrugged. "I'm always getting challenged by guys smaller than me because they think they have to prove something. Since I only mildly want to carpet the ground with you, and since you're a friend of Kat's, or rather nosey neighbor of Kat's as she put it, I'll refrain from any violence on your person."

Jurgen's knit brow made it clear he didn't understand. "I think it's time someone taught you that you can't come into our village and steal our women."

"Really?" Why did he suddenly feel as if he were in an old spaghetti western? The question was, should he be John Wayne or the Lone Ranger? "I didn't realize I was stealing anyone. In fact, I thought I was doing you a favor by riding as the Headless Horseman. I expected maybe a thank-you card, not a threat."

Jurgen's face turned to one of confidence as he looked to his right and left.

Braeden glanced to both sides and silently groaned. Shit. Three more men had come into the barn and they were obviously ready to kick ass, his in particular. The strangeness of the scene was the period clothing the men wore. The breeches with suspenders and loose shirts with handkerchiefs tied about the neck made for unique brawling apparel. All three had dark hair and two wore it in short ponytails. It appeared he would be fighting the founding fathers' sons instead of modern-day men.

He hated this. It was senseless and someone could be seriously injured, including himself. Braeden smiled as he heard Daredevil snort and stamp his feet. At least the horse had his back.

Jurgen picked up the pitchfork.

The situation suddenly became a lot more serious.

"Don't worry, we just need to mess with your face a little so you don't look so much like Brom." Jurgen swung the pitchfork toward Braeden's head.

Self-preservation came into play fast. Braeden grabbed the handle as it came at him and twisted it before slamming the pitchfork against Jurgen's side.

The man crumpled to the ground, but two took his place.

Braeden threw down the pitchfork and crouched, ready for the next attacker. Both moved to his sides, splitting his attention. He backed up a step. The man on his right stepped too close to the stall and Daredevil chomped on his ponytail.

The other man took advantage of the distraction and threw a punch toward Braeden's face. He ducked and the man's momentum sent his hand into the stall door.

Jurgen was rising, rage clear in his eyes, but Braeden couldn't spare a moment as the other man lunged at him. With practiced ease he kicked out, catching the man in the gut. Braeden spun just as the pitchfork came at his neck. He shielded himself with his forearm and felt the bite of the prongs as they scraped through his skin.

"Halt!"

He glanced toward the open doors at the back of the barn. Ludo stood there with some kind of rifle in his hands pointed directly at Jurgen.

"You four men get out of here before I have the town throw you in stocks." He gestured to the front with the gun. "Go!"

Jurgen's three buddies started walking toward the exit, but Jurgen wasn't easily cowed. "He threatens our way of life and you defend him?"

"The only threat to life in here is this flintlock and the only life threatened is yours. Having a man come to the village for festival is no threat."

"But Katri—"

Ludo stamped his hard boot on the floor. *"Godverdomme! Katrina is a grown woman and she can make her own decisions. Just because you don't like them doesn't give you the right to take them away. Now get out of here. My finger control ain't what it used to be."*

Jurgen's gaze moved to Ludo's hand where it clearly shook. He blanched. Giving Braeden a final scowl, he turned on his heel and strode from the building.

Braeden leaned against the stall wall. "Thank you."

Ludo let the rifle barrel fall toward the ground. "My pleasure. Jurgen's been a little out of sorts lately. Not sure what we're going to do about him."

"Maybe he just needs a different woman to occupy his obsession."

"Maybe. Damn, but my hand is shaking bad. Good thing I never loaded this flintlock or someone might be dead now."

Braeden swallowed hard. "It wasn't loaded?"

"Nah, my reputation from the war is enough for these men to fear me."

"Which war?"

Ludo ignored the question and strolled forward. "Are you hurt bad?"

He'd forgotten about the pitchfork already, but now that Ludo pointed out his wound, it stung like hell. "I don't know."

"Come over to my tack room and we'll treat that. It looks bad."

Daredevil nudged the back of his head. He grinned despite his pain and turned around. "You did great, boy. You deserve this." Gingerly reaching his right hand into his pocket, he brought out the apple. Shifting it to his left hand, he gave it to the horse.

Ludo rolled his eyes. "You two are like different branches of the same tree. Come."

Braeden gave Daredevil one last pat. "See you tonight, boy."

Kat wiped the perspiration from her forehead before pumping more water into her bucket. As she lifted it to lug into the kitchen, the bell at the front desk rang. Setting the bucket down where she was, she strode to the kitchen door.

The visitor rang the little bell again. By the saints, didn't anyone have patience anymore? It had to be a Newtimer. Just as she put her hand out to push open the door between the kitchen and main room, the bell rang again.

"Will you give a person—" She stopped. Braeden leaned back against the desk with a smile as wide as the Hudson River.

"I couldn't wait to see you."

Self-consciously, she tucked in the stray strands of hair about her face. "I wasn't sure you would be back. The rumor is that Stephen is here to be the Headless Horseman."

His smile fell. "What? No. He just needed to talk to me about some important news he had from a good friend of mine." Braeden straightened and walked toward her. "He couldn't reach me by phone so he came here. I'm not even sure he'll stay to see the ride tonight." He'd reached her and cupped her face with both hands. "I couldn't wait to see you again."

As his lips descended to hers, a stirring of need filled her, both physical and emotional. Once he made contact and his tongue breached her lips, she melted. Her body took over and she looped her arms around his neck.

He explored her mouth with confidence, his tempered strength surrounding her. He pulled back to kiss the side of her lips, her cheek, her jaw. "I missed you."

His whispered breath sent tingles of excitement spiraling from her ear into her heart. "I just saw you yesterday."

He lifted his head to gaze into her eyes. His had darkened to mahogany. "But I wanted to spend the night in your bed."

"Sleeping?"

He laughed. "No. Exercising."

She leaned back in his arms. "How can you exercise in my bed?"

"Ah, let me count the ways."

She shook her head. Maybe the man was mad.

"You really don't know what I'm talking about, do you?"

"Should I?"

He stepped back, taking most of the heat with him. "What's going on?"

"Huh?" She frowned. "What do you mean?"

"I mean this whole village disappears. There's nothing modern within miles of this spot, I get attacked by four men still dressed in eighteenth-century clothing and I'm defended by a horse and a man with a flintlock, and now you have no clue what I mean by exercise in bed." He ran his hand through his hair, bringing her focus to a white bandage wrapped around his forearm.

She stepped forward and grabbed his hand. "You've been hurt."

He pulled away. "It's nothing. I'll have it checked when I get home."

She made for his arm again, but he pulled it out of reach. "Braeden, who attacked you? What happened? If you've been cut, we need to clean it. I have turpentine."

"Turpentine? Don't change the subject."

She crossed her arms over her stomach and backed away from his anger. "What is the subject, exactly?"

He studied her, his keen eyes measuring, analyzing, trying to read her thoughts, and she looked away.

"Where do you live?"

Ah, that was the subject he wanted to know about. "Why do you want to know?"

"Damn it, Kat. Don't answer a question with a question. You said you would tell me when no one was around. I don't see anyone, do you?"

She examined the room to stall for time. She wasn't supposed to tell him. If she did, she put their whole village in jeopardy. Their way of life could change. That was if he even believed her. Everyone who stayed at the inn was at the festival, so if no one walked in, there would be no reprieve. She held her breath as she brought her eyes back to Braeden.

"I live here."

"That much I figured out."

She dropped her arms. "You did?"

He sighed, clearly frustrated. "Yes, I did. It's your grandmother's inn, which you run. You have a bedroom in it with every worldly possession you own including a Victorian mirror, which I might point out is not from the late eighteenth-century period you're so proud of, and your parents live farther down the main road on the farm you grew up on."

Not happy that he'd concluded so much when she'd taken such pains not to let him know, she put her hands on her hips. "So then why do you keep asking me?"

He rubbed the side of his face with his hand. "Because this entire village disappears Sunday night. The buildings, the stalls, even the litter is gone."

"Oh."

He gestured toward the door. "Last year I woke up on the ground, bare-ass naked to the cold night air and the sound of crickets."

She chewed at her bottom lip. She'd assumed a more modern version of her inn would have been in its place. No wonder he was irritated. "Last weekend."

"Last weekend what?"

She dropped her arms and took his hand. "Let's go into the parlor."

He pulled her against him. "I don't want to go into the parlor. What I want is to take you to bed, but not just today. I want to be able to take you to bed next week too and the week after that."

She laid her head against his chest. His simple statement had her heart pounding in her chest. She wanted that too, but it was impossible.

"Kat. Tell me the truth." The deep sincerity of his voice required only one answer.

She leaned her head back and stared into his eyes. "The truth is, for every week of Oldtime, the time I live in, a year goes by in Newtime, the time you live in. The only overlap is this one weekend."

He stared hard at her, but she kept his gaze, determined to prove her words.

He nodded and she released the breath she'd been holding.

"I can see you honestly believe that, but that's impossible."

"No. It isn't. Not in Sleepy Hollow."

"Kat, I know you think—"

She pulled out of his arms. "It's not about what I think, Braeden Van Brunt. It's about the facts." She started to pace. "First, you yourself said you saw something the night you rode as the Headless Horseman. Second, you yourself woke up on the ground last Sunday. Third, I know all about your uncle and his father and his father before him because I helped them find their way as the Headless Horsemen." She stopped pacing and stared at him.

"You're beautiful when you're agitated."

Ugh. The man was impossible.

"Okay. Okay." He put his hands up in front of him. "Stop growling at me. And let's suppose what you say is true, then—"

A yell from outside startled both of them. Kat picked up her skirts and ran through the kitchen, Braeden right behind her. As she stepped outside, the cause of the yell was obvious.

"Oh Max."

Braeden helped the young man to his feet. "Are you okay?"

"I think so. Who left that bucket in the middle of the yard?"

Kat flushed. "I'm sorry. I was bringing in water when I had an impatient visitor." She threw an annoyed glance at Braeden.

Max brushed himself off and started to walk toward the inn. "Ouch."

She ran to him. "What is it?"

"My ankle."

Braeden looped Max's arm around his shoulders. "You must have twisted it. Come on. We'll get you inside."

Kat held the door as the two men went into the inn. Max, unlike Braeden, fit on her long settee just fine. After Braeden left to get his truck, and she settled Max with some of her precious ice at Braeden's insistence, she went outside to retrieve her bucket.

It was gone.

A shiver slithered up her spine. Could her telling Braeden about Oldtime have put the village at risk? Was Max's accident just the beginning? She shook herself mentally and searched the yard. It could simply be that a dog ran off with it. She had others.

Still, as she walked into the house, she glanced behind her one more time. Was this a warning to her about her own selfishness? That she should never have told Braeden about Oldtime?

~~*~~

Braeden walked into the stable for the second time that day, only now it was night and he wore the Headless Horseman costume and carried a new-and-improved pumpkin head. He switched the battery-operated jack-o'-lantern on. It was still too small for the body he sported in the costume, but at least he had something.

Once again, Daredevil was tethered outside the back door of the stable. The horse's soft nicker as he came closer welcomed him. The night was much colder than last year and he swore he could smell snow in the air.

Jumping onto Daredevil's back, he kicked the horse into movement.

Daredevil knew what to do and how to do it. Like an expert, he galloped through the streets. Braeden reveled in the powerful mount beneath him and this time, just before heading onto the forest path, he turned Daredevil back toward the village center and had him rear. As the horse's hooves pawed the air, Braeden let out a full-throated laugh.

When Daredevil hit the ground, they raced down the forest path. Braeden slowed the horse ahead of time to avoid being hit with branches. The opening in the woods with the church was just ahead. Braeden anticipated his ride in the open. He would be watching this time for the strange apparition.

As he and Daredevil cleared the trees, the horse reared. Braeden held on, dropping the pumpkin again, but his gaze swept the clearing for the ghost.

It was there. It laughed.

Daredevil raced the white steed whose feet never touched the ground. Sure of his mount's abilities, Braeden concentrated on the ghostly figure, looking for wires or reflections or something to explain how it was done.

When the ghost laughed again, Braeden focused on the man's face and caught his breath. It was as he remembered, a somewhat blurred mirror image of himself. On they raced, the horses neck and neck as Braeden searched for clues.

When Daredevil hit the bridge, the apparition vanished, the fading sound of the ghost's laughter echoing along the little brook.

Braeden reined in Daredevil and tried to make him turn around but the horse refused, prancing and neighing. Maybe Daredevil knew something he didn't. Not ready to tangle with the unknown in the dark of night, Braeden let the animal have his way, and they trotted back to the stable.

When they arrived, he jumped from the horse and Ludo appeared from the tack room. "Everything go well?"

"Perfectly, though I think this horse has a one-track mind."

Ludo stepped forward and took the reins to guide Daredevil into his stall. "That be true. What did he do now?"

"He wouldn't turn back." Braeden pulled off the chest piece and set it down next to the stall wall as Ludo started to brush Daredevil. "I dropped my head and the horse wouldn't let me return for it."

"Uh, it looks to me like you still have your head." Ludo raised a brow, but didn't pause in his brushing.

"Not my real head. I lost the jack-o'-lantern. I need to go back and get it." Braeden started to pull the black silk shirt off, but stopped. It *was* cold.

"So you won't be wanting any of my fine whiskey?"

Braeden chuckled, his throat remembering the rough burn of the alcohol from last year. "I'm sure your whiskey will put hair on a man's chest, but I'm happy with what I have."

"That's right. You fit in so well here, I keep forgetting you're from the big city. I do have a bottle of scotch from 1776."

"You do?"

Ludo winked. "I do."

Braeden looked out the open barn doors he'd come in from. He wanted to see Kat but couldn't get the pumpkin head and have a drink and expect her to still be awake.

Ludo finished the brushing and placed the brush on a wall beam. "You can always go back there in the morning to find your head. I'm thinking a little nip might warm your insides for the trek back to the inn."

Braeden nodded.

The stableman grinned. "Right. Have a seat."

While Ludo searched for his scotch, Braeden moved the costume to the sawhorse near the front of the barn. Then he pulled off the black gloves and sat on a hay bale.

"Here you go." Ludo handed him a tin cup and poured in a healthy portion of scotch. After giving himself a similar amount, the stableman lifted his cup. "To the Headless Horseman."

"The Headless Horseman."

As their cups clinked together, Daredevil neighed.

Ludo looked over his shoulder. "Ah, go to sleep, you beast. You had your run for the day."

Braeden could tell Ludo loved every horse in the barn and Daredevil in particular. He took a sip of the scotch, familiar heat gathering in his limbs as the smooth liquid went down. "That *is* good."

"Yah."

They sat in companionable silence. The sounds from the village center had died down soon after he galloped through, so the crickets took over the night. They reminded him of the night he woke on the ground. He studied Ludo. He seemed like an honest man, and he'd come to Braeden's defense earlier that day. He glanced at the inch of white bandage that peeked through gaps in his black shirt where it buttoned at the wrist.

"Ludo, can I ask you a question?"

The man nodded, taking another sip of his drink.

"Have you ever heard of something called Oldtime?"

The stableman's demeanor changed. "Yah." The man didn't move, nor did he look at Braeden.

"Have you heard that for every week of Oldtime, a year of Newtime passes?"

Ludo set down his cup. "She told you."

"Yes, she told me what she believes."

"It's true and glad I am she told you. I've been sidestepping my tongue all day."

Braeden took another drink as he tried to wrap his brain around the fact that Ludo, for all intents and purposes, was a perfectly sane stableman. Then again, Kat was down-to-earth herself. So how could they believe in two different time periods existing together?

Ludo stared hard at him. "But you better not tell anyone besides me that you know. This be a superstitious lot and they will start blaming every little mishap or odd happening on the fact a Newtimer knows."

"So you believe this too?"

"Yah. And everyone else in the village too because it's true. Every weekend we hold the festival, but we've seen the changes in the people who attend. We even had one of our own test the bounds of this time twist."

"Time twist." Braeden ran his hand through his hair. He liked Ludo, but the man was crazy if he thought there was some kind of time discrepancy between one piece of land and the rest of the world. It was impossible. "How did the 'villager' test this time problem?"

Ludo leaned forward, his elbows on his knees, the material beneath them worn thin. "Don't get me wrong. Kolbus Van Bueren didn't plan to test the boundaries of our village. The poor old man was quite the drunk." Ludo raised his tin cup and took another sip before continuing. "One Sunday night, Kolbus stumbled along the road here and passed out beyond the village limits. It was only a year after Brom disappeared, but that would be some fifty Newtime years. The next weekend for us, we found his skeleton, with pieces of his clothing still on it. We buried him at the church anyway. A man's body shouldn't be left to rot, no matter how little labor he did in his lifetime. That's just not right."

Ludo's story matched Kat's. Braeden did the math in his head while the stableman paused to refill their cups. Though the calculation came to the same conclusion, he still didn't believe the time differential was real. That these people had some strong superstitions was true, but that there was a time issue, he couldn't accept. Since they wouldn't agree on that subject, he turned it to another that had been niggling at his brain.

"You said it had been a year since Brom disappeared."

Ludo nodded.

"Jurgen and his friends said they wanted to mess up my face so I wouldn't look like Brom. Who is or was Brom?"

Ludo shook his head. "To be truthful, Abraham Van Brunt, or

Brom Bones as many called him, was a wild man. Everyone loved him, but he was reckless. He had your exact frame. Big, broad and tall. He had the same black hair but it was longer. He's the one who first pretended to be the Headless Horseman and scared that schoolteacher, Ichabod Crane, away. Ichabod was afraid of his own shadow and believed all the tales told around the hearth. He'd been after the Van Tassel farm as sure as I'm a stableman." Ludo shook his head. "But Brom took care of that. He led that group of men you encountered in all types of mischief. When he disappeared, Jurgen became the leader."

"Van Brunt?" His family connections to this small place in New York seemed to be growing.

"Yah. Brom would be an ancestor of yours. Not surprising you look so much like him. You gave me quite a start when you first came to the stable. I thought I was seeing the ghost of Brom Van Brunt." Ludo released a quiet, uncomfortable chuckle.

At the mention of a ghost, the image of the apparition he'd seen on both his rides came to mind. "You say that as if you've seen ghosts before."

Ludo shrugged. "May have."

"Have there ever been any sightings near the church?"

"Well, of course." Ludo grinned. "That's where the real Headless Horseman is. He runs around at night looking for his head, but always goes back to the grave by morning. Why? Have you seen him?" The man's face lit with excitement.

"No, I haven't seen that particular ghost."

"Eh, just as well. He's a very old ghost, but there are lots of others, as many Oldtimers will tell you. Even Kat has seen a few."

Kat. Braeden glanced at his wrist for the time, but he'd taken his watch off as Stephen had instructed. "Do you know what time it is?"

Ludo shook his head.

Braeden swished the scotch around in his tin cup before gulping it down. "I need to get back to the inn."

"Yah." Ludo stood and held out his hand. "I hope to see you again next festival."

Braeden shook hands. "I hope it's a lot sooner than that."

"Not likely."

Braeden smiled and shook his head even as he gathered up the costume before striding from the barn. The time issue the festival workers appeared to believe in was beyond crazy. He'd just have to prove them wrong.

Walking through the dark, quiet village was peaceful. He liked the slower pace of Sleepy Hollow Village. There was something to be said for slow. Then again, the warmth in his veins from the scotch was making him mellow and contemplative. That was some smooth stuff.

He opened the door to the inn to find a lantern burning on the registration desk. Taking it with him, he crept down the hall, trying not to make any noise, but the damn floorboards creaked, sounding as loud as gunfire to his ears. But when he stealthily opened the door to Kat's room, he found her sound asleep.

Setting the lantern on the end table next to the bed, he carefully put down the costume and quickly disrobed. He was anxious to finally view her naked body and see if it was how he pictured her in his mind based on what he'd seen so far and the places he'd touched. Slipping under the heavy quilt, he eased himself next to her. She slept on her side, facing away from him, and his chest touched her back.

Ugh. Cloth. Granted it was soft, but it was also thick. Still, it should be easier to remove than the whalebone contraption she always wore.

He snuggled his hardening cock against her rounded ass and sighed. The material she wore might be a barrier, but it was soft and sensuous. No wonder she wore it. Did it help her pleasure herself? He yawned. It must be late.

Wrapping an arm around Kat's waist, he pulled her tighter against him. She mumbled in her sleep but didn't wake. He kissed the skin of her shoulder where her nightwear had slipped down. The scent of freshly baked cupcakes filled his nostrils, making him smile. Moving his hand upward, he cupped her heavy breast in his hand and moved his index finger over the peak.

He yawned again. The heat from the scotch combining with the warmth of Kat's body and the heavy quilt that covered them relaxed him more than he wished. He kissed her hair, still in her flyaway braid, and rubbed his cheek against it. Its silkiness, like the rest of Kat, was comforting, warm and soft.

Closing his eyes, he filled every sense with Kat…and fell asleep.

Kat moaned as need spiraled down from her nipple where a soft rubbing caused it to peak. She opened her eyes to find large fingers brushing over the material of her warmest shift. The white bandage around the wrist identified her lover.

She pressed her chest against the moving fingers, liking the way the soft material slid across her. Braeden must have sensed she was awake because he began to press soft kisses along her neck and shoulder.

As her quim swelled, she noticed the hard cock pressing against her butt and she moved her hips backward.

"Ah, Kat. You're so hot."

She wanted to tell him to take off the quilt, but her mouth was dry from the cool night's sleep and it was too much effort to form words when the nips he gave her ear sent delightful tingles down her spine.

Braeden's hand moved from her nipple and she moaned, but when it descended over her stomach and down to her thigh where her shift stopped, she held her breath. He did not disappoint. Slowly, he pulled the material to her waist before stroking down over her abdomen and mons. He paused.

"I want you, now." His breath caressed her ear and she lifted her leg in invitation. With little effort, he pressed his hard cock between them and touched her opening.

She waited, breathless for his penetration, but instead, his hand brushed aside her curls to find her pleasure point. "Yes. Please."

His fingers found her opening and brought moisture up to her hard nub and circled. He moved too slow. She grabbed his wrist without thinking.

"Oww."

She let go quickly. Heat rose to her cheeks. "I'm sorry."

He chuckled behind her, the vibration running from his chest to his cock. "It's okay. Did you want me to stop?"

"No, I wanted you to go faster."

Again, she felt his body move with mirth, but he kept it silent as his fingers traveled back to her opening and once again encircled her nub, this time with much more friction.

"Yes." Her hips pressed back against his cock, but still he didn't enter her.

"Come for me, Kat. I want to feel you break apart in my arms."

The friction increased and the shocks of pleasure reached her core like hard rain, faster and faster, blending into one another, building upon each other, closer and closer.

Braeden's hand kept the pace steady as her body climbed toward fulfillment and a constant pleasure. Suddenly, his hips pulled back and he speared his shaft deep inside her.

She splintered into a thousand pieces around him. His finger pressed her nub down as his hand pinned her pelvis against him while he rocked into her, sustaining her pleasure, holding her at her peak. Then he thrust deep and held her still while his seed filled her, sending her flying higher. Every nerve ending vibrated with satisfaction.

They lay connected, spent, each trying to catch their breath. That he'd been as lost as she made her feel a bit better.

"Damn, woman, you make me lose control."

She grinned, having already surmised that. "I know."

"Don't be flip with me. All I have to do is move my hand."

She stilled, but her heartbeat sped up at the thought of what he might do, her nub throbbing beneath his fingers.

"I'll take your silence to mean you'll behave."

Despite his threat to pleasure her again, which she was more than willing to test, she had to respond. "If I behaved, you wouldn't be here right now."

"Vixen." His mouth on her neck surprised her, but even as he sucked, causing her limbs to melt, a tension built inside. His hand moved up her body, latched on to her breast where it pinched her nipple. The pleasure-pain of his fingers and mouth had her moaning her surrender. Without warning, his hand and mouth released her. Before she could voice her disappointment, he rolled her onto her stomach, his body on top of her, his hardening cock still inside.

He brushed aside her braid and licked the back of her neck. Pinned as she was by his weight, she was helpless to do anything. He pushed her legs farther apart with his before he sucked hard where the back of her neck met her shoulder. She'd never felt anything like it. Her sheath tightened around him as her helplessness increased, spiking her pleasure.

He leaned on one arm while his other hand burrowed beneath her body, grabbing hold of her breast and squeezing.

"Oh Lord." Her juices flowed, bathing the hard cock deep within her, but she couldn't move.

Braeden's hips pushed against her ass and his cock slid farther inside. The heat where they joined flared. In her position, she couldn't tense, couldn't push, couldn't do anything but lie there and be taken.

And Braeden took her. His mouth moved to the other side of her neck to suck hard again. He kept himself on his forearms while both thumbs brushed over her nipples even as his hands squeezed and let go. His hips pulled away and she couldn't help a whimper, but he thrust back in, filling her and teasing her need, giving her sparks of excitement while she could do nothing in response.

He licked the base of her neck and as he started to suck, he ground his hips, pushing them deeper into the mattress, rubbing her nub against the sheets. Her need climbed, her sheath sucked at him.

Braeden pulled back before sending his cock deep, shooting pleasure through every nerve ending. He groaned as he squeezed her breasts and pumped into her again. Holding her tight as his hips and hands pumped again and again, he increased his rhythm and her orgasm strained to be released.

Though her helplessness was frustrating, it brought a new sexual tension, but she couldn't maintain such a level of stimulation and not come. It wasn't possible. Or was that the point? Instead of reaching for release, she relaxed, allowing the sensations to come as they would.

Braeden sensed her capitulation and growled. His thumbs and

forefingers found her nipples and squeezed, and she let the pleasure flow through her. He began to thrust in earnest, pushing against her butt with his abdomen, shifting them across the bed sheet…and she reveled in every erotic feeling. The prolonged sexual pinnacle held her enthralled until he slammed one final time and she shook with her release.

Floating on pleasure, she hung there as Braeden, grasping her across the chest tightly, filled her. She felt his shudder even as her body cooled, satisfied in a way she never dreamed possible.

His hold loosened and he turned her head so he could kiss her. It was a sweet kiss, the perfect ending to a fulfilling experience. He pulled out and rolled onto his back, snuggling her against him.

She nestled into him, her head on his shoulder as his hand cupped her hip. His strength surrounded her, protected her. She wanted to analyze what had happened and why she felt so complete, but her body wanted to sleep and she easily gave in.

# Chapter Nine

Braeden enjoyed having Kat on his arm again. It just felt right to be escorting his woman through Sleepy Hollow.

*My woman.* He liked the sound of that.

"Max and his grandmother live about a half mile farther along this road." Kat brought them to a halt.

"And I need to go to the church to find my head."

She smiled at him, her blue eyes sparkling with deviltry. "I know precisely where your head is." She lowered her lashes and looked down at his pants.

He laughed. "It appears you have a one-track mind. I like that."

"I thought you would." She wrapped her arms around his waist. "You need to bend down if you're going to kiss me goodbye."

"I think we are going to need to buy you stilts."

She squeezed his ass, hard.

"Ow. Okay, okay." Lowering his head, he brushed his lips against hers, intending to simply say goodbye as she suggested. But once he felt her unique softness, he needed more. He opened his mouth in invitation and she accepted, sweeping her tongue inside. He tightened his arms around her, tilting her head with one hand to better taste her.

"Ahem."

Braeden opened his eyes to find a short old woman in black staring at them. He raised his brow and ended the kiss.

Kat opened her eyes. "Why did you stop?"

"We have company." He nodded toward the stranger.

Kat whipped around and a becoming blush rose into her cheeks. "Dame Vandend. What are you doing so close to the festival?"

The older woman harrumphed. "We need bread and with Max unable to walk, it appears I have to buy it myself."

"That makes sense. I'm sure Hans will be happy to see you."

The woman ignored Kat and peered at him. "Who are you? You are not Brom."

He stepped to the side and bowed. "I'm Braeden Van Brunt, at your service, ma'am." Kat's elbow into his side had him stifling another sound altogether. Obviously, he'd said something wrong.

The old woman's brows furrowed. "A Van Brunt descendant." Her gaze shifted to Kat. "He's the one, yah?"

"Yes, he is and he was just on his way to the church, and I was on my way to your house to see how Max is doing."

The old woman's face softened at the mention of her grandson. "He will be glad to see you. He's got no one but me for company during festival."

"Then I better get going. You too, Braeden. Don't forget I need you to stack the split wood and move that block for me."

It was clear Kat was in a hurry to part ways with Mrs. Vandend, so he took the hint, but he would question her later. "Nice to meet you, Dame Vandend."

The old woman waved her hand in dismissal before trudging by them. Kat squeezed his hand before she too strode off, only in the opposite direction. Braeden stood and watched the sway of her hips and the swing of her braid for a time. He really liked her.

He turned to head down the path into the forest but paused when he found Dame Vandend had stopped to stare at him. Perplexed by her sudden interest, he nodded once in acknowledgment. She didn't respond, so he continued on his way to search for his lost head.

It wasn't far to the church, but it seemed so without Kat by his side to make everything fun. That's what she did. She brought fun into his life. Something he'd denied himself after Reed was hurt. His whole carefree, unattached life had changed that day. Gone were the one-night stands, replaced by college courses. Trips to bars were replaced by trips to the hospital and then the rehabilitation center. Money that had been spent on concerts and trips went into paying off student loans and making investments. He hadn't deserved to have fun.

So why did he think he deserved it now? Because Reed would have his own place? Maybe even land a job? Because Reed was moving on so he should too?

What the hell was he even doing in Sleepy Hollow around so many people where he could hurt someone else? What if something happened to Kat?

That thought halted his steps. A chill permeated his body and then moved on and disappeared. The dark overhanging branches of the narrow path felt like a metaphor for his life. Dark, colorless, alone. But Kat was his sun now. He wanted his life to revolve around her. With her, he didn't have to think about holding back every touch.

He was only here for the weekend, or longer if she let him stay. He could prove to her there was no time difference. Then they could see each other more, learn more about each other. He'd learned a lot about his own strength over the last decade. Maybe, just maybe it was safe to have a life again, only now with Kat in it. The question was, would she be interested?

The exciting possibility had him striding toward the clearing ahead, which at this time of day was in full sunlight. It should be easy to find his pumpkin now.

But twenty minutes later, though he'd found Daredevil's tracks, he couldn't find a big orange pumpkin anywhere. Granted there were many orange and brown leaves on the ground, but a big orange ball would stand out. He must be missing it.

Tracing Daredevil's tracks back to where he reared, Braeden made the motion of dropping the pumpkin and then searched the leaves a foot at a time. As he brushed back a pile of them, he felt something small and hard. Rummaging through the light leaves, he grasped the object.

A double-A battery. He had to be close. Kneeling, he sifted through the immediate area. He found the second battery that provided power for lighting the pumpkin, but no pumpkin. Finally, he stood and studied the ground.

The pumpkin was gone. It was too big for a squirrel, but a black bear could have easily carried it off. Strolling back to the horse tracks on the path, Braeden studied the ground. There were other tracks there as well. Shoe prints from what looked like a woman's shoe. He followed them until they reached the steps of the little church.

Slowly, he pushed the door open.

A woman swept the area at the front. Her back was to him but he could hear her humming. It certainly wasn't a hymn from the jaunty sound of it. It was more like something a person would hum after having the kind of sex he and Kat had. The kind that made a person feel as if it were going to be a great day.

Her sweeping brought her around the stairs of the raised pulpit, so he strode up the aisle, a row of pews on each side. "Hello."

"Ack!" The woman brought her hand to her chest and lost all color in her face. He stepped toward her and she sidled behind the stairs. "Evils spirits spare me."

Braeden stopped and put his hand out, the reason for her fear finally coming together in his mind. "I'm not Brom. I'm Braeden Van Brunt, the current Headless Horseman. I didn't mean to scare you."

"Oh my. I'm sorry." She moved her hand from her chest and brushed back the dark strands that peeked from beneath her cap. "I had heard you were here, but I didn't realize how similar in looks and build you were to Brom."

She walked out from behind the altar and gave him a curtsey, the scent of roses preceding her. "I'm Nora Addens. I was just sweeping up after the service."

"I see." He watched as she fidgeted with her skirts. It was a telltale sign someone hid something or was nervous and he would guess both. "I didn't realize this church had services during the festival."

She leaned the broom handle against the wall. "Oh yes, but they are very early. People have to get back to the square before the crowds return."

He nodded to show he understood. "I was wondering if you might have seen a pumpkin by the path when you came to church."

"Oh, I didn't make it—uh, no, I didn't see anything, but Mein Gelen, he has a number of pumpkins for sale. All sizes."

He smiled politely. "Thank you. I will keep that in mind. Have you seen anyone else out here?"

Now he was certain she hid something because her cheeks took on a rosy hue. "No, I came after the service and there was no one here."

So another person had "slept" in this morning. He grinned. "Thank you for your help. I need to get back, then."

She nodded without looking at him, but didn't say another word.

He let himself out of the church and strode toward the cemetery. People had commented he looked like Brom one too many times. It was time to learn more about this supposed ancestor of his. Of course, if what Katrina and Ludo believed was true then that would explain why people in the village mistook him for Brom. He halted. But for that to be the case then that meant there really was a time twist, as Ludo called it. He shook his head and continued to the gravestones. There had to be another explanation. Maybe Brom was a distant relative from another branch of the family.

The tombstone of the Van Brunt ancestor he'd seen with Kat was easy to locate. There were quite a few others nearby, but none of them with the name Brom Van Brunt, Abraham Van Brunt or even Brom Bones. He leaned against the largest headstone and ran his hand through his hair. He had hoped he'd find the man's grave because with a date of birth he could do an online search to see exactly how they were related, but it looked as if he was denied even that. All he had was a lot of questions. He dug into his pocket and pulled out the batteries. A lot of questions, two batteries and two missing pumpkin heads.

Kat sat across from Max, his foot on a bench as he reclined in a tattered, stuffed chair. She hadn't been to his house in a long time and had forgotten how run-down it was, or perhaps it had become more so.

"So you didn't bring me a waffle?" Max's pout was that of a young man who had long been spoiled by his grandmother despite the status of their finances.

"No, I didn't. Ria had a large crowd of Newtimers, and I wasn't going to wait in line. Besides, my guess is the more you miss my cooking, the sooner you'll be able to return to work."

He grinned. "You're probably right about that."

"After you left, I went outside to retrieve the bucket and it was gone."

"Gone? But I just tripped over it. It was still there when I hobbled into the house."

She leaned forward. "Are you sure you didn't kick it or anything?"

"I'm sure. Maybe one of the children picked it up, or even a Newtimer who wanted a memento."

"Maybe. I hadn't thought of that and there have been more people wandering behind the inn."

"That's because of your beau." Max winked.

"Maxwell Vandend, Braeden is not my beau. He is a friend, not that it is any of your concern."

Max shook his head. "Not according to Liesbeth. She told me Janna and Ria said he likes you and you him. She said even Nora isn't going to try to marry off one of her girls to him, and you know Nora will do anything to find those girls a husband." He shivered.

"You would make a good husband."

Max turned bright red. "Nah, I'm too young." He looked away.

He wasn't too young. Her own mother and father had been married two years by the time her papa was Max's age. She had hoped he would have mentioned Liesbeth as a reason not to marry Nora's girls, but by not doing so, he told her a lot. He really didn't know the poor woman existed. Maybe she could help him notice her.

"Has anyone come to visit you today?"

He thought for a moment. "No, not today."

"Are you bored? I could bring over a few books I have." She did feel guilty for leaving the bucket in the yard.

"Not at all." Max reached into the space between the bottom cushion and the wing of the chair. "I've been reading books on here." In his hand was the flat machine Stephen had given him.

"You still have that? Why didn't you give it back to Stephen before he left yesterday?"

Max cocked his head. "Because he gave it to me. Why would I give it back?"

"Because it's from Newtime. We aren't supposed to bring Newtime objects into Oldtime."

"Why?"

Kat stood and paced to the end of the small parlor. "Because it's important we keep Oldtime pure, separate from Newtime."

"So you want to be separate from Braeden?"

"What?"

Max crossed his arms over his chest. "Braeden is from Newtime. You don't want him in Oldtime?"

She stalked toward him. "Braeden is not an object, he is a person."

"I know." Max's bravado deflated. "But I don't see why we have to keep living on the outside. People from Newtime get to buy our goods and bring them home, so why can't we do the same? Objects don't disappear when the time splits. They stay with the owner. I understand we can't live in Newtime, but why not adopt some of the advances that have been invented to make life a little easier? You, my grandmother, even Jurgen are constantly harping on keeping Oldtime pure. Why?"

"Why?" Kat stared at Max, knowing how it felt to be his age, on the verge of life as a true adult. She had been in love, planned a wedding and life with Brom, but he had moved on after they were separated, never knowing he could have come back. He didn't waste his life on the past. He threw himself into Newtime, of that she was sure. And she had been waiting. Was that what she was doing? Still waiting? Was she adamant about keeping Sleepy Hollow exactly like it was the day Brom disappeared so he could return when he no longer existed? Did she want to keep Sleepy Hollow as it was so she could keep her memories of him alive since that was all she had?

"Kat?"

She refocused her attention. "I know it's frustrating for you. Maybe we can talk about this at Monday's meeting."

Max's eyes lit up. "Really?"

"Of course. You know anyone can speak. We will just have to make sure you have a turn." She looked at the small machine he had in his hand. "But until then, you better hide that from your grandmother. She wouldn't be happy to know you have it."

He nodded eagerly and stuffed the reader back between the cushion and arm of the chair. "Right."

She bent low and kissed his forehead. "I have to get back to the inn. I will have Braeden do your work. Rest and get better because I will need you next weekend for festival."

Max grinned and she took her leave.

Braeden opened the door to Kat's bedroom to find her tying the neckline of the loose garment she wore to bed. Her hair was barely plaited from a long day of it escaping its confines. The glow of the lantern next to the bed lit her night clothes, teasing him with her curves.

She glanced up and sucked in a breath. Her attraction to him, when she allowed it to surface, made him feel as if he were her dream come true. He stood straighter, keeping the lantern he held behind him and a tight grip on the towel that lay low on his hips.

Her gaze covered his body and his cock responded. When she finally met his eyes, she swallowed. "I could have warmed up some water for you."

"That's okay. You can warm me up now."

Her mouth shut at his statement, and he smirked. For such a tough lady, she could be so sexy when caught off guard. "Would you unbraid your hair for me, Kat?"

"My hair?"

He smirked. "Yes, your hair. You know. Those long, blonde strands you keep tied at the back of your head."

"Why?"

Had no one made love to this woman? Had no one ever shown her how beautiful she was? "Do you have a hairbrush?"

"Of course." All bustle again, she moved to her chest and pulled out an old hairbrush. "Do you need it?" She glanced at his head.

He probably did, but that wasn't what he wanted it for. "In a minute."

He set down the lantern, picked up a straight-back chair that sat against the wall and placed it facing the armoire. Opening the floor-to-ceiling piece of furniture, he centered the chair across from the large oval Victorian mirror. "Sit."

Puzzled, she started to obey.

"No, wait."

She froze in place.

"Take your nightgown off."

"My what?"

"That long shirt you're wearing."

"You mean my shift?"

He nodded.

"But I don't have anything on underneath."

He let his smile grow. "Exactly."

The blush that rose to her cheeks transformed her from beautiful to a glowing goddess. "I can't do that."

He stepped next to her and took the brush from her hand. "Yes, you can." Without giving her a chance to think, he grasped the edges and lifted the garment over her head. She raised her arms and allowed him to have his way.

She was all curves, and seeing them for the first time all at once was breathtaking. He moved the nightstand closer to the chair so the lantern would illuminate her clearly. Then he took her hand and guided her to sit, forcing himself not to touch all the places he craved. This was about her.

Once she was seated, he moved the other lantern from the floor and set it on her bureau. When he turned back to look at her, she was bathed in a yellow glow.

Her gaze met his and the uncertainty he witnessed made him want to crush whoever had made her think she might be anything less than gorgeous. He forced his body to relax. She could simply be shy.

Best way to help that was to distract her. Without hesitation, he unfolded the towel from his hips and set it on the floor to the side of her.

"Braeden." The word was a whisper.

"Yes." He stepped in front of her, his cock as hard as permafrost and level with her mouth. It was almost too much to ignore, but he kept his control. He lifted her chin, forcing her to move her gaze to his face. "You're lovely, Kat."

Her brows furrowed. "Really?"

"Look for yourself." He stepped aside.

She did. He watched as she studied herself in the mirror. Did she see what he saw, substantial breasts with dark, rosy areolas? Did she see the softness of her pale skin and the way it tightened inward at her waist before flaring enticingly to her hips? Her legs… Damn, her legs were fully shaped and begged him to nestle between them.

She moved her gaze away from the mirror and looked at him. "I've never looked before."

His cock jumped as multiple images flashed through his mind of the two of them with a mirror over a bed. He had to control himself. He squeezed the brush in his hand and focused on what he intended in the first place. "Sit back and watch the mirror."

She did as told for a change.

Kneeling on the towel next to her, he pulled her braid to the side and untied the leather at the end. He threw the tie toward the chest, anxious to see the transformation that was sure to come. The silken strands unwound themselves with little help from him. The softness against his fingers had his cock jealous, but he somehow kept his concentration. Gently, he ran the brush through her hip-length hair. The strands glowed in the lantern light, their pale color appearing a deeper yellow. He imagined they were thrilled to be free.

Carefully, he brushed every one multiple times from scalp to tip, enjoying the fine silk against his hands. He glanced at the mirror and found Kat had closed her eyes. She looked as if she were ready to purr. He continued to brush through her hair until it flowed like liquid gold. Dividing it in two, he lay half over each shoulder. It fell against her breasts and teased her thighs.

Kat's eyes opened.

He pointed. "See. That's you."

He left the brush on the floor and rose to stand behind her. Watching her look at herself fascinated him. He'd never been with a woman who was so ignorant of her own beauty. Kat could have passed for Lady Godiva. The thought of her naked on Daredevil's back had his cock leaking pre-cum. Shit, he would take her that way too if he had any say in it.

"I'm pretty." The words, spoken so softly, almost in awe, fell from her lips and straight into his heart.

"Yes. You are." He put his hands on her shoulders, unable to resist touching her for one more minute. The silkiness of her fluid hair over her soft skin was too erotic to ignore. He let his hands follow her hair down, over her breasts and waist to her thighs. Gently, he pushed her legs apart and whispered in her ear, "You're beautiful here too."

Kat's gaze flew to his in the reflection. "I don't think—"

"Look. I want you to look at yourself. I want you to see these folds of pink."

Hesitantly, she lowered her gaze in the mirror.

He brushed her pale curls upward and moved his fingers to show her. "Here is your clit, which is hard with excitement. And this," he spread her inner labia, "this is where I enter your tight pussy. Do you have any idea how good it feels to be inside you?"

When she didn't answer, he moved his gaze from between her legs to her face. She was staring at herself as if mesmerized. He had to show her more. Slowly, so she could see, he moved one finger toward her opening. At the moist juices he found, he breathed easier and gradually inserted a finger inside her as she watched him do it.

Her lips parted and her breaths whispered past his arm.

While his right hand began a slow glide in and out, he used his left to stroke her nipple, rubbing the soft strands of her hair across it. He couldn't stop staring at her as she watched him do what he wanted to her body. It was a powerful spell he was caught in, and he didn't want it to break.

A tiny moan escaped from her lips and he kissed her temple, but didn't take his eyes off her reflection. He changed his pace between her legs and pulled out to circle her clit with his wet finger.

Her reaction was swift. Her eyes widened and her breathing increased. He slid back inside her and brought his finger out again to repeat the circular action.

Kat gripped the seat of the armless chair as he continued his erotic assault on her body. Even as his right hand worked her pussy and clit, his left attended to her nipples, first one, then the other, while he dropped light kisses along her neck.

Her head tilted back, but he pressed his hips against it. He sucked in a breath as his hard cock connected with her silky strands. "Don't close your eyes. I want you to see yourself come."

Even as he said the words, her body tightened in response. The muscles in her thighs and stomach became more defined. She was close. But she kept her eyes open.

He applied more pressure to her clit and rolled her nipple, while his cock set a rhythm of its own against her hair. But as her tight walls squeezed his finger hard, he used his other hand to stroke her nub, building her pleasure. Her legs opened wider and then shut hard upon his hands as her whimpers of ecstasy filled his ears and tightened his balls.

He needed to be inside her where her pussy held his finger tight. He'd never needed a woman before. Not like this.

Unable to bear it, he pulled his finger from between her thighs and her eyes opened.

He caught her gaze in the mirror. "And this is what you look like when you're satisfied."

She looked at herself then. Her mouth formed an O but she didn't speak.

Did she see her own radiant beauty, the flush in her cheeks, her still-hard nipples, the moist, pink pussy? He brought his finger to his mouth and sucked, closing his eyes as he savored her own unique flavor. When he opened them again, he found her staring at him as if she could devour him. His cock jumped.

She gave him a shy smile in the reflection before she rubbed her head back and forth across his erection.

"Kat, you will make me come right here and I don't want to."

She tilted her head to look at him directly. "What do you want, then?"

"I want to be deep inside your tight sheath and come until I have nothing left." Her flush reminded him she liked to know what he would do.

The clock in the hall chimed eleven and she suddenly stood, her hair sweeping behind her to touch her ass. Damn, he'd yet to fully appreciate that particular asset. Maybe he could do so now.

She turned and faced him, but his gaze moved to the mirror where her full butt curved away from the ends of her hair, making him want to grab her there and never let go.

"Go to the bed." She raised her hand and pointed.

He could give her a hard time about her bossiness, but his cock had other ideas. "Were you not happy with my performance?" He spoke as he stepped toward the bed.

She put her hands on her hips. "Are you begging for a compliment?"

He grinned. "Maybe."


Kat let her gaze roam over Braeden's chiseled body. How could he be so built, so confident, and wonder if he pleased her? He must have felt her pleasure. As the image of his finger buried deep inside her filled her brain, so too did anguish fill her heart. "You pleased me well. Now it's my turn. Lie down."

He raised one brow but obeyed, crossing his arms behind his head, legs crossed at the ankle.

She bit her lip. She'd only ridden a man once and something about Braeden had her instinct telling her it would be good. But more than that, she could control how close they could be. She only had an hour left with him and she wanted to be touching him every moment.

Approaching the bed, she stared before running her hands over his pectorals, across his hard nipples, down his rippled stomach until she reached his proud cock. She grasped the base and kissed its tip.

He held his breath but she didn't take him in her mouth. Instead, she brushed her hair over the head.

"Kat."

She ignored him. Instead, she crawled onto the bed and pushed his legs apart. Kneeling between them, she lowered her head so her hair enveloped his length.

"Oh God." His guttural words had her heart skipping a beat.

Moving her mass of hair to one side, she gently wrapped it

around his cock. His entire body tensed harder than a cannon. Slowly, she raised her head and watched as her hair first tightened and then unwrapped from him.

"Kat. I'm going to come."

She smiled as she wound her hair around him again, this time holding the end. Then she pulled her head up, tightening her silken sheath around him.

"Oh shit." Braeden's hands fisted in the quilt as his body arched toward her. Pleasure filled her heart and new moisture pooled between her thighs, but this was for him, not her.

She loosened her hair's hold by bowing her head, but no sooner had he taken a breath than she raised her head again.

This time he yelled and his body shuddered as he bowed up from the bed and came into her pale strands. She squeezed her hair harder around him, loving that she could please him.

When he finally lowered his hips to the bed, she let go of her hair and it unwound from his cock.

"Wow."

Yes. That was the word for him. She crawled over his body until she could lie on his chest, her legs nestled between his.

He brought one arm around her, pressing her wet hair against her back. "I didn't mean to get you dirty."

She shrugged. "I don't mind as long as it felt good."

He tilted her head back to look at her. "Are you begging for a compliment?"

"Absolutely not. I know you enjoyed that."

He chuckled, a sound she loved hearing. Actually, she loved many things about him. Maybe a few too many.

He bent his head and kissed her lightly on the lips. "I could make love to you all night."

She stiffened at his words. They didn't have all night. They only had…how long did they have? She listened for any sound from the grandmother clock. It chimed every fifteen minutes. How long had it taken? How long did they have left?

"Kat. What is it?"

She pushed herself up to kneel between his legs. "We don't have much time left."

"What are you talking about? We have all night if we want."

She shook her head. "No, we don't. It's Sunday. At midnight you will disappear and I won't see you for another year of your life."

He stared, uncomprehending.

"The time issue? Between our two eras? Remember?"

His face grew serious. "You sincerely believe I will disappear at the stroke of midnight."

"I do."

He cupped her cheek. "If what you say is true, then I suggest we make love again right away."

A flare of excitement grasped her heart. "But how can you? You just—"

"Came? Yes, I did. But you sitting there between my thighs, looking so lusciously delectable, has got me wanting more."

Kat glanced down. By the saints, he was already hard again. She returned her gaze to his face.

"What can I say? You do that to me." He moved his hands to her thighs.

Warmth suffused her body at his words and she wasted no time. Pushing herself forward, she straddled his hips.

He moved his legs together while she rubbed her wet labia up his hard cock.

"Ride me, Kat."

Yes. She wanted to ride. To have him to herself. To keep him to herself.

The clock in the hall chimed fifteen past the hour. "Yes." Placing her hands on his hard chest, she lifted her hips high and slowly lowered herself onto him. His cock spreading her made her moan, but she continued her leisurely decent until she was completely impaled. She wriggled a bit, trying to get closer, pushing down on his abdomen, making him slide just another half inch.

*Not enough.* She pushed herself up to sit straight and melted as his cock tip touched the end of her sheath. "Yes. I want all of you inside me like this."

Braeden's chest muscles tensed and he grasped her hands in his. "You're so tight. I have to move. Come with me."

She loved the fullness of him inside her and didn't want to lose it, but she couldn't deny him. She nodded.

Without warning, his hips lifted her and the pressure inside increased, sending shards of pleasure from her core to her extremities. "Braeden." His name was but a whisper as her breath was forced from her lungs.

Her body tensed as he lowered his hips but raised her hands in his. His arms bulged with tense muscles as he grasped her. "Ride me."

And then she understood. As his hips pushed upward again, she held his hands as she tilted her hips, rubbing her nub against his flesh as he pressed into her. Flashes of exquisite excitement streaked through her body in ragged edges, like lightning in the night sky. As Braeden lowered his hips again, she rocked back, still held steady by their joined hands. Oh Lord, it was too good.

He increased their pace and she rode him as he wanted, her body tensing in anticipation with each thrust upward and igniting as his cock pushed her beyond limits she'd never explored.

She watched his hard body grow tighter even as her own was shredding with pleasure. His eyes closed as he concentrated on lifting her, enjoying her, until his face tightened.

Her sheath constricted in readiness and his shout released her even as his seed flooded her. *Complete. Finally complete.* The thought flitted by as her body spasmed over his. Her hips moved beyond her control as she milked every last drop of him into her and soothed her sensitive clit in his liquid.

He pulled her down on top of his chest and wrapped his arms around her. "What do you do to me, lady?"

With her ear pressed to his chest, she could barely hear him above the rampant beat of his heart. She tightened around him and his breath caught.

"Whoa, there. Let a man enjoy the moment."

She smiled against his chest. She hadn't meant to do it, but it felt right.

He stroked her back, which helped her relax, but reality intruded. She lifted her head and stared into his darkened eyes. "I don't want you to go yet."

He pulled her hair to one side and smoothed it down her back before he responded. "Yet? You mean you want me to go later?"

"What?"

"You said you didn't want me to go 'yet'. I figure if you never wanted me to leave, you would have simply said you don't want me to go."

Even as he said what was supposed to be a joke, she could see him struggle with his thoughts.

"No, I meant that I want you to stay—"

The grandmother clock sounded 11:45 p.m.

She stared at him, desperately trying to keep her tears away.

Maybe if she held him tight enough. She pulled her hips up, disconnecting them, and slipped to his side. Wrapping her arm across his chest and leaving one leg between his, she laid her head on his shoulder.

His arm came around her and locked her against him as he closed his eyes. Within minutes, his breathing grew even.

She listened to the silence of the night and the heartbeat of the man she didn't want to lose. What did that mean? How could she care so much for him? She loved Brom with all her heart, but now that feeling was like a treasured toy from childhood, always loved but no longer relevant. Did that mean she loved Braeden?

She tensed. What good would that do her? She'd be left heartbroken again. Even if he did return, he'd grow older in just months of Oldtime. Despite the hopelessness, she continued to hold him tight. Her heart wouldn't listen to reason. She wanted him to stay. There was time later, when he was gone, for her to take out that treasured toy again and bask in the memory of her first love.

The clock in the hall bonged. She closed her eyes and concentrated on the feel of Braeden's body, his warmth and the steady cadence of his heartbeat. Through every stroke, she kept her ear pressed to his chest until the last bong ceased.

# Chapter Ten

Braeden's steady heartbeat continued.

She hesitantly opened her eyes, afraid her mind played tricks on her. The black hairs on his chest greeted her as they raised and lowered with his breathing. She squeezed his body against her in joy and he mumbled in his sleep.

He was still in Oldtime! He was still with her! Happiness filled her soul. The last time she'd been so filled with joy was the morning of her wedding day. That fateful day that time split in two.

Why was he still in her bed? He'd disappeared last weekend even though he was in the very same bed. Frowning, she stared at the bedpost as if it could answer her. Why was this Sunday different?

Oh darn. The village. This wasn't right. What would everyone say at the meeting in the morning? What did it all mean? Worried now, she glanced at Braeden's relaxed face. He was so handsome in his own way, not as rounded as Brom. The lines of his face, hands, even his muscles were more defined. Of course, she was the only one to really see this.

His overall personality spoke of control and yet he was somewhat retiring, almost hiding away from life, while Brom would attack it. Once again the question came, but now it was more important. Now it was whether she loved Braeden for who he was or did she love him because he replaced Brom for her? She gazed at him. Her heart said it was him, but her head kept asking the question and she couldn't answer, even to herself.

Laying her face back on his chest, she closed her eyes. Maybe after a good night's sleep in his protective arms, she would know her own heart. At least, she hoped so.

Braeden watched Kat's fidgeting as he finished his coffee. She was like a hummingbird, flitting here and there about the kitchen. He'd finally made her sit down to eat, but after a few bites, she did nothing but fold and refold her napkin. He placed his hand over hers. "Worrying won't change anything."

She pulled her hand away and sat back. "I'm not worried."

"Yes. You are." He raised his hand as she was about to argue. "You haven't remained still for a full second since we woke. Tell me why you're worried about the villagers' reaction to my being here this morning. Is it because you fear they will know we slept together? We don't have to let them know that particular detail."

"No. Yes. No, I mean, I don't want them to know that. I'm unmarried and it is not accepted. But that is not why I'm worried."

"Then why?"

Her gaze met his for a moment before she was folding her napkin again. "It's hard to explain to a Newtimer how our village works."

He grasped her hand again. "Kat."

"Ugh." She stood and paced the small confines of the kitchen. "I guess the more you know, the better prepared you'll be."

She wrung her hands, an action he'd never actually seen a woman do. He found himself growing more concerned and determined to protect her, from her entire village if he had to.

"You need to know this town is very superstitious. For over four years Oldtime, that's more than two hundred years Newtime, this village has disappeared from Newtime on Sunday at midnight and no Newtimer has ever been here on Monday morning. That you're still here attests to the fact something has changed, and no one will think the change is good."

"Hold on. You honestly believe I was supposed to disappear last night."

She nodded.

He couldn't accept that smart, intelligent, hardworking Kat believed her village disappeared from his time. "And the rest of the villagers believe the village disappeared last night, and so I shouldn't be here?"

She nodded again.

He shook his head. "Then maybe we should check and see if it did or didn't. You're basing your belief on the fact I'm here." He couldn't believe what he was about to say, but he could think of no other way to reason the situation out. "What if we are still in my time as opposed to me disappearing with you into yours?"

She stopped pacing. "You're right." She started pacing again. "But even if that were true, you're still an anomaly and that is never good here."

He stood and grabbed her arms. "Let's figure out which it is, okay?"

"How?"

Good question. As he hesitated, her shoulders slumped. Shit, he hated to see her so defeated. Hold on, there was a way. "If my truck is still parked in the dirt lot, then we are in—what do you call my time?"

"Newtime."

"Okay, and if my truck is gone, either someone stole it or we are in…"

"Oldtime."

He grabbed her hands and held them tight. "Whatever is happening, according to your village, we will face it together." He didn't think anything was happening, but Kat's nerves were real and for such a spunky woman, that bothered him.

"Why? It's my fault. Why would you stand with me?"

He dropped her hands and cupped her face. "Because for the first time in my life, I have found a woman who tempers my strength and I can relax, be myself. That intrigues me. Besides, I believe I had something to do with last night as well. You didn't have sex all by yourself."

Her cheeks flamed red beneath his hands and he couldn't resist. He brought her lips to his in a gentle kiss, then pulled her to him. He needed to comfort her.

She pulled away. "Fine. Let's go see what time we're in."

Now that was the Kat he knew and lov—liked. He liked her a lot. Yeah, that's how he felt about her. "Okay."

He pushed the kitchen door open so she could precede him into the main room.

"I better fetch my cloak and cap. It's cold this morning. The water had ice on it when I went outside earlier." She headed for the hallway to her room.

"Damn, I forgot to bring a coat. All I have is the cape from the Headless Horseman costume."

Kat stopped in midstride. "No." She turned to face him. "Don't wear that. I have a chest upstairs in the front bedroom filled with clothing guests have left behind. Why don't you check that and see if there's anything large enough, though I doubt there will be anything long enough."

"Good idea." He climbed the stairs, careful to duck his head, and found the vacant room with the chest. After laying everything aside except what appeared to be an old brown blanket, he pondered the pile of clothing. There wasn't a single modern item in it. In fact, he had no idea what some of the items were supposed to be. Did Kat only allow villagers to stay at her inn?

Reaching into the bottom of the chest, he lifted out the brown material. As it unfolded, it was clear it was some kind of gentleman's coat made of wool. It was a bit worn in places, but it appeared large enough. Placing his arms through the sleeves, he shrugged it on. It had a high, folded-over collar and the sides buttoned at his chest, but then they cut away sharply at his waist to give him tails in the back. It reminded him of the tuxedo that he wore once to a company event.

He returned the other clothes to the chest before taking a quick look around to see if there was a mirror, but the room boasted neither that nor an armoire. He'd have to check it out in Kat's later.

He shook his head as he descended the staircase. It concerned him that Kat believed there was some kind of time warp in Sleepy Hollow. It would just be his luck to discover the only woman he connected with had hallucinations or some other psychological problem.

He slowed as Kat came into view, her eyes wide and her face pale. He looked over his shoulder. Shit. He'd seen that look a number of times before.

"Brom." The word was torn directly from Kat's heart and issued from her lips as if pulled out by the man on the stairs. The love and loss associated with him welled up inside her chest until she couldn't breathe. Tears gathered in her eyes and she wrapped her arms across her stomach, sliding down the wall at her back until she sat like a spring puddle on the floor.

"Kat!" Brom rushed toward her and she closed her eyes, unable to look at him. Not Brom. It wasn't Brom. It was Braeden. Braeden in Brom's old frock. *God in de Hemel*, where did he find that darn coat?

Braeden grasped her shoulders and she opened her eyes to look into his concerned gaze. Tears flowed down her cheeks.

"Kat. What is it? Are you okay?" He brushed at her tears before folding her into his arms.

How could she accept his comfort when she couldn't distinguish him from Brom? It was wrong. She pushed away.

"What is it? What's wrong? You look like you've seen a ghost."

"I did."

"You mean Brom, right?"

Startled, she nodded, not willing to divulge too much. Why hadn't she used the material of that coat to make something else long ago? Probably the same reason she'd never cut into the wedding dress still hanging deep in her armoire. She couldn't seem to sever her ties to Brom.

"Do I look that much like him?"

She studied him and laid her hand on his cheek. "Yes, but you're very different. I'm sorry. I was just startled. You are wearing his frock."

He looked down at his sleeve. "Oh, so he must have left it when he stayed here. It's a nice coat, though I noticed it's a bit worn in the elbows."

She gave him a tremulous smile. "Brom was rough on his clothes."

He stood and offered her his hands. "Are you better?"

She nodded as she placed her hands in his and he pulled her up. "Let me just wash my face and then we can leave."

Without waiting for a response, she fled back to her room and used the pitcher of water to cool her face and bring some semblance of reason to her mind.

What were the villagers going to think? Would it be better for Braeden to wear the cape of the Headless Horseman? She bit her lip as she tied her cloak. No, the cape would be far worse. Better to face the resemblance head-on.

Striding back to the reception area, she ignored the hiccup in her heart at seeing Braeden in Brom's frock and straightened her back. If she couldn't even look at him in that coat, how would she face the villagers?

"Are you ready?" He bowed as he extended his arm for her.

No. Definitely not Brom, who would have taken her by the hand and dragged her outside. She grinned. "I am."

They stepped out into the crisp, cold air of an early winter. The area before the inn was quiet because people had already begun to gather at the town square. After a quick glance in that direction, Katrina focused her gaze the other way, toward the stables.

They hadn't walked far before Braeden's vehicle came into view. Usually on a Monday morning, there would be nothing there. She nudged Braeden to stop. There was no reason to go to it.

"My car means we are still in Newtime, right?"

She looked up at him. "Yes."

"And you say this has never happened before."

"Yes." He looked quite handsome in the coat. Handsome in a different way from Brom. Though she was sure no one else would realize it. There was no doubt his car had already caused a stir. She sighed.

He lifted her chin. "It's not the end of the world."

"Actually, it just may be with my village. We better join everyone at the town square. It's time for our Monday morning meeting."

He dropped his hand and raised his brow. "Your whole village has a meeting every Monday?"

"Of course. Doesn't yours?"

He stared hard at her. "No."

There was a strange look in his eye as if he thought she'd gone mad. "Don't look at me like that, Braeden Van Brunt, until you have been through one of our meetings. Then you will understand." She tugged on his arm. "We shouldn't be late for this. We are bound to be in the middle of it."

He finally moved, his one stride equaling two of hers. "Why would we be in the middle of all the trouble?"

She shook her head. "Not the middle of the trouble, the middle of the circle. What do you all do in Newtime?"

"Probably more than you want to know right now."

"True. We need to focus on our defense."

He slowed. "Our defense? What is this, a trial?"

"No. Not a trial, but they will be asking you questions because you aren't supposed to be here and neither are we."

He let her pull him along at a faster rate, but he obviously had no idea what they were about to encounter.

As they drew closer, the loud buzz of conversation trickled to complete silence.

Jurgen stepped aside and swung his arm out toward the center at their approach. "I believe it's your turn." He pointedly looked at Braeden's clothing.

Kat scanned the crowd, noticing it was bigger than usual and all eyes were on them. Some were in shock. This wouldn't be pleasant. She nodded at Jurgen and started to withdraw her arm from Braeden's.

"Uh-uh. I go where you go. We're in this together."

"But only one person is allowed in the place of speaking at a time."

He continued to grasp her arm. "If they want answers, they have to take both of us."

Surprised, she stared. Her whole body warmed at his protective stance at the same time it cooled with the knowledge of the conflict soon to come. His gaze was resolute and it was clear he would have his way. She really didn't have any say. "Fine."

His raised brow of amusement didn't better her mood, but it did get her backbone in place.

They walked to the center of the circle and she faced them toward her mother out of respect. Instead of the chattering that usually ensued when someone took the center, everyone remained quiet.

She took the time to look at each of them. They all stared at Braeden. Of course. The frock. How could she have forgotten already? How could she have—she had. She'd forgotten he reminded her of Brom. He was Braeden.

She smiled inside as her heart warmed with confidence. She looked up at him to find him gazing at her. "Are you ready?"

He nodded and raised his head to stare at the villagers.

She disengaged her arm from his. "As you are all aware by now, we are still in Newtime. Also, you can see Braeden Van Brunt has remained here as well." She took another quick scan of the crowd to see if Dame Van Brunt was there, but the older lady was still home recovering. That was probably for the best. "The question is, why? Why are we still here?"

"It's because of him!" Jurgen pointed at Braeden. "Ever since he came here, things haven't been right."

"What?" Kat put her hands on her hips. "Since Braeden has come, our attendance at the festival has increased. Didn't you hear people talking about the Headless Horseman and how real he seemed last year?"

"Yes, I did, and that is just one way in which he has changed things. You've changed, coming out to the festival when you never used to. That isn't normal. And strange things have begun to happen. Just this morning, the Aldershoe sisters almost had their woodpile fall on them. Right, ladies?"

The ladies in question nodded vigorously before one of them spoke. "That's right. Marieke went outside to bring in another log for the fire because it is so cold. She took one off the top and the whole pile fell away from the house for no reason. She jumped back just in time, but still fell on the ground." The lady in question absently rubbed her hip.

Kat's stomach tightened as people started to murmur and lean toward each other. Murmuring was never good at a town meeting.

"And that's not all." Jurgen stepped forward. "Ludo's papa's dog is sick."

The murmuring grew. "And don't forget, Max tripped on a bucket."

Kat swung around but couldn't find who had said that. "Max's injury happened before today. That has no relevance."

"But it does." Jurgen stared hard at Braeden. "It is ever since he came to Sleepy Hollow that things have gone wrong. He's brought change and mishap. What if it continues? Will we start aging twice as fast? Will we have seasons again? Do we have enough food put away for a winter? We can't allow this to continue. We must stop it."

Kat threw her hands up. "Stop what? What is there to stop? We don't even know how we managed to stay in Newtime instead of reverting back to Oldtime."

"Yah. You had congress with him." Dame Vandend's voice came from behind them. Kat stepped around Braeden to face the old woman, who sat on a bale of hay as usual. Braeden remained silent but positioned himself behind her, showing his support without interfering.

Everyone grew quiet. Did they hear that? She glanced at her mother, who didn't look shocked. The last thing she needed was for Dame Vandend to repeat what she said. "How would you know what the cause was?"

The old woman smiled gleefully. "It's the curse."

The villagers all covered their hearts with their hands, protecting them from what might be uttered next. Kat controlled herself from doing the same. Braeden wouldn't understand. "What curse?"

"It's the curse that stopped us from continuing on the same time path with the rest of the world. Only by you having congress with a Newtimer could we stay in Newtime past Sunday's witching hour."

Kat felt her whole face heating.

Braeden lowered his head and whispered, "What is congress?"

She closed her eyes for a moment as embarrassment overtook her. Opening her eyes again, she watched his face as she spoke. "It means what we did last night, just before midnight."

He stood straight again and grinned at the old woman. By the saints, were all men so cocksure? But then Braeden's grin faded. What was wrong now? Oh wait, but last weekend they had—

Braeden's deep voice sounded loud as he addressed Dame Vandend. "Then why didn't the village stay in Newtime last year?"

This time Kat kept her gaze on Braeden, unwilling to see the disapproval, snickers or even jealous looks of her fellow citizens.

Dame Vandend chuckled. "You must find fulfillment together every day to keep the village in Newtime. Otherwise we disappear again."

Braeden nodded as if it all made sense, but Kat wanted to crawl inside him and not come out. What would her neighbors think now?

"Well then, that's easy." Jurgen's sneer was strictly for Braeden. "All we have to do is get him to leave and we can go back to Oldtime."

"No!" Kat spun and glared. "We don't know if that would be worse. Braeden may be the key to lifting the curse. Going back to Oldtime means we are still cursed."

Ludo stepped forward. "Katrina does have a point. If being in Oldtime is the curse, then Brom—I mean Braeden—could be our redemption. I knew there was something special about him when he got along so well with Daredevil."

No one had ever been able to ride Daredevil except Brom and Ludo. The crowd was silent for a moment before the usual chattering started. Kat sighed at the sound, never so happy to hear it.

Janna added to the melee. "And my chickens laid two extra eggs today. That's definitely a good sign."

As others shared positive experiences, Kat dared to glance at Braeden. His stare was only for Jurgen, who returned it with a glare.

"Don't worry about Jurgen. He'll do what the village wants."

Braeden shook his head. "I'm not so sure."

"I am. He—"

Ludo stepped in front of them and held out his hand. "We need to be in Newtime. I know many who will be happy with this." He glanced behind them and Kat saw a smiling crowd coming toward them.

Braeden shook Ludo's hand. "I'm pleased to be able to help." His grin reminded her of why they were still in Newtime and based on the people gathering around them, it might become an uncomfortable topic of conversation.

She took the opportunity of the Alder sisters greeting Braeden to slip through the growing crowd. She spotted her mother still standing in the same place and reluctantly approached her.

"Katrina." Her mother took her by the hands. "I'm happy for you."

She raised her brows. "You are?"

"I am, but he looks so much like Brom. Are you sure he is the one you care about?"

"Yes, Mama. I'm sure." She smiled and her mother pulled her in for a hug.

"Good. We shall see where this leads."

Kat nodded and her mama left to join the crowd around Braeden. Her mother's final words caused a lump to form in her throat. Where could her relationship with Braeden lead? What did the change to Newtime mean? And would she and Braeden only have each other for as long as they were intimate, as Dame Vandend said?

At the thought of the old woman, she studied the crowd and those left milling about the square. The hay bale was empty.

How did Dame Vandend know so much about the curse?

Braeden smiled and shook people's hands but he noticed Kat slip away. He understood and felt bad he hadn't fully appreciated her position when the old crone had said the village stayed in Newtime because they had sex. It was hard to take any of it seriously when he firmly believed there was no such thing as Oldtime and Newtime.

He also noticed, while listening to Janna and Ria offer their assistance in keeping the village in Newtime, that Jurgen and his friends had slunk off in different directions. Every bone in his body said they were up to something he wouldn't like.

People had begun to disperse when the woman he'd met at the church approached him. Nora was her name, though he didn't remember her last name.

"Thank you for giving us hope."

He studied her this time, her rose scent reminding him they'd already met. Her hair was brown, as were her eyes, but there was no distinguishing feature. However, all together her face was quite pretty. The few white streaks in her hair and crinkles around her eyes and mouth told him she was older than he'd first thought. "I'm not sure what I've done, but if I've helped, I'm glad."

She placed her hand on his arm. "You have helped me. You have given me hope that someday we can rejoin your time."

He was about to brush away her comment when he noticed tears in her eyes. This was a monumental event for her. He needed to respect that. "I hope that's the case, Ms…"

"Addens. Nora Addens."

"Now I remember, Ms. Addens."

She patted his arm as she nodded before turning away and joining two young ladies who had been waiting for her. Her emotional response bothered him. It was too elemental, and there were too many people who believed there were two different timelines. It was something he needed to investigate further.

When no one else approached, he strode toward Kat's inn. She would be the perfect person to help him uncover what was happening here. As he drew closer, he smelled chocolate cupcakes. It reminded him that she hadn't had much breakfast. Was she making cupcakes for breakfast? He took a deep breath in. No, that smelled like Kat and her closet. Shaking his head, he opened the main door of the inn. The smell was much stronger inside.

"Ow! By the saints, watch what you're doing."

Braeden didn't like the sound of that. Stepping into the kitchen, he halted. Kat carefully poured what appeared to be steaming liquid into a small bottle. Her concentration was so focused that he didn't dare move. When she put the hot pot down, he let the door close behind him. "What happened? Are you hurt?"

She started at his voice and stepped back, tripping on the chair leg behind her. As her arms spread to try to catch her balance, he scooped her up.

"Ow!"

"You're hurt."

She sucked at her wrist. "Not badly. I just burned myself."

"Let me see."

"Let me down."

He grinned. Holding her in his arms was too pleasant. "Show me your burn first."

She scowled at him, then moved her arm so he could see. It was already puckering. He kicked out a chair from the table and sat her in it. "Do you have ice?"

"Yes, but that is used for special occasions. Why do you need ice? I need butter. Nora should have some made for the festival."

"Never mind. Stay here." He strode outside and grabbed the new bucket next to the water pump. Without hesitation, he filled it and brought it back into the house, bringing in a gust of winter air with him. Moving another chair next to her, he placed the cold water on it. "Put your hand in there."

"What?" She grasped her hand closer to her chest. "That water has to be frigid."

He knelt and gently took her arm. "Trust me?"

Her gaze showed her uncertainty, but she nodded.

Guiding her arm over the bucket, he quickly immersed her hand and wrist.

"Ow! That hurts too."

"Wait."

Her eyes watered and his gut wrenched at her pain. If he wasn't sure it would soothe and help her heal, he couldn't do it. He would never hurt her, not even accidently. The realization settled comfortably in his chest.

"I don't feel the burn anymore."

Her wonder wrapped itself around him and made him feel like the greatest hero to walk the earth. Unable to resist, he kissed her.

Tentatively, she kissed him as if she knew something had changed for him.

He pulled back and gazed into her eyes. It was said the eyes were the windows to the soul. If that were true, her soul was as beautiful as she. And what did she see in his? He shuttered his gaze and lifted her hand from the bucket. "We need to dry this gently and then you can wrap it if you like."

She shook her head as she stood. "No. I don't want anything on it right now."

In his position on the floor, his head came to her stomach and he had to tamp down the urge to wrap his arms around her waist. She stepped away to dry off her wrist and he rose.

"It was my own fault. I knew better than to try to do the pour over the oven."

Braeden stayed where he was, not sure how close he wanted to be to her at the moment with unresolved feelings for her running rampant inside him. "What are you making?"

"Purple aster."

"You're making a flower that smells like cupcakes?"

"Cupcakes?" She wrinkled her nose as she patted her wrist. "What are cupcakes?"

Braeden's haze cleared. "You don't know what a cupcake is?"

She hung the cloth she'd been using and faced him. "I know what a cake is and a cup." Her face brightened. "Are they cakes baked in cups?"

She wasn't joking. How could she not know what a cupcake was, especially when what she was making smelled like a chocolate cupcake or brownie? "Do you know what a brownie is?"

"Of course. They are the wee ghosties that haunt Scottish crofts, but what has that to do with purple aster?"

A chill ran up his back at her answer. "Do you know what chocolate is?"

"Now you're just teasing me, Braeden. Don't start talking about chocolate unless you have some. It's far too delicious and too expensive to speak of if you don't have any." She continued to clean up her mess after capping the bottle.

He needed to find out when cupcakes and brownies were invented. A doubt had started in the back of his mind and he didn't like what it could mean. He needed to find a spot with cell service as soon as possible.

Kat finished washing her pot and set it on the counter to dry on a cloth. "I'll let that cool and put it away later."

"What is that?" He finally focused on the small ceramic bottle with the stopper.

Kat blushed. "It's what I use for perfume. It doesn't cost anything to pick the flowers and usually I don't burn myself in the process." She grimaced, obviously embarrassed by her mishap.

Of course, perfume. That was why her armoire had the scent of brownies. Why she smelled good enough to eat. He definitely had to do some internet research. "I need to go into town where there's a signal for my phone. I have to call my brother and my employer."

"But you will be back?" She crossed her arms over her stomach, going from the confident Kat to the vulnerable one within seconds.

He stepped close to her and laid his hands on her shoulders. "I will be back before the sun goes down." He wiggled his brows. "You heard what the old crone said. I have to make you happy in bed if I want to continue to stay here."

Kat wrapped her arms around his waist. "No. What she said is we need to find fulfillment together. She means we have to, I mean you have to…"

He grinned and cupped her face. "She means I need to be deep inside you when we both come." Kat's blush made him chuckle. "I promise. I will be back in time to make love to you. You have the rest of the day to decide where. After all, we have already christened your kitchen table, your bed and your mirror."

"Oh." Her suddenly rapid breathing gave him all the promise he needed, but to be sure, he pressed his lips to hers in goodbye. She tasted like coffee and he couldn't resist coaxing her to open for him. He pushed his tongue inside and savored the sweetness of Kat and the bitterness of the coffee on her tongue. Pressing her against the sink, he devoured her mouth, enjoying her lush curves as they crushed against his body.

She tasted so good he wanted more. He wanted to be inside her and stay there forev— He broke off the kiss at his thought. Kat remained in his arms, her breathing fast, her lips reddened from his onslaught. Gently, he moved away, unhooking her arms from around his waist.

She opened her eyes like one in a daze, but there was no manly pride in it for him. Only the need to get answers so he could be sure to hold on to her. He couldn't explain his near panic that he might lose her, and he didn't plan to stay around and analyze it either. Without a word, he strode from the kitchen, grabbed the coat and pushed his arms through the sleeves as he exited the inn.

The cold air had him buttoning up, but it didn't take away the anxiety he felt. Heading for his car, he noticed a wall of fog not far down the road. He glanced back the way he'd come. It was a clear sunny day. Clicking the car starter, he increased his pace. As he reached for the door handle, a black horse and rider came out of the fog, headed straight for him.

He threw himself over the hood to land on the other side. Quickly, he knelt to look over the car for where the rider went, but all he caught was the horse's tail as it disappeared into the forest. "Shit."

Braeden stood and brushed himself off, still watching the forest for any sign the rider might return. After it was clear that would not be the case, he walked back to the driver's side door and paused. Mud had been scraped along its side. If the rider's boot hit his door, then he could have been trampled under the horse's hooves. Was someone trying to kill him or would they have swerved at the last minute?

He sat for a moment in the warming car before a glance in the rearview mirror showed the fog creeping over it. Heeding his inner voice, he stepped on the accelerator, turned onto the dirt road and headed into the mist toward what he hoped was civilization and the answers he needed.

# Chapter Eleven

Braeden parked his car and jumped out into the darkness. The village of Sleepy Hollow was quiet. No lanterns lit his path, but a bright half moon made it possible to see. He raced down the hard-packed earth that served as the main thoroughfare and opened the door to the Sleepy Hollow Inn.

The sight that greeted him made him smile. Kat, dressed in what she called her shift, had fallen asleep on the settee. Probably waiting for him, scared he wouldn't return, but he'd make it up to her.

He'd lost track of time in the library while using their computers as his phone charged in a wall nearby. He'd finished with as many questions as answers, but his gut told him that as farfetched as it sounded, there might be some kind of time glitch in Sleepy Hollow. The fact was, cupcakes weren't in existence until the early 1800s and brownies, the kind he loved to eat, didn't appear until the late 1800s. But how could Kat not know what those were and yet know about cell phones and eReaders? It was a mystery he planned to solve.

That, and who had tried to run into him with a horse. It still rankled that someone would put a horse in such danger, never mind himself. Still, he would rather deal with that than Kat being hurt. His gut tightened again as he remembered the look on her face when he'd set her hand in the cold water. He really cared for this woman, and the more it appeared she wasn't crazy, the stronger his feelings grew.

Though he'd rushed from the library when he noticed it was dark outside, he'd been stuck on the highway due to an accident. Sitting in the traffic jam had made his need to return as strong as his need to find answers had been earlier in the day. He'd learned so much and now he had to make Kat his again. All he'd thought about while he sat in his vehicle, crawling along a foot every few minutes, was her. Not just her, but her delectable body with her full breasts, muscled legs and rounded hips. He kept seeing her face when she came, and the need to claim her again pushed him to his limits.

He glanced at his watch. 11:10 p.m. He wasn't taking any chances.

He avoided the creaking floorboards that would give him away. With as light a touch as possible, he pulled the thin material over her head. She murmured in her sleep and her brow drew downward.

Without taking his gaze from her ripe body, he stripped, throwing his clothes on the settee across from her. His hard cock sprang up, anxious to be sheathed inside her lush form. He knelt and nudged one of Kat's legs to the side. Softly, he spread her folds with his fingers and licked from her opening to the top of her clit.

"Huh?" Her single noise didn't signal her waking, so he continued.

Her taste made him crave more. Licking again, he stopped at her hardening nub and circled it, then nibbled at it until it turned bright pink.

She moaned and spread her legs wider.

Yes. His cock moved and his balls tightened. He stroked his

tongue downward until he pushed it into her pussy and explored. She grasped his hair while her juices flowed over his tongue. It was too much. His need clawed at him, his cock so hard it was painful.

"Kat, wake up."

She rolled her head back and forth.

Great. Maybe sexing her awake hadn't been his brightest idea. Carefully, he lifted her off the settee and laid her on the braided rug that covered the parlor floor.

Kneeling between her thighs, he tried one more time. He bent over her left breast and sucked it into his mouth, rolling the nipple with his tongue. Perspiration gathered at the base of his back as he held himself in check, barely.

But Kat pushed her chest harder against his mouth and brought her knees up. "Yes."

He couldn't wait any longer. He let go of her nipple. Positioning himself at the entrance of her pussy, he pushed his cock into her in one hard stroke.

Kat's hips pushed upward, though her eyes remained closed.

He was ready to come, but he needed her with him. Leaving finesse behind, he pulled out and pumped into her hard. Her body moved upward on the rug, away from him. Gritting his teeth, he positioned his hands on the floor above her shoulders.

"Kat. Come for me." He pistoned his hips down, filling her until he hit her cervix. Her shoulders moved against his forearms, but he had her tight.

Her eyes fluttered open. "Now?"

"Yes. I need you to come with me. I need you tightening around me, hugging me to you. Can you do that for me?"

"Oh Braeden. Yes." She wound her legs around him, tilting her pelvis and taking him deeper.

"Yes, Kat. Like that."

He pulled back and thrust again, and again, and again. His body trapped hers, keeping her against him, but her excited whimpers egged him on to fulfill her need.

Harder he thrust, pounding now as her sheath pulled at him to stay inside her, pulsing against his cock as it moved in and out.

Every muscle in his body drew tighter until he lost control, slamming into her.

His orgasm hit him against his will, forcing his come from his body as Kat's sheath grasped him in a viselike grip, her cries of ecstasy drowned out by his shout. Satisfaction filled his body and his heart. A feeling of being where he was supposed to be threaded its way into his brain.

He moved his arms to Kat's sides and lowered himself to his elbows.

"Oh." Her moan and tightening sheath had his body tensing for a moment.

"Are you all right?" He kissed her lips.

"I am now. I thought— I thought you weren't coming back."

He gazed into her pale-blue orbs and was lost. He felt her heartache and cursed himself for being a thoughtless jerk. "I'm sorry. I lost track of the time and then the traffic was backed up and—aw, hell. I was an idiot." Kat's nod had his male ego stiffening. "Well, you didn't have to agree so fast."

"Yes, I did. You were an ass to worry me so."

He stared in stunned silence before chuckling. Her honesty was definitely one of her charms. He pulled out and knelt between her legs. "You're right. I was an ass, and I promise never to worry you like that again."

She nodded regally, her braid to the right of her head, barely recognizable as a braid, her lush naked form sprawled before him like a willing sacrifice and yet she behaved like a queen. What wasn't there to love about her?

He froze. That was a good question.

"Braeden, what's wrong?"

He shook his head. "Nothing."

"Really?"

"Really." He squatted and picked her up in his arms, the feeling of contentment in his heart filling his soul.

"Braeden!"

"What?" As he walked toward her bedroom, for once he was happy for his overdeveloped muscles. She weighed less than his barbell, making it easy to maneuver inside the door and gently lay her on the bed. He didn't waste a second. He lay next to her and pulled her close. The need to touch her, physically stay connected, remained strong.

"Braeden. What's wrong?"

The grandmother clock in the hall took that moment to announce the hour. Midnight. He shivered. Could he have really lost Kat for a year because he was too engrossed in a computer? "That was too close."

She wrapped her arm over his chest. "I agree."

"Let's make love earlier in the day next time."

"Make love?"

He grinned in the darkness, pleased no one had said this to her before. "Have congress."

"Oh." She yawned. "That sounds like a fine idea."

Braeden grinned.

Kat worried her bottom lip as she and Braeden approached the Van Brunt farmhouse. Dame Van Brunt was much better, but the cold had been keeping her in. As much as Kat didn't want her former "almost" mother-in-law to meet Braeden, it might be the only way to convince him that there were two different timelines. He had plied her with so many questions over breakfast, she had determined they had to make this stop before going for a private lunch in a small meadow she wanted to show him. At least the blueberry muffins she carried appeared to be a good excuse for a visit.

"Now remember, you will be a surprise to her." She glanced up at Braeden's face to be sure he listened. "She may even think you're her son."

"I understand."

"And don't repeat anything Dame Vandend said. I don't want to worry her."

"I won't."

"And if she—"

"Kat." Braeden halted, her arm in his causing her to stop as well. "I'm well aware that I look a lot like Brom."

"Not to me."

He nodded. "I understand that you, more than anybody, see the difference, but at first it was a surprise to you too. I have had plenty of people turn white and stutter to a stop in my presence. I'm ready."

She swallowed. He thought he was ready, but a sinking feeling in the pit of her stomach told her the day wasn't going to go as planned. "Fine."

He raised his brow, but consented to commence their walk. When they reached the house, they stood upon the porch and she knocked.

"Yah. Yah." The older woman's shuffled step could be heard.

Kat pulled her arm from Braeden's. Dame Van Brunt had seen her and Brom arm in arm too many times. It would be best if she saw Braeden separately.

The door opened and the old woman's welcoming smile changed to an open mouth before her eyes rolled back and she started to fall.

Braeden moved fast, brushing by and catching Dame Van Brunt before she hit the floor.

"Oh dear." Kat hurried inside. "I was afraid of something like this. Let's put her on her settee. I will find some water and try to revive her." As Braeden laid Dame Van Brunt down, Kat strode outside to fill a pitcher of water. When she came back in, she dampened a cloth and gently stroked the older woman's face.

As the lady's eyes opened, she clasped a hand over her heart and stared wide-eyed at Kat. "I saw Brom." Her voice was raspy with emotion.

Kat squeezed her hand, but shook her head. "No, you saw Braeden. He is a Newtimer and he is right here."

The woman's gaze moved to the side. She swallowed hard.

Braeden bowed. "It is a pleasure to meet you, Mrs. Van Brunt."

She glanced at Kat, then back to Braeden. "Yah, you are not Brom."

He knelt next to her and she tentatively touched his face. She shook her head. "*Niet*, you are not Brom. But you are big like my Brom."

Braeden smiled. "Yes, I have been told that. I understand he is an ancestor of mine, so that must mean we are related in some way. Perhaps you're a very great-grandmother of mine."

Her fingers continued to touch him. When she reached his biceps, she grinned. "Yah, strong like my Brom too."

"Glad to know it has been a family trait." He glanced at Kat and grimaced.

Dame Van Brunt's hand dropped into her lap and her face fell. "I still miss him."

Kat took the older woman's hand. "I know you do. I don't know how you get along here all by yourself."

Dame Van Brunt patted Kat's hand and returned her gaze to Braeden. "Jurgen and the boys come over and help sometimes. If you see him, could you tell him there's a break in the fence?"

"Maybe Braeden could fix it." Kat glanced at him to see the softest expression on his face as he looked back at Dame Van Brunt. "Do you think you could help?"

"I would be happy to." He rose to his full height and Dame Van Brunt leaned her head back.

Kat pointed to another door. "You will find tools in the barn in the back."

"I noticed your fence is wood. Are there any additional rails?"

Dame Van Brunt shook her head. "I don't think so."

"I'll take a look and see what we require. Kat and I can stop by Jurgen's if we need to." Braeden walked to the door, but hesitated. "You'll be here, right, Kat?"

"Yes. Dame Van Brunt and I are going to have some of these blueberry muffins I brought."

At her reassurance, Braeden exited the house. Now that was odd, nice, but uncharacteristic of him. Kat shrugged and turned back to Dame Van Brunt. She was still staring at the door Braeden had exited.

"It is a shock at first, isn't it?" Kat put her hand on the older woman's and Dame Van Brunt grasped it tightly.

There were tears in her eyes. "Yah. He is not Brom, but he

makes me miss him more." She turned her head to look at Kat. "Does he make your heart ache for Brom too?"

"At first, yes. But Brom had his life and his family. Braeden is a testament to that."

Dame Van Brunt's eyes grew intense. "And you did not. You like this Newtimer."

Kat nodded.

"He is not Brom."

"No, he isn't. He is different in many ways, ways I admire." Ways she loved, but she didn't want to insult Brom's mama.

Dame Van Brunt studied her, a habit so much like Braeden's that she grew uncomfortable.

"You brought muffins? Yah?"

The change in subject had Kat smiling. Dame Van Brunt was known for her appetite. "I did."

The two of them moved to the small kitchen and Kat made herself at home there, preparing coffee and pulling out plates while the woman who was supposed to have been her mother-in-law sat at the table.

When the coffee was ready, Kat poured before lifting the cloth off the basket.

"You are too good to me." Dame Van Brunt licked her lips as she gazed at the basket of muffins, breads and koekjes.

"You deserve it."

They each helped themselves, and the older woman closed her eyes with her first bite. She was not heavy, just big, and she did enjoy her food. "This is lovely. You need to be someone's wife."

Kat waved the comment aside. "I'm too busy with the inn for that. Did you hear we are still in Newtime?"

"Yah. I also hear it has to do with your Newtimer. Jurgen told me."

The man was becoming more than an irritation. "He isn't happy. He won't understand I don't love him."

"And you love this man?"

She started. "I-I don't know."

"But you like him a lot."

She took a bite of muffin to avoid the question.

Dame Van Brunt stared hard at her. "You have congress with him."

Kat's cheeks heated and she quickly took a sip of coffee. The whole darn village knew they coupled and it made her uncomfortable, but for Jurgen to have told Brom's mama was inexcusable.

"It is all right. You need to live life too."

Kat swung her gaze to the old woman's face. "I do."

"You do work, not life. You need love. You have my blessing."

"But I didn't—"

"Did you hear about the *schurk* on the black horse?"

She shook her head at the change in topic. "What? There's a ruffian on a horse?"

Dame Van Brunt nodded sagely as one who knew more gossip than her guest. "Yah. He trampled through Jurgen's garden. This is not good."

Kat stiffened. She'd been knocked down last week by a man on a black horse. All they needed now was another supernatural event and her village would be sure to be rid of Braeden. "It's probably someone playing a prank."

"That could be. Or it could be the spirits warning us of hard times to come."

"I doubt it's spirits. We haven't seen spirits in years." Braeden's concern after his first ride came back to her and a chill ran up her spine. Had he seen a spirit?

A loud banging behind the house interrupted her thoughts.

Dame Van Brunt reached her hand into the basket again. "Yah, your man, he is a good one."

Yes he was. But could she keep him? Would Sleepy Hollow let her?

Braeden threw aside the two old pieces of wood that had made the bottom horizontal bar of the fence section. Strolling into the barn, he was surprised to find new railings. Dame Van Brunt must be unaware of the new wood stacked inside. He sawed the wood to the length he needed. Working with it reminded him of his days after high school when he and Reed would build houses during the day and raise hell and pick up women at night…until he'd slept with the wrong woman and injured Reed emotionally, physically and mentally. He dropped the saw as the small piece of wood fell to the floor. He stared at it, his memories as painful as they'd been the day he'd tried to stop Reed from leaving. He could still see himself grabbing Reed's arm, his friend falling, and the loud thump of his head hitting the concrete.

He took a deep breath, trying to dispel the images from his mind. Grabbing the rail, he strode outside with an axe. Focusing on the task at hand, he fitted the wood into the holes on each post. It was a snug fit. With the back of the axe, he knocked the piece into place. Reed had been good at wood. Maybe he would find a job in finish-work again.

Braeden kicked the old boards aside so he could step back and view his work. It looked odd. The entire fence was rotting away. Most of the wood had softened with decay, and the new plank appeared out of place.

He shrugged. It was fixed and that was what his very-great-grandmother wanted. He paused at the thought. For that to be true, what Kat had said about the timelines would have to be factual, an idea he no longer dismissed. So if it was, then what?

He turned to pick up the broken rail to place it near the woodpile when he noticed a strange impression in the wood. With the two pieces lying together as they would have been whole, there was a definite indentation. Squatting, he moved the two halves tight against one another. It was a boot mark. The wood was so soft that the bottom of a man's shoe was clearly visible stamped across the break. Someone had kicked this fence in.

For what purpose? To prove how old it was? Just looking at it was enough for that.

"I planned to fix that."

Braeden looked over his shoulder to find Jurgen walking toward him. "You don't have to now."

The man scowled. As Jurgen stopped, Braeden noticed even his hands were clenched. "We don't want you here. We can take care of our own."

He stood to remind Jurgen of his large stature. "So you mentioned when you attacked me in the barn. But I'm here and I plan to stay a long while."

"Why? So you can be Brom for Katrina? It's wrong. You need to let her go."

"What do you mean Brom? I'm not Brom, and she is quite aware of that."

Jurgen's mouth turned up to one side in a nasty smirk. "Is she? The man she was going to marry disappears on her wedding day and then you arrive over four years later looking just like him? I doubt *she* even knows what she's feeling."

Braeden froze. Kat had meant to marry Brom Van Brunt? His heart started a march in his chest as his body tensed.

"But if you don't mind her loving you for her long-dead betrothed, then I guess that's your decision. She could even marry you in the dress she sewed for her wedding to Brom. She probably still has it. Me? I'd never take a woman who loved someone else."

The shrewd calculation in Jurgen's eyes brought Braeden's fighting instincts to the fore. "Kat is well aware of who I am, just as Dame Van Brunt is. So try your mind games on someone else."

Jurgen's shoulders slumped but he wouldn't give it up. "You can think what you will, but when she calls Brom's name in the dark one night, you'll know where you stand." He turned and stalked off, back the way he'd come, his boot treads in the soft earth very similar to the one on the fence rail.

Braeden didn't utter a word, his throat refusing to work. All the signs fell into place. Kat's shock when seeing him in Brom's coat. Her not wanting him to stay at her inn. His stomach tightened as if he'd just been gut-punched and nausea took hold. The betrayal was worse coming from her, the one, the only one he didn't have to control himself with. The only one who had seen past his body to who he was.

He sneered. Who he was? She hadn't seen who he was at all. She'd seen who she wanted to see, her long-dead bridegroom! The hurt melded with heated anger and he stalked to the house. Throwing open the door, he stood on the porch. "Kat." The word came out as cold as he felt.

She saw him from the back room where she sat and jumped up. Saying something to their hostess, she quickly made her way toward him.

"What is it? Are you all right?"

"No. Come." Grabbing her hand in a viselike grip, he pulled her outside and down the road.

"Braeden, what's wrong? What has happened?"

He didn't look at her, but kept them moving. "I had an enlightening conversation with Jurgen."

"Jurgen? What did he say?"

"He said you were planning to marry Brom. He said Brom disappeared the very day of your wedding. He said you're with me because you're still in love with Brom and think I'm him."

Her gasp gave him a small amount of satisfaction, but then she tried to pull away. "Braeden, I think I can tell the difference between my dead betrothed and you."

He stopped and looked at her. "Can you? Then why didn't you tell me you were engaged to Brom?"

He started to pull her toward the inn again before she could form a word. He had one goal in mind to confirm everything.

"I didn't tell you because I didn't want you to think what you're thinking, especially when I hadn't decided what my feelings were yet."

They were at the back door of the inn, and he let her go. "And what exactly are your feelings, Katrina Van Tassel, fiancée of Brom Van Brunt?"

Kat put her hands on her hips, her eyes flashing. "And what are your feelings, Braeden? I have yet to hear how you feel about me."

"How I feel about you right now is that you betrayed me. You led me on. Let me think you enjoyed my company when all the while you were pretending I was your late lover!" He yanked open the door and stomped inside, making a beeline for her bedroom.

"Braeden!"

He ignored her and entered her room. Reaching her armoire in three strides, he threw both doors open, hard. One cracked.

"Braeden, what are you doing?"

The scent of brownies flooded his senses and he paused for a moment. Her scent. The woman he had thought he—the woman who couldn't see beyond a ghost. With anger spurring him on, he pulled clothes out and threw them to the floor.

"Braeden!" Kat grabbed at his arm and he shook her off, but even in his anger he was careful not to hurt her. With her it was instinct.

He growled, "Don't touch me." He continued to pull material and clothes, cloaks, shawls, even blankets out of the armoire.

There it was. White material with delicate embroidery along the neckline and shoulders that declared it a wedding dress. He pulled it from its home and held it before her.

Her eyes grew round.

"Were you hoping to wear this again?" His fingers dug into the material. "Perhaps you wanted to wear it for me so we could recreate your long-lost love story?"

Kat stepped back and shook her head. "No. I kept it as a memory, nothing more. It was all I had left of the happiest time of my life…until I met you."

He stepped toward her. "You mean until you met the man who could be Brom for you. I thought you were different. I thought you liked me for *me*." He gave a hopeless chuckle. "You *were* different. You liked me for the ghost I could be."

Emotions played across her face like a movie, so when her brows furrowed and her hands found her hips again, he had fair warning.

"Now let me tell you what I think. I think you want me to imagine you're Brom because then *you* don't have to figure out how you feel about me. I know how I feel, but do you? Yes, in the beginning I had a hard time separating you from Brom because when I love, I love with my whole heart and you reminded me of having lost my heart forever."

He opened his mouth to argue, but she raised her hand. "No, it's time you listened. As we spent more time together, I learned how different you were from Brom, not just in looks, but in your personality. You are a gentleman while Brom was a wild man. You're considerate and caring of my needs while Brom was mostly about himself. Oh yes, he loved me in his way and did think of me, but not with the focus you have."

"If I'm so different, why didn't you tell me about your relationship with Brom? You hid it." He sounded like a little boy and he hated it, but he couldn't take it back.

"I didn't tell you at first because I needed to figure out who it was I loved. If I was still in love with Brom, then I would have to tell you. But I realized when we stood in the town circle yesterday, that it was you I loved."

He lowered the wedding dress. "You love me?"

She bit at her lip and nodded. "Yes."

Shit. What was he supposed to think now? He ran his free hand through his hair. She loved him. So she said. He looked shrewdly at her. "You're sure you have the right man?"

Her eyes watered as she gave him a tentative smile. "Yes."

She loved him. Him. A warmth settled around his heart and he took a calming breath. "You're absolutely sure it is me?"

"Absolutely."

A joy he'd never felt before blanketed his brain. He dropped the dress and took the step to reach her. Cupping her face between his palms, he stared into her eyes. "You love me."

"I love you."

Gently, he brushed her lips with his, her softness his undoing. Deepening the kiss, he clasped her hard against him, tilting her head to enjoy her taste. When he lifted his lips from hers, her eyes remained closed.

"You have to tell me everything."

# Chapter Twelve

Kat stopped at the edge of the small clearing deep in the woods behind the church. She loved this spot. It was just beyond the village boundaries, but it was safe for the day. She and Braeden would return to the house to make love long before midnight.

He squeezed her hand. "You're right. This is the perfect place for lunch and dessert."

"I didn't bring any dessert. Do you want me to go back to get some?"

He pulled her into his embrace. "No. You will have to be my dessert."

She frowned, not sure what he meant until his tongue licked the side of her neck. The heat of understanding filled her, making her flush. She pushed him away. "Can your brain only focus on one thing?"

He chuckled even as he spread the quilt on the ground. "No, but I like focusing on you."

"I think we should concentrate on having our lunch." She stepped onto the quilt and sat. "Are you going to join me?"

"In a minute."

Curious, she watched him as she emptied the contents of the basket.

He walked the perimeter of the little meadow, facing the trees beyond. When he returned, he joined her on the ground.

"What were you doing?"

"I was listening for a horse."

"A horse?"

He chose an apple and bit into it. "Yes. I had a horse nearly run me over yesterday. I think it was on purpose. Being here on the ground would make me an easy target, so I thought it best to be sure we were alone."

Kat dropped her plate. "Was it black with a black-hooded rider?"

"Yes. Have you seen it?"

"Yes, it knocked me over last week when I walked home from Dame Van Brunt's. She told me a horse like that trampled through Jurgen's garden. This isn't good."

"No, it isn't." His brows lowered. "I thought the person was after me, but if he is harming others, then we need to find out who it is and why he's doing this."

Kat picked up the plate again and sliced into the cheese. "I think we should bring it to the next town meeting."

Braeden took another bite of his apple. She couldn't help watching his neck muscles as he chewed. Everything about the man was strong.

"Why are you so muscular? I thought you typed on a computer all day."

He took another bite and swallowed before answering. "I have no choice. I grew up like this. I have to work out or my muscles burn. It's a curse that keeps my body hard and my strength difficult to manage."

With any other man she would have considered his statement

a joke, but Braeden was serious. "I wonder if that has anything to do with the time curse of Sleepy Hollow. Dame Vandend said we were cursed. I think that woman knows a lot more than she has told us."

Braeden tossed his apple core into the woods. "I agree. We need to pay her a visit. But first, I want to know what happened with you and Brom."

The bread and cheese in her mouth suddenly tasted like a mud bog. Swallowing as best she could, she followed it with the water she'd brought. "Don't you want to eat?"

"Not until you tell me what I want to know."

She placed her plate on the quilt and clasped her hands. "Brom was my intended. The day of our wedding, he disappeared."

"He jilted you?"

"No! He disappeared. He was on his way, according to his father, but as usual he'd forgotten something. This time it was his hat, and he wanted to be perfect for me." She gazed down at her hands. "He ran back and his father continued to the church. When Brom didn't arrive, everyone looked for him. At first people thought as you did, but after weeks, we grew concerned. It wasn't until we realized we were in a different time than the rest of the world that we understood Brom was gone forever."

He lifted her chin to study her. Did he see the pain she had endured? Did he see her broken dreams? "You loved him." His thumb stroked her cheek.

She looked away. "Yes."

"Then how can you be sure you love me?"

She snapped her gaze back to his. Doubt was clear in his eyes. "Because you are not like him. You don't even have the same eye color. To be honest, the only similarity you have is your body. It's as tall and broad as his, but otherwise you're a completely different person."

It was clear he wasn't convinced.

"You're the only other man I have ever given myself to since then."

His eyes widened at that. "How long ago did Brom disappear?"

"Over four years."

"And you haven't had sex all that time?"

Her cheeks heated. "No."

"Well aren't we the pair?" He chuckled. "I guess we need to make up for that."

"I guess." Excitement flitted along her skin at the look he gave her.

"Stand up."

Confused by his request, but curious, she did as he asked.

Braeden rose and walked behind her. "I want to get you out of that dress and see your beauty in the sunlight."

"Here? In the open?"

He put his hands on her shoulders and squeezed. "Why not? There's no one here."

She spun around. "But someone might come."

"So? The whole village already knows we make love. Otherwise it wouldn't still be in Newtime."

A strange thrill raced to her core and she wondered at her wantonness. "But knowing and seeing are different."

He reached for her but she stepped back. His look turned predatory. "True. If they see, they have a choice. To turn around and leave us our privacy or to watch. Either way, it doesn't affect us."

She swallowed hard and glanced behind him at the trees. Someone might watch?

He moved toward her again and she stepped back a few more paces, shaking her head. "I don't think this is a good idea."

His grin widened. "Oh, but I do." He walked forward, his long strides closing the distance.

Panicked yet excited, she turned and ran for the trees. She'd just made them when he caught her. "Oh no. You're not getting away from me." He pinned her against a large pine. "I want you. Now."

"But what if—"

His mouth against hers stopped her protest while his hand cupping her breast caused her lips to open in pleasure. His tongue plunged in, ravishing her mouth as his hand kneaded her breast and his body pinned her against the tree, making escape impossible.

When his lips left hers, his breaths were as short as hers, and she could feel his pounding heart.

"I'm not waiting until the last moment to come with you. If making love to you will keep you here, then I want to do it now. I don't want to lose you."

Her heart pounded at his words and her body surrendered. She wrapped her arms around his neck. "Please, Braeden, make love to me."

He groaned. "I promise I will make slow, leisurely love to you, but right now I need to be inside you. Let me in?"

His need fueled her own and she nodded, knowing she was ready. He unzipped his pants and his hard cock sprang forth. Her sheath contracted at the sight.

"I swear, I'm going to see all of you in bright light soon, just not now."

She smiled even as she lifted her skirt to bare her naked pussy to his gaze.

Another groan followed before he positioned himself at her entrance and slowly speared her. "Wrap your legs around me."

"What?"

"Do it." The harshness of his voice belayed his need and she lifted one leg around his waist. He caught it with his hand and he slipped inside her farther, causing her to squeeze him.

"Don't. Not yet." His breathing was rough. "Your other leg."

She held on to his neck and pulled her other leg up around his waist. His cock slid to the hilt and then he pushed his hips farther, pinning her between him and the tree once again. The shocks of pleasure sped from her core to every extremity.

As he rocked his hips out and in, excitement built, and her body tensed around him.

"God, you're so tight."

"You're so big."

"Good point." His smugness did nothing to lessen her enjoyment. In fact, it made her hotter, tighter as he pumped into her, filling her with every stroke.

His strength excited her even as his hardness pressed deep within her. His hips increased the rhythm, driving into her steadily, her pleasure building into a tight ball.

"Oh God, Brom."

Braeden stilled.

She pressed against him. When he didn't continue, she opened her eyes. "Braeden? Why did you stop?"

His eyes were hard. His face unreadable. He pulled from her and dropped her legs.

Her cry of loss was soft. She stumbled before grabbing on to the tree, her legs weak, her body crying for satisfaction. "Braeden? Is someone here?" Her gaze swept the little clearing.

"Yes. Brom is here."

She snapped her head back to him. "What?"

"You called Brom's name."

No. She couldn't have. But in his eyes was the truth. Oh Lord. "Braeden, if I did, it was only because we were just talking about him. You are nothing like him. Not at all."

His eyes held no softening. "You said I'm built like him. I guess I must feel like him too."

"No." *God in de Hemel,* she could see what he felt, what he thought. "No. Brom never did this with me. He wasn't as strong as you. Or as patient. It was nothing more than our last conversation. Truly."

He studied her face before looking down to push his soft cock into his jeans and zip them up. "Maybe your body knows more about what it loves than you do."

He turned and stalked across the clearing, away from her.

She ran after him and grabbed his arm. He stopped and she felt his muscles shake beneath her hands.

"Let go." His tone brooked no disobedience, but she held on anyway.

"No. I won't let you go in this state."

He yanked his arm from her grip but caught her as she started to fall backward. "Leave me."

She shook her head, tears gathering in her eyes. "I can't. I love you."

His eyes held no warmth. "Not smart. I should have told you. I hurt those who love me." He spun on his heel and stalked off into the woods.

Her heart hurt so much, she pressed her fist against it to try to stop the pain. "Braeden! Please!"

She watched as he disappeared into the depths of the forest, his unique scent still clinging to her clothes. He couldn't be gone. He had to come back. He had to.

But the pain in her heart said otherwise, and she crumpled to the ground as sobs racked her body.

Braeden slowed his pace and surveyed the forest. Where the hell was he? He turned in a circle and examined each object. He'd seen this area before but not from this angle. He cocked his head and listened. No sounds but the chickadee and the rustle of a light breeze in the air.

What did it matter if he found his way back? What would he do when he arrived there? He couldn't compete with a ghost. No one could. A live man he could deal with. A dead man he couldn't fight.

He ran his hand through his hair. He'd believed her when she said she loved him. Maybe she believed it herself. Just his luck to find the one woman who could look beyond his body, but couldn't see past her own dead lover.

He fisted his hands at the reminder. She'd said she'd only been with Brom besides him. He wished she'd had others, but instead he was compared to her first and only. He should walk away.

A noise in the wood brought his attention back to his surroundings. In the distance, he could see the black horse approaching. This time he'd be ready for him. If he stayed—

Pain shot through his head at the same time a loud crack sounded in his ear. He struggled to remain upright as the trees spun around him.

"Idiot. Can't you even knock a man out properly? Give me that."

Braeden turned toward the voice, but a second blow caught him on the side of the head and the world went black.

~~*~~

Braeden moaned as he became aware of a throbbing pain in his head. Touching his hair, he felt leaves tangled in it. He gently pulled at them and opened his eyes to find dried blood on his fingers. Shit, how long had he been out? He'd bet Jurgen had something to do with the large bump he now sported.

He sat up. The earth whirled and tilted and he closed his eyes again, fighting nausea. He focused on the darkness behind his lids until his stomach settled. Once more, he opened his eyes, thankful the world had righted itself. Scanning the area around him, it was clear he'd been dragged. He was near the road into Sleepy Hollow, but hidden from it by bushes. Grabbing on to the tree next to him, he slowly lifted to a standing position. The ground didn't move much this time, and he breathed easier. He might very well have a concussion.

He focused his sights on the road. The question was, which way led into the village and which way out? He didn't like how unsteady he felt. Breaking a dried branch off the pine tree he leaned against, he used it as a walking stick and gingerly made his way to the roadside.

The sun shone brightly, but was positioned in the west, which meant it was late afternoon. He must not have been out that long. Moving west toward the village, he was surprised by how quiet the area was. Only the chatter of birds broke the silence.

As he made the bend in the road, his car came into view. That was a welcome sight. At least he was headed in the right direction. He hoped Kat had… Damn, Kat. His chest tightened, his thoughts running riot in his brain, causing the pounding in his head to grow louder, deafening.

He stopped walking and closed his eyes again. He needed to

relax, think about something pleasant. Kat's full lips formed in his mind. Their soft lushness beckoned him. He snapped his eyes open. Not exactly what he'd wanted to think about, but the pounding was a bit more bearable. Continuing toward his car, he focused on the road beyond it. It seemed deserted. His breath caught in his lungs.

The village was gone.

"No." He threw down the stick and ran, ignoring the pain in his head.

It couldn't be.

He slowed to a stop in front of what should have been the Sleepy Hollow Inn and stared at the empty space. The field swayed with dried grass and dizziness overwhelmed him. He fell to his knees. "Kat." The word tore from his throat in an anguished whisper.

Realization dawned through the pain in his head. He'd been unconscious a full day. Jurgen had taken the decision out of his hands. Maybe he should be thanking the man. What more could they have said? Kat had a stranglehold on her past as strong as the curse that kept her in the 1790s. What place did he have there?

Slowly, he stood and walked back to his car. He crawled into the backseat, not willing to risk driving, and lay down. There was no rush. All he had to return to was his penthouse, his job and the occasional visit to family. The once-a-month visits to the stable were one activity he could look forward to. That was something.

## *Oldtime—Wednesday*

Kat strode toward the Vandend farm, her temper barely in check. She had two reasons for her visit and she planned on being successful with both. Marching up the steps to the old porch, she banged on the wooden door. Max swung it open and she narrowed her eyes at him. "As I thought. Your ankle is fine. You need to come back to work."

He backed in and avoided her gaze. "I planned to tomorrow. I was just making sure I was completely well."

She reached around him and pulled the thin square machine out of his hand. "I'm sure you were, once you finished whatever you were doing with this."

"Please." He looked over his shoulder. "Don't let Grandmama see it. She hates anything Newtime."

"I'm not liking it much either when I have no one to fill the root cellar, stack the wood or clean the windows."

"Right." He lowered his voice. "Give it to me and I will go to the inn posthaste."

She glared at him a moment longer, then nodded once. As soon as it was in his hand, Max was as good as his word. He brushed past her out the door and strode down the lane.

Now for the tough job. "Dame Vandend. Are you here?"

"Yah. I'm in the garden."

Kat walked through the small, dilapidated house and stepped through the open back door.

Dame Vandend wasn't tending to her garden. Rather she sat on a chair in the middle of it, a bottle of whiskey on the bench beside her and a glass of the amber liquid in her hand.

Some example she was for poor Max. The man wanted nothing more than to be involved with Newtime and his grandmama wanted everything to stay the way it was. Unfortunately, time eventually took its toll, and the woman would be sorry for her laziness one of these days.

Kat strode to the bench and sat. "I want to know about the curse."

The older woman cocked her head. "Which curse?"

"There's more than one? I want to know about the one you mentioned at the last town meeting. Where you said the village was cursed to stay in Oldtime and only by Braeden…" She swallowed down the pain of his name. "Braeden and I having congress with each other would we stay in Newtime. That curse."

"Oh."

"You know a lot more about why we remain in Oldtime. It took me a while, but I finally put the pieces together. You want us to stay in Oldtime. Why?"

The old woman took a sip of her whiskey before turning her intense gaze on Kat. "Don't you want to stay in Oldtime? I thought you preferred we keep our ways pure."

"That was before I knew being in Oldtime was a curse. I thought we were special, but then I hear we are being punished somehow."

"Not punished." Dame Vandend readjusted her significant seat. "How can living longer than any other people in the world be a punishment?"

Kat lowered her brow. "So that's it. You want to live beyond your rightful time. That's why you like this curse?"

The old woman's smile was crooked. "It's not such a bad thing, no?"

"Yes." Kat looked to the sky and took a deep breath before refocusing. "If this is a curse, that means there must be a way to break it."

"What?" Dame Vandend stiffened, almost to the point of sitting straight.

"What can we do to break the curse?"

The woman's lips closed tight.

Kat stood, her agitation growing. "Do you realize what this

curse has done? Nora's daughters are looking at a life with no love, no husband and no children. Your own grandson, whose mind is smart and could easily invent any number of the objects found in Newtime, is stuck in this time, forced to be a laborer or farmer."

"That's honorable work."

"Yes it is, but his mind is ready for bigger challenges more suited to him. And who would he grow old with? Have a family with? All he can see is what he can't have and will never be happy in the 1790s."

The older woman looked down and took another swig of her whiskey.

"Why did you call me maiden at the first meeting after Braeden arrived?"

"Because you are, were. Your Brom didn't marry you and never will." The woman gave her a shrewd look. "You may think you have found him again but he is gone, generations now. You will never have him back."

"I don't want him back. Yes, I loved him but he left, had his own life with the family we were supposed to have and never looked back. I don't want him. I want Braeden."

"Then why do you hold on to Brom?"

"Why do people keep telling me that? I don't—"

"You do. The curse will never be lifted while you do so."

Kat stilled. She had something to do with the curse? "What do you mean?"

The older woman shook her head and took another sip of whiskey.

Kat gripped the edges of her gown in frustration, wishing instead to shake Dame Vandend until she spoke. "Fine. But you think about what kind of life you are forcing on others as you idle your way beyond the years you should have had. Don't forget after you're gone, and no one knows the way to break the curse, you will condemn the rest of us to live it out until perhaps only your grandson is left, living here alone."

The old woman looked at her with her last statement, but pursed her lips.

Beyond frustrated, Kat turned and stalked out the gate in the backyard fence, slamming it back as she opened it. The old wood shattered but she kept walking.

There had to be a way to keep the village in Newtime permanently. She'd failed to keep it in Newtime temporarily. Her heart lurched at the memory of her and Braeden's last time in the forest. He hadn't come back. They could have talked, but he never returned. She couldn't accept he was gone forever.

Her gut told her Stephen would be at the festival next weekend. She wasn't sure she could face him. She loved Braeden so much, the pain of losing him was like gangrene in her soul. It far eclipsed what she'd felt after losing Brom and she didn't know what to do.

Reaching the inn, she opened the kitchen door and stepped in.

"Katrina." Her mama's sympathetic voice greeted her. She stood next to the table with open arms and offered the comfort only a mother could.

It was too much to resist. Without a word, Kat stepped into her mother's embrace.

"I'm so sorry. What happened?"

She held on to her mama's warmth a moment longer and then stepped away. The sadness in her parent's gaze almost tumbled the limited control she had. She swallowed hard. "I called him Brom."

Her mother's shock undid her. Kat collapsed into a chair and put her head in her hands as the tears fell and the pain of the moment swept through her again.

Her mama hugged her from behind. "There, there. We will figure out how to fix this."

Her mother took the seat next to her and Kat wiped her eyes with her sleeve. "I don't think this can be fixed."

"Tch, tch. Of course it can. You love him, yah?"

She nodded.

"And he loves you, yah?"

She shrugged. He cared for her, at least until she called him Brom.

"I'm sure he does." Her mother patted her hand. "Now why did you call him Brom?"

"We were just talking about Brom. Braeden asked me to tell him everything and so I did. Then…" She paused. She almost couldn't say it, still shocked it had happened. "We were having congress when I called him Brom."

Her mother's look turned serious as she rose from the table, which made Kat worry all the more. It proved there was no way to ever bring Braeden back. She covered her face with her hands, unable to bear the situation she'd made for herself.

"This is serious, Katrina. Fixing it may be…difficult."

The sounds of coffee being prepared reached her ears, but her stomach tightened. Her mother rarely called anything difficult. She worried her lower lip, desperately holding back tears.

While the fire caught, her mother returned to the table. "Why did you call him Brom?"

"I don't know." She lowered her hands. "I thought it was because we had just been speaking of him, but he didn't believe me."

Dame Van Tassel shook her head. "No. That is not why. You

still hold on to Brom here." She put her hand over her chest. "You have to let him go. You must make peace with him."

"But I am at peace." Kat rose and put the coffee on the heated surface. "He's been gone for more than four years. He had a family and children. What more can I do?"

"Yah, he left you and had a wonderful life, but Kat, you have not left him."

She leaned against the cupboards and crossed her arms over her stomach. "I—"

"No. You have not left him. In fact, you resent him for having that life, don't you?"

She looked at her feet. "Yes. I do." She lifted her gaze to the window and envisioned them walking along the lane. "We had such beautiful plans. We were going to have a family, run Papa's farm, grow old together."

"But that didn't happen. He disappeared into Newtime."

"Yes. I'm sure he saw it as a great adventure. I can see him enjoying the sights and sounds of a different time. Oh, I'm sure he came back, but we were gone. Brom would never have the patience to wait a year to find us again."

"Precisely, and yet you had the patience to wait. And after you realized he had made his own life with a new wife, you held on to the past, keeping it alive, keeping it authentic." Her mother raised her brow.

Had she? Was that what she'd done? Was that why she'd been so adamant that Oldtime stay pure? Was she as guilty as Dame Vandend in that respect?

Her mother joined her and pulled cups from the cupboard. "You still hold on to him. You kept his frock."

"But I had forgotten I kept it."

Her mother stared at her before continuing to place the cups and spoons on the table. "And what else do you still have? The wedding dress. Yah?"

She turned away from her mother's shrewd gaze and lifted the coffeepot to pour.

"Is there more you have held on to in addition to your dreams?"

When she'd completed her task, she sat and faced her mother. "Yes. I have the ring he made from a vine. I have the blanket we used when we got caught in a rain storm. I think I still have the poem he wrote me." She sat in stunned silence. There were other items she'd kept from their time together as well.

Her mother patted her hand. "You need to let him go, Katrina. Whether you can repair the damage you have done with Braeden or not. You will only find happiness living in the present, not the past."

She lifted her gaze in wonder at her mother's wisdom. She hadn't expected to learn more at her mother's knee at the ripe age of twenty-eight, but obviously, she had much more to learn. "Thank you, Mama. I understand now."

"Good." The older woman spooned in a large amount of sugar into her coffee.

Somehow she needed to determine how to expel Brom from her life and embrace the present.

It would not be an easy task.

# Chapter Thirteen

November—Newtime

Braeden wrapped his arms around Kat's lush body, pulling her back against his chest, her rounded ass cupping his erection. The water splashed from his tub, wetting the marble floor. He didn't care. He wanted to be inside her.

He palmed one breast and played with the nipple until it was a tight nub. He kissed the bend of her neck and she tilted her head, giving him more access. "I want you, Kat."

She wiggled her butt against his cock.

"Wench," he growled. Lifting her, he floated her over the tip of his cock and eased her tight pussy onto him. When he'd filled her, she sighed and leaned back against him, splaying her legs wide across his. The warm water caressed them as he moved his hand down over her belly to find her hidden folds where they connected.

"Take me." Her words were but a whisper but they sped through his body like a command.

He used his finger to make slow circles on her clit while he brought his other hand up to squeeze her breast. She tightened around him as he played with her body, her hips grinding against him.

His balls constricted as his cock pushed into her, lifting her with his thrusts.

"Oh God, Brom."

His eyes opened wide, male laughter filling his ears. He stared into the darkness of his room for a moment, catching the vestiges of sound. The chill of her betrayal cooled his heated body, causing him to shiver. "Computer, low lights. Seventy-eight degrees."

The lights came on and the air-conditioning ceased. He sat up.

He'd heard that laughter before. It was full, boisterous, yet scratchy. He ran his hand through his hair and winced. The bump on his head was still tender. According to the doctor, he did have a concussion.

Looking at the clock, he groaned. Midnight. Not again. He stared at the nightstand drawer where he'd thrown her comb. He should throw it away. He couldn't live the rest of his life with sex dreams about Kat, especially if they turned to nightmares. He needed to get laid. He needed to forget about her. He needed a drink.

Rising, he shivered, his body still sweaty from his dream. He stepped into his closet and grabbed his old terrycloth robe. Shuffling into the living room, he manually hit the light switch for a change. He reached behind the bar for the cognac, but changed his mind and pulled out the scotch instead. After pouring a shot, he settled himself into his leather La-Z-Boy.

The aroma of scotch reminded him of his last night playing the Headless Horseman, coming back to the stables to have a drink with Ludo. It still boggled his mind that a whole village could disappear and reappear. If he hadn't seen it with his own eyes, he'd never have believed it.

He should tell Stephen. Shit. He would have to meet with Stephen to tell him he wasn't going to be the Headless Horseman anymore. He hated giving it up, but he wouldn't go near Sleepy Hollow again. He took a sip of the scotch, savoring the amber liquid across his tongue before swallowing. The relaxing burn eased the nightmare away as it made its way to his stomach. There was nothing like a good single malt.

What year was Ludo's? It was revolutionary times. How many people could say they had scotch that old? It would have been nice on the colder nights to have had a bit of scotch or whiskey before the ride, but Ludo was never in the barn then. That was a bit odd, but then again, what wasn't odd about Sleepy Hollow?

He raised a brow and took another sip. Riding Daredevil was pure pleasure, but he could ride at the stables he'd found. Still, there was no horse like Daredevil, except perhaps the white one he and Daredevil raced across the church meadow.

Braeden sat up and put his glass down hard on the side table.

The laughter. That's where he'd heard it. The ghost on the white steed, but what did that have to do with Kat? Why the laughter? Why—

"Fuck. It's Brom."

It made sense. The ghost looked so much like himself, it had to be Brom. Brom was the original Van Brunt to play the Headless Horseman and scare Ichabod Crane from Sleepy Hollow. But if Brom had lived in Newtime, why would he haunt Sleepy Hollow?

Kat. Kat wouldn't let him go. That had to be it. So not only had Braeden been dealing with a dead man, but a ghost as well.

He lifted his glass and leaned back in his chair. He definitely owed Jurgen a thank you for knocking him out. He was better off never stepping foot into the weirdness that was Sleepy Hollow again.

## *Newtime—December*

"Braeden, you have to go see him."

He stared at his brother, shocked by his anger. "Why is this so important to you?"

Stephen stalked across the room, though pacing was usually Braeden's forte. "It's not important to me, it's important to you. You need to see Reed."

Braeden looked outside at Stephen's children roughhousing in a pile of snow. He remembered the two of them doing that when they were young. So much had changed. "I helped him find his apartment and I will see him at Christmas. Why now?"

Stephen stopped in midstride. "You helped him find the apartment with internet searches. That's not the same as sitting down and talking to him. Besides, he asked for you."

Braeden swallowed. "Why?"

"I think he wants to thank you for all you've done and make you stop. He wants to be on his own now. I'm not sure, but based on what he said last week, that's my hunch."

Braeden rubbed the side of his face. He didn't want to see Reed. As much as he loved him like a brother, he was always afraid his friend would remember what happened and that he'd been the cause.

Stephen sat on the ottoman across from him. "You told me Kat wouldn't let go of her past, right?"

He stiffened. What did Kat have to do with Reed? "Yeah."

"Well, I think it's time you confronted yours. You need to tell Reed what happened."

"What? No. That's crazy. What good will that do?"

Stephen leaned his elbows on his knees. "You look like shit. You have bags under your eyes, your hair is a mess and your clothes are far from their usual neatness."

He ran his hand through his hair. "I haven't been getting much sleep."

"Why?" Stephen stared at him with a determined look Braeden recognized. Shit. He hated that look. Stephen was like a cat with his prey when that gleam appeared in his eyes.

There was no way he would explain he had sex nightmares about Kat every night at midnight. He wasn't going to tell him about the sleeping pill that didn't work, or the fine cognac that couldn't keep him asleep or even his new penchant for single malt scotch, which unfortunately didn't work either.

"Okay. I'll go see him."

"Tomorrow."

He waved his hand. "Yeah, tomorrow."

Stephen grabbed his wrist, his wiry strength a surprise. "I mean it, Braeden."

He nodded. He'd go. He'd confess and lose another important person in his life. "And you will play the Headless Horseman next year."

"Agreed." They shook hands and Braeden rose to leave.

"Do you want to say hi to the kids?"

Braeden shook his head. "No. They're having fun. No reason to interrupt that."

Stephen smiled. "We used to do that. Do you remember?"

"Yeah, I do, but that was before life got complicated."

Reed looked good, like his old self. His streaked blond hair had grown to his normal length, past the collar, and his physique had filled out. He wasn't so thin and willowy anymore. If it wasn't for the pauses as he searched for the right word, or the stiffness in his left arm, the average person wouldn't have a clue he'd almost lived his life out as an invalid, incapable of caring for himself or thinking for himself.

Braeden met his friend's gaze. "This is a great place. You deserve it."

Reed handed him an iced tea and sat across from him on the matching couch. "I do deserve it. I worked very hard to get where I am. At first, I didn't…think it would happen."

Braeden swallowed. The fact Reed had to do any work to have his own apartment hurt. He deserved so much more.

"But then my new…physical therapist wouldn't accept it when I said 'I can't' and a lot changed."

"I need to thank him, then."

"Her. And no need. As she says, it's just her job."

"She sounds more like a miracle worker to me."

"Yeah, there is that." Reed smiled, just like he had before the accident.

Braeden relaxed. "So what are your plans now?"

"I'm going to go to college. You made such a…success of yourself, I've decided I should give it a try."

Shit, Reed had changed a lot in the last year. "That's great. Just let me know where and I'll send the tuition check immediately. When are you going?"

Reed took a swallow and avoided Braeden's gaze. When he put the glass down, he stroked the moisture from it as if it were the focus of his attention. "About that. I'd prefer you didn't pay for it. I want to do this on my own."

A tightness settled around Braeden's chest. "But why?"

Reed finally looked at him. "Because you've done enough for me. Far more than any friend would do. I don't even know why you kept our…friendship going when it was two years before I remembered who you were and another before I could recall most of our time together."

Sweat formed at the base of Braeden's spine. He couldn't lose Reed again. He gave a choked chuckle. "Hey, we were best buds. You're still the only guy I'd dare tell anything to. Look at those emails I send you. Do you think I'd tell that stuff to just anyone?"

"So you'd tell me anything?"

Braeden took a swallow of the ice tea, his throat suddenly dry. "Sure."

"Then tell me what happened."

"What happened where? You mean at Sleepy Hollow? I think I filled you in on most of that."

Reed sat back and folded his arms. "No. I want you to tell me how I got…hurt."

"I told you. It was an accident." His whole body felt warm and he wished he'd worn a t-shirt instead of a sport shirt.

"Yes, you did. But how did it happen? How did I hit my head on the concrete bench in the park?"

Braeden couldn't look at Reed. The flush of fear that overtook his body at the memory of that day took his breath from him. His heart raced as the image of Reed, lying on the grass, blood oozing from his head became clear in his mind. He had to get help. He stood as air rushed back into his lungs and glanced at Reed, then strode to the window, feeling eighteen all over again.

He ran his hand through his hair and took a deep breath. It was time to confess. Time to confront his own past. He turned to Reed. "We argued. When you tried to leave, I freaked. I thought you were done with me. You were the only person who knew me and liked me for who I was. When you started to walk away, I panicked."

He looked past Reed, at the doorway to the kitchen, anywhere but at his friend. "I tried to stop you from leaving. I was strong even then. I didn't realize my own strength. I yanked you back. You fell and hit your head. There was so much blood. I thought you were dead."

He turned away, the memory of the day still as sharp as a diamond's edge. "I called 9-1-1 and tried to get you to wake up." He gripped the windowsill. "I thought if I could get you to wake up, you would be okay. But you wouldn't open your eyes. I begged and yelled, but you were out. When the ambulance arrived, the EMTs scowled at me as if I'd killed you. They wouldn't let me in the ambulance. That's when I called your parents."

He still remembered the look on Reed's parents' faces when he walked into the hospital with Reed's blood on his clothing. They railed at him, but he'd been too scared Reed would die to notice.

"Braeden." Reed's calm voice forced him to look at him. "What did we argue about?"

Shit. He stared at the ceiling as if he could get help to stop the torture that was long overdue. He deserved this. These years helping Reed get better were borrowed time. Time to hold on to a friend he loved who, in the end, had wanted to walk away. It looked like the time had come. He might as well face it like a man.

He met Reed's intense look with his own. "It was over a woman."

"What about her?" Reed continued to stare.

"You had been dating her for three months but wouldn't introduce us. You really liked her. Until then, we had thought it a blast to go to bars, pick out a couple of the ladies for the night and take them home, but we didn't always go out together."

He ran a hand through his hair again and came back to sit on the couch opposite his once best friend. He stared at his drink. "That day you finally told me her name. You were confident in how she felt about you and were going to introduce us. The problem was, I had slept with her two nights earlier. I didn't know. She didn't act like she was in love with someone else. I didn't want to tell you but I had to. When I did, you were hurt and angry, rightfully so, but then you said you didn't want to have anything to do with me." He lifted his gaze to meet Reed's. "You said I was a freak. For the record, I still am."

Reed sat still as stone. Braeden braced himself for what would be the end of his last relationship outside his family, if hiding behind the computer could be called a relationship.

"I know." Reed's soft voice caught his attention.

"You know I'm a freak. Yeah, so do I."

Reed shook his head. "No. I know what happened. I remembered it almost a year ago."

"What?" Braeden frowned. "You remembered before I visited you last Christmas and didn't say anything?"

Read gazed thoughtfully at him. "Yes. At first, my anger… fueled my need to get better. I wanted to kick your ass, and I saw how much larger you had become. So I had to work hard."

"You're welcome to take a swing at me now. You look a lot stronger and honestly I'm not sorry you are."

"Neither am I. But then I was talking to my physical therapist about the…event and I couldn't remember her name."

"Your therapist?"

"No." Reed rolled his eyes. "The woman I'd been so in love with."

"Rhonda."

"Ah. Yes." Reed took a sip and contemplated his iced tea. "I don't remember what she looked like or the feelings I had for her."

Braeden sat forward, his elbows on his knees. "Maybe that's because of your injury. Maybe I stole that from you too."

Reed shook his head. "No. I remember some of the other

women we took to bed." He smirked, looking just like he used to back in high school. "But she is…vague. I've come to terms with it, and I think she means so little to me now because you mean more."

Huh? Braeden stared at Reed as if he'd gone off the deep end. "I think you may have had a few too many drugs. I slept with the woman you loved. I didn't know it, but I did and I hurt you."

Reed crossed his hands behind his head. "I think that says a lot more about her than it does you. She knew." He winked. "Still, I'm not going to bring any woman I'm in love with anywhere near you until I marry her. Nothing personal."

This couldn't be happening. Braeden's heart lightened but his brain refused to accept what Reed said. "But I physically hurt you. You have been in medical treatment for almost a decade."

"Yeah. Medical treatment you paid for. And like you said, it was an accident. Actually, I need to…apologize."

"What?" Braeden swallowed the lump in his throat as all his worst fears started to dissipate.

Reed lowered his arms and turned serious. "I'm sorry I called you a…freak. I remembered that too."

"Ah shit." Braeden stood and grabbed Reed up into a bear hug, still careful not to let his excitement cause him to squeeze too tight.

When he let go, he noticed the water in Reed's eyes matched his own and he stepped away, but he couldn't get the shit-eating grin off his face.

Reed smiled too. "So what's this I hear about you not leaving your penthouse for weeks, and only…visiting family twice a year?"

Braeden's face fell and he exhaled. "Stephen."

"Yup. You said you'd tell me anything."

"Not without a beer."

Reed grinned as he walked toward the kitchen. "I can make those arrangements."

## *Oldtime—Thursday*

Kat set the burlap bag on the ground beside the church. It seemed the appropriate place to say goodbye. Sitting on the front steps in her wedding dress, knowing Brom was gone, was burned into her memory as clear as any wood carving. She needed to burn that wood.

She looked around. The spot was perfect. She could see the church steps, the cemetery and the bridge just to the right of the church. Brom had proposed to her on the bridge. It was one of the few romantic things he'd done. The softness in her heart dissipated as resentment flared. Had he been more romantic for his next betrothed when he proposed to her? Had he settled down, become quieter, or had he been a loud old man, happy with his wife and children? Her gut told her he'd been the latter.

She lifted the bottom of the bag and dumped the contents on the ground, then sat on the bag. The morning had been chilly and the dead grass was not much of a buffer between the bag and the earth. She arranged all the articles into a pile. At the bottom was Brom's frock. She laid the vine ring on top and then a dried flower from their first walk alone. She added the book she'd given him for Christmas that he never took with him, always claiming he preferred to read at the inn, but as she'd come to know him, it was clear he wasn't a reader.

A twig snapped in the woods and she halted her movements. Looking over her shoulder past the graveyard, she saw a deer standing among the trees. She watched it blink and sniff the air. Not happy with the scent, it bounded away. She sighed. She loved the deer that visited the forest. Brom had focused on hunting them, unable to see their beauty beyond meat. She added a ripped waistcoat he planned to throw away, but she'd asked to use the material and then held on to it. Other mementos followed, including the poem she'd written him. She'd been surprised at how much she'd kept. Lastly, she reverently covered the pile with the wedding gown she wore to wait for him to be her husband. She could never bring herself to cut into it. This was better.

She reached into her pocket and dug out the little packet Max had given her. She discovered she wasn't the only one holding on to items of value, except while hers were from the past, Max's were from the present. She rose and stepped back. He'd shown her how to make the matches light on the small strip, having her try a couple.

"Goodbye, Brom. I loved you, but I need to live my own life now. In the present, or as present as I can get. There's more to life than your memory."

With practiced precision, she lit the match and threw it on the gown. It caught immediately. Tiny flames spread along the white cotton and in minutes, a small fire warmed the air. She reached her hands toward it. Small black ashes floated above the fire in the heat before gently falling to the ground. It was hard to watch the beautiful gown she'd spent so many nights sewing go up in flames, but the reason for its existence was no longer relevant.

Mesmerized by the flames, she felt nothing except the light breeze that rustled the dead leaves along the forest floor. The sound of the church door closing broke her reverie. "Hello?"

"Katrina?" Nora's red head peeked around the wall of the church.

"I'm just saying goodbye."

"What are you burning?" Nora approached cautiously.

"Memories."

Nora gave her a quizzical look before turning her attention back to the fire. She held her hands over it. "Oh, this feels good. It's so cold in the church."

"Why were you in the church?"

"Just getting it ready for the weekend." Nora kept her attention on the fire. "People are talking about how we are back in Oldtime. We assume you and Braeden didn't, um, decided not to…

"We had a fight."

"Oh. Do you think Braeden will return to play the Headless Horseman?"

Kat crossed her arms over her stomach, the pain in her heart too harsh to bear. "No, I don't."

"I'm sorry. You seemed so happy." Nora put her hand on Kat's arm.

Kat's throat closed and she nodded before returning her gaze to the dying flames. She should have done this long ago, but she'd never been like Brom, taking life by the tail and swinging it around. She was slow, methodical, taking each step carefully, at least until Braeden.

"I'd best get back and see how the girls are doing with the bread. Do you want to walk with me?"

Kat watched the smoke reach for the sky. "No, I'm going to stay until the fire is out." She glanced at Nora. "I don't want to take a chance it will run across the churchyard and into the trees."

"Very well. Don't stay too late." Nora lifted her skirts and started down the path toward the village.

Kat stared at the flames, holding back the tears at the reminder that she would never see Braeden again. She sat back down on the burlap bag and poked at the fire with a stick. Would Braeden quickly find someone else now that he'd given up on her, like Brom had? How could she erase her feelings for him? They were so new, too strong.

She had to live in the present. If her terrible mistake with Braeden taught her anything, it was she had to live now, and the first order of business was to lift the curse and help the people of Sleepy Hollow acclimate to Newtime.

She poked at the dying fire again, causing ashes to rise from the now-glowing red coals.

"I found you." Jurgen's voice as he walked across the bridge surprised her.

Lovely. He was probably searching for her so he could gloat. She ignored his approach and set about covering the smoldering ashes with dirt she dug with her stick.

He came to a stop on the other side of her little pile of ash, his tone kindness itself. "I've been looking for you. Your mom's table is complete. Would you like to deliver it with me?"

She didn't glance up. "No."

"But I'm sure she would like to see you."

She raised her gaze to his. "We spent all day together yesterday. Is that enough?" She threw down her stick and stood, irritated with Jurgen always needing to tell her what she should do. How did he know he had all the right answers?

He took a step back and put his hands out in front of him as if to ward her off. "Oh, I didn't know. I just thought if you wanted a ride, but if you just had a nice visit…"

He too held on to the past too tightly. He kept thinking he could have her when she didn't want him. She fisted her palms as her anger simmered. He wanted to keep them all here in Oldtime, especially her. "You need to understand something. Just because Braeden is gone doesn't mean I'll turn to you. In fact," she pointed at him, her finger shaking, "I am going to make every effort to discover how to lift this curse so we can live in Newtime with the rest of the world, because that is where we should be. This village should have disappeared long ago. It should have changed, the people should have had generations of family, and life should have continued."

"Now, Kat. You don't mean that." His voice was placating, irritating her even more. "You're just upset, but you'll come to see—"

"No. You're wrong." She advanced on him and he stepped back. "We are under a curse. That means being in Oldtime is a punishment for something. It is payment for something we did or someone did. It means—wait. That's it. We have to determine what we did and somehow undo it."

She grabbed the empty burlap bag from the ground and strode toward the path, leaving him behind. "Dame Vandend said it had to do with me. I need to figure this out."

## *Newtime—October*

Braeden sat in the back with the kids, their excitement for trick-or-treating catching.

"Uncle Braeden, why don't you come with us on Saturday?"

He chuckled and it felt good. "Because I don't have a costume."

"You can be the bad guy."

Michael covered his mouth with his hand. "Yeah. Luke, I am your father."

The boys laughed at the imitation of the character's deep voice.

Stephen turned in the front passenger seat of the van. "Or he could be the Headless Horseman."

"Yeah!" The boys started to pretend to ride horses using the pumpkin buckets they brought for the weekend as the disembodied heads, but Braeden tensed as he stifled the thread of exhilaration that wound through his body at the idea.

He stared hard at his brother. "I believe that's your role from now on."

"I'm more than happy to leave it in your capable hands, especially because I know how much you like to ride that devil horse."

"He's not a devil horse. He's perfectly well behaved."

Stephen snorted. "Yeah, and I'm as old as Grandmother. There's a reason he's called Daredevil."

Braeden looked out the window, the scenery a blur, but Kat filled his mind as she did every waking hour and every night at midnight for the past year. His resentment had long passed and in his heart was a dull ache that roared to life at night. Everything about her returned with a vengeance then. Her smile, her body, her kindness, her drive. She always had something to do. Was it motivation or a need to fill the time?

He couldn't fault her for her willingness to get her hands dirty. Her only fault was she still loved Brom. He'd hoped he'd found a woman who would love him for himself, but so far, that was not to be. At least he visited his family more often now. He had Reed to thank for that. He grinned. What would Reed think of Kat?

His eyes caught the highway sign as it sped by. *Sleepy Hollow.* What? "Stephen!"

The whole car quieted at his yell, but Marilyn kept driving, driving toward Sleepy Hollow.

His brother turned around again. "Yes. I'm right here. You don't have to yell. I think you've been spending too much time with my kids."

The boys giggled but Braeden didn't laugh. He was too focused on trying to breathe as icy fear sped through his body and froze his lungs.

"Braeden? What is it? You're as white as the Catskills in winter."

He struggled to relax his chest enough to pull in much-needed air. "You said you were going to visit friends for Halloween."

"We are."

"Then why are we headed to Sleepy Hollow?"

Stephen glanced at his wife before meeting Braeden's gaze. "Our friends live in Tarrytown. After years of coming to the festival, we've made a few good friends nearby."

"You failed to mention that."

"I thought I did. How else can I ride as the Headless Horseman since you won't?"

Braeden broke eye contact with his brother and stared at the roadside as it sped by. The trees were bare of leaves, much like his soul, stripped, exposed to the elements, only for him there was a blizzard brewing.

The boys began their chatter again, oblivious to the pain of their uncle. Braeden hoped they never experienced what he'd gone through, kept going through.

Stephen interrupted his thoughts. "You can stay at the hotel. There's no reason you have to visit Sleepy Hollow unless you want to ride again."

The midnight ride on Daredevil called him. It was as if he were drawn to Sleepy Hollow. As the car sped closer, the pull grew stronger. By time they reached the hotel, his muscles were strained to their limits.

As soon as he dropped his bag in his room, he told the family he was headed for a walk and left. Marilyn's show of concern for him made his muscles tighten even more. She validated every feeling he had. Without a backward glance, he strode from the hotel.

His strides ate up the sidewalk, freeing his muscles to move, releasing the built-up energy pulsing through his body. He didn't pay attention to where he headed. He simply walked. After an hour, he looked up to find a road sign welcoming him to Sleepy Hollow.

He stopped and stared at it as if it were a monster that had suddenly appeared in his way. He tried to turn back, but he couldn't make the first step. The need to continue on was like the burning of his muscles when he hadn't exercised in weeks. It had to be appeased.

Running his hand through his hair, he glanced back the way he'd come. He couldn't go back. With his brain reconciled to the idea, it took his body half a second to respond. His legs carried him past the sign and into Sleepy Hollow.

# Chapter Fourteen

Newtime—October/Oldtime—Friday

Braeden found himself standing in front of the stables, the scent of hay enticing him forward. The sound of a horse from inside fired his reflexes, and he stepped into the dimly lit barn. Without thought, he strode forward to Daredevil's stall. The wily horse was already waiting for him and nickered as he approached. "How have you been, boy? I've missed you."

"Yah, probably more than he missed you, I'd guess." The rough voice behind him was well known and well liked.

Braeden stretched his hand out to stroke the stallion down his neck, but he turned his head to greet Ludo. "It's good to see you."

"Yah, and you. Does this mean you will be riding tomorrow night?"

"Yes. No. Ah shit. I don't know."

Daredevil swung his head away and shook it.

"Tch, tch." Ludo stepped to the horse and gentled him with a touch. "I don't think your horse is happy with your reply."

Braeden moved away. "He's not my horse."

"No, but he'd like to be. He was Brom's horse. No one has been able to ride him besides me until you came, but I can't handle him at a gallop anymore. My bones ache."

"You're the only one who can ride him?"

Ludo nodded.

Hell. If he didn't continue his role as Headless Horseman, Daredevil was doomed to sedate walks about town until one of Stephen's kids grew up. He didn't like that at all. The horse was meant to run.

"Come." Ludo lumbered away toward his tack room. "Have a drink. The setting sun is causing a nip in the air."

Braeden peered out the barn doors and noticed Ludo was right. The day had turned a blustery gray that darkened by the minute. He should let his brother know he wouldn't make dinner. He looked back at Daredevil, who watched him. Shaking off the horse's uncanny stare, he pulled over a hay bale and sat.

The stableman poured and they drank in companionable silence for the first two sips.

"You will have to see her." Ludo's comment, though vague, was clear and Braeden didn't pretend not to know what he meant.

"Will I?"

"Yah."

He took another sip of the scotch. "What good will it do? She still loves a dead man, and I don't want half her heart. I want it all."

Ludo stroked the side of his tin cup. "If you want her, then you should fight to have her. Would you give up so easy if you knew Jurgen was courting her?"

"Has he been bothering her?" Reflexively, Braeden crushed the tin cup in his palm.

"I don't know. I don't see either of them much."

"If he has caused her any trouble, I promise—"

"Promise what? You aren't here all week and if you stay in Newtime, you will age much faster than Jurgen."

Braeden stared at the mashed metal in his hand and slowly bent the cup back into shape, careful not to spill the liquid inside.

"If you loved her, you'd do what it takes to claim her whole heart. Trust me, being a part-time lover is not the answer."

Huh? What did old Ludo know about… Oh, that was why he was never at the barn at midnight. He was with his own female friend. "Who is she?"

Ludo stared out the barn doors at the growing darkness.

"Ludo? Who is it you care about?" He couldn't say the word "love", for that would mean that was what he felt for Kat and he couldn't go there. Not with her in love with a ghost.

The other man threw back the rest of his scotch and hissed. He set his cup down and interlaced his fingers before meeting Braeden's gaze. "Nora."

"The widow with the two young ladies?"

At Ludo's nod, Braeden whistled. "You have good taste, my friend. So why not ask her to marry you? I don't see a time glitch or a ghost standing in your way."

"I can't. She is only with me because she has no other options. I could never tie her to me, especially if there's a chance we could someday live in Newtime. If that happens, she could choose whoever she wanted and not be stuck with me."

"What? That's the craziest thing I've ever heard. Has she said she wants to find someone else?"

Ludo shook his head, his own conflict clear in his dark eyes.

Braeden raised his brows. "So where did you get the idea she is with you because you're her only option here?"

"Because she is always talking about getting the girls married in Newtime. I figure once she has accomplished that, she'll start looking for a man herself. I would just be in the way."

"Hell, you're more twisted up than I am." Braeden shot to his feet. "You just sat here and told me to fight for my woman, even against a dead man, while you aren't willing to fight for yours against an improbable future man?"

Ludo chuckled. "Hmm, I see what you are saying."

Braeden raised his cup. "Here's to us both. I, for one, am done running my thoughts into circles. It's time to claim what's mine." He swallowed what scotch was left, slammed the misshapen cup on the hay bale and stalked out.

The cooler night air freshened his spirit as he marched toward the Sleepy Hollow Inn. Lights inside illuminated the packed-dirt road and his feet slowed. Kat was everything warm and right. He had to force Brom from her heart.

He didn't want to have her only in dreams as he had for the past year. Luckily, over time, the nightmares and Brom's laughter had faded, and he'd been left with sweet, sexy dreams of Kat. He'd come to look forward to them, going to bed earlier in the hopes of longer dreams. In a way, he'd been no better than Kat. Living in a dream world, but his could become reality if he had the guts to take what was his.

Opening the door softly, he stepped into the inn and tapped the bell at the counter.

"Braeden." The tortured whisper escaped Kat's lips as she stared at the back of the man waiting at the counter of her inn.

He must have heard because he started to turn in her direction.

Panicking, she retreated two steps and swung around the corner of the hallway, plastering herself against the floral wallpaper. Her heart beat faster than the day she met him, and she folded her arms across her stomach as heat swept through her body and hope ignited in her soul.

It couldn't be him. She peeked around the corner. Yes, it was. He was here. She ducked back against the wall and tucked her stray strands of hair into her braid. She groaned as she looked at the blueberry stains soaked into her apron and onto her dress from making pies earlier. She should change.

The bell rang again.

"Hold your horses, I'm coming." Irritated at his impatience, she strode into the entryway. Her steps faltered as Braeden gazed back at her. She tried to restrain herself, but as soon as the corner of his lips quirked upward, she lost her control. She ran to him and he swept her into his arms.

Oh Lord, he felt so good. She pulled her head back from his shoulder and kissed him with everything she felt for him.

His tongue met hers and he drank from her mouth like a bee from a flower.

She riffled his hair as she inhaled the forest-like scent that was him alone.

He pulled away and gently set her down. One hand stroked the tears of happiness from her cheeks as the other held on to her waist. "I missed you."

She grinned like a darn fool. "I missed you too."

"I missed you more."

"You did not."

"I did. For me it has been months, while for you only a few days."

She sighed. "True. But it was I who hurt you. I was the one who made you angry. I was the one left behind. Again."

He lifted her lowered head. "I didn't stay away. Someone hit me from behind. By the time I regained consciousness, it was the next day and the village had disappeared."

"Jurgen."

"That was my thought as well."

She held tight to his light sweater, a new anger starting a slow burn. "It's time that man learned his place."

"Whoa, it's never a good thing to back a man into a corner. I think we should first make sure it was him. I was distracted by the sight of the black horse and rider heading toward me, which I had thought was Jurgen, but now I don't think so. We need to investigate."

She agreed with a slight nod, but in the back of her mind she planned a rather scalding cup of coffee for the man. If he hadn't hit Braeden, then they might have been able to reconcile. "Can you forgive me for what I did?"

She stared at him, anxious to see forgiveness in his eyes, but that wasn't the case. Something like determination appeared instead. She stepped back, but he kept his hand on her.

"Kat. You need to let Brom go. You need to let your past go. It's time to move forward, live in the present." His eyes pleaded with her as much as his words. He truly cared for her. He looked away. "Sometimes to do that you have to confront your past. Something I learned to do this last year."

"But Braeden, I—"

He put his finger to her lips.

She mumbled anyway. "Bub Ib albreaby bib."

"Shh. I think I know how you can confront your past and let it go, but you have to trust me. Can you do that?"

She nodded, but his finger remained where it was.

"Good." He smiled.

Her heart sped and her body flushed. Without thinking, she stuck her tongue out to lick the finger over her lips.

He jolted back, wary.

His reaction sent fear sliding through her body. "What's wrong?"

"Let's just wait until we're sure we have a future as well as a present."

She didn't like the sound of that but was willing to accept it… for now. "Fine. So did you need a room for the night?" She smiled shyly.

He ran his hand through his hair and she barely kept herself from sighing at his tousled look.

"No, I have to get back. I arrived with my brother and walked here, but he will be wondering where I've been."

He was leaving? "I don't understand."

"Honestly, I hadn't planned to be here, but I promise I will be back tomorrow, and I will ride as the Headless Horseman." He pulled her against him once again, hugging her to him as if he were afraid to let go.

She grasped him around the waist, anxious yet unwilling to push him but needing to feel him close. She'd been the one to ruin their courtship. She had to take what he could give right now. When he pulled away, she reluctantly let him go.

He took her hand and walked to the door. "Trust me when I say I want this to work for us."

"I trust you, but that's because I love you."

His face tightened and fear settled against her heart. "I will see you tomorrow." He gave her a chaste kiss goodbye and slipped out the door.

She stared at the closed portal as doubts assailed her. His withdrawal was palpable. Did he fear her calling him Brom again? Did she?

She searched her heart for the answer. Only Braeden was there and she grinned. She *could* win him back.

But first she had to get him to admit he loved her in return. That he desired her was clear, but that was also where his hesitancy stemmed from. Maybe some feminine wiles would help. Though what hers were, she wasn't sure. Perhaps it was time to ask for help.

Before she lost her nerve, she walked back to her room, donned her cloak and headed outside. Her fast pace helped keep her warm as she strode toward the village and the beginnings of the festival.

As Braeden strapped on the torso of the Headless Horseman, he hoped the crazy plan he thought of after talking to Ludo last night would work.

Kat's sultry look during the day had his cock in a constant state of readiness, but every time he thought to act upon his need, the memory of her calling Brom cooled his ardor.

It was as if she'd purposefully enticed him. The dress she wore to the festival when they met with Stephen's family was one he'd never seen before and it fit her curves in all the right places. When it became warm, she'd pulled off her shawl, as she called it, and exposed her low square neckline along with her bountiful assets.

Opening her armoire, he used her mirror to hook the black cloak around the neck of the Headless Horseman's frame. He paused and inhaled the scent of warm brownies, which only made his hunger for her stronger. He could have resisted all the beautiful, tantalizing things about her today if she'd kept her hair in her usual braid, but with her flaxen strands loose down her back with only a ribbon to keep them away from her face, he'd been lost.

He couldn't help finding secluded spots throughout the day to kiss and touch her.

He didn't put it past her to be seducing him. Even those around him had been set back by her appearance. As he pulled on the black gloves of the costume, he grinned. Watching Jurgen's reaction had been perfect, but the best had been when Irwin Crane hadn't realized it was Kat. As they walked by, she said hello and for once, Irwin had been struck dumb. For Braeden, it had been Kat's soft giggle in response that melted his heart. For such a beautiful spirit, she was rarely appreciated.

The door to her room opened and she entered. "Is this how these pants are supposed to look? I thought they were a skirt until I put them on. They're quite strange."

Braeden stilled. She twirled around in the wide, black gaucho pants he'd found at a secondhand store. The pants were snug on her curvaceous ass, but spread wide from the juncture of her thighs. The pale-blue silk blouse he'd purchased matched her curious eyes, and her sunlit hair continued to move after she'd stopped spinning.

He cleared his throat, which had suddenly gone tight. "Yes, that's how they are supposed to fit. Come here."

"I can't see you. Where's your head?"

He flipped the drape over the frame before reaching for the buttons at her neckline. He buttoned one more.

"Is that how far up it's supposed to go? From what I've seen of Newtimers, most of the women have the shirts unbuttoned farther."

"That's fine for them, but tonight, you need to be buttoned up. I also need you to put your hair back into a braid."

Her bottom lip came out to pout. Where the hell had she learned that? All he wanted to do was suck on it. He moved his gaze away.

"But I thought you liked my hair down."

In a split second, he was holding her by the shoulders. "I do. I like it for me. But I never want you to wear it down in public again."

Her startled expression at his touch became hard. Her back stiffened.

Ah shit. He tried a more cajoling tone. "Please. I want that to be special, for just the two of us." He stroked her cheek with his thumb, barely keeping himself in check. If he gave in now, he'd never be sure of her.

She turned her head and kissed his palm. "Fine."

He breathed a relieved sigh and stepped away, the feel of her lips still burning his hand. Grabbing the new-and-improved pumpkin head from the bed, he tested its contours for the best hold. Stephen had outdone himself this year. The pumpkin's face moved and cackled, as well as lit up. He liked the texture of it better than the others too, and it was finally big enough. He would watch where he left it this time.

"Is this better?" Kat held her arms out for inspection, her long hair neatly braided and resting over her shoulder.

"You're perfect."

She blushed prettily. "So, now will you tell me why I had to dress like this?"

He threw the drape back over the frame and took her hand in his. "Come and I will show you."

They walked behind the inn and the pub and all the shops that lined the road. When they came to the end of the buildings, he slowed and crept along the side until they reached the dirt road, directly across from the stables.

He squeezed her hand and whispered, "It wouldn't do for the Headless Horseman to be seen before his ride."

She nodded in the darkness, her top half in the pale silk clearly visible in the limited light of the quarter moon.

Again, he hoped his plan worked. Swallowing hard, he looked both ways to be sure no stray pedestrian was anywhere near before they sprinted across the road into the barn. As usual, Ludo wasn't there, for which Braeden was thankful. The last thing he needed was for the man to talk him out of his insanity.

Daredevil waited outside in the back and raised his head as he caught their scent.

She whispered, "He likes you, doesn't he?"

Braeden didn't reply. His biggest concern was whether Daredevil would like Kat.

She stepped around him to pet the horse. The blasted stallion nuzzled her neck! So much for being worried about her riding with him.

She looked up at him as if she could tell where his face was. "Daredevil and I are old friends. I'm so glad he likes you too."

"Since you two already know each other, we can get going. Up you go."

"What?" She stepped back.

"I said up you go. You're going to ride with me tonight."

She shook her head. "I can't do that."

"Why not?"

"It's just not done. Never been done."

He put his gloved hand on her shoulder. "You won't be seen by anyone. This cape and drape will cover you. Why do you think I bought you black pants and had you wear black boots?"

"But no Headless Horseman has ever taken someone with him."

Her statement gave him pause. Not because he knew it to be

untrue, but at the fact she had known all the Headless Horsemen before him. His uncle, his grandfather, his great-grandfather. That knowledge was hard to accept.

"Braeden?"

"You're wrong." He raised his brow as one who knows all as if she could see him. "My brother has taken Marilyn with him a few times. That's where I got this idea."

"He has?" Her eyes lit with excitement.

"Yes. And weren't you the one telling me on our stroll today that tradition was nice but it shouldn't stop us from moving forward and living in the present? Isn't that why you and Max are planning to prepare the villagers for better integration with Newtime?"

Her arms came across her stomach and she worried her bottom lip.

He squeezed her shoulder, unable to move closer with the Headless Horseman frame. "Please, Kat. Come with me."

She hesitated, but finally dropped her arms and straightened her back. "Fine."

He loved hearing that word pass her lips. He wanted to kiss her, but couldn't because of the costume.

"Good. Now, up you go."

For such a short woman, she pulled herself up and over Daredevil's back with little help from him. He kept forgetting how strong she was from her manual labor at the inn. Handing her the pumpkin, he gathered the reins and hoisted himself up behind her.

Daredevil pranced but Braeden kept him steady. "Okay. Hand me the pumpkin and pull this drape over you."

"Oh Lord. I can still see. This is magic material." The wonder in her voice pleased him.

He chuckled. "No. It's just different from anything you have known. Now hold on to the pommel. Daredevil takes a fast pace and usually rears at the end of the square."

"I'm ready."

He grinned. His tough Kat was always ready. Giving Daredevil his head, they flew down the road toward the village. Once in sight of the people, Braeden turned on the pumpkin. Screams and squeals followed them as he headed through the crowd, the pumpkin making faces. When they reached the end, he turned Daredevil toward the square and laughed loudly as the horse reared.

When Daredevil came down on all fours, Kat gave a huff and they were off again. They continued along the path where a few brave souls waited, but once past the final festival goers, he slowed the horse to a stop.

"Okay, you can lift the drape now."

Kat threw the material aside and turned to look at him. Excitement radiated off her in waves. "By the saints, that was fun! I didn't know that was what it was like. No wonder you Van Brunts have loved playing the Headless Horseman."

He laughed. He couldn't help himself. The sheer exhilaration of the ride coupled with Kat's joy had him feeling more alive than ever. Certainly a lot more than the original Headless Horseman, may he rest in peace.

"Now I understand why Brom loved it too, but I can't see living every life moment like that." Kat placed her hand on his chest. "That's what Brom was like. Everything was big, brash, a competition, a reason for excitement."

Braeden looked down at her and threw the pumpkin head into the trees. This time he made a note of where he could find it, nowhere near the church, then grasped her hand against his chest. "I enjoy this ride for the specialness of it. I'm not an adrenaline addict. I don't crave this feeling on a day-to-day basis."

She leaned her head against their hands. "I'm glad."

A spot near his heart loosened a bit. This woman was all he wanted. If only he could have her completely. Looking over her, he could see the opening to the clearing in front of the church. He took a deep breath. "We still have more work to do, but you can stay undraped for this part. Daredevil is going to rear again and when he does, I want you to scream this time."

She sat forward. "You want me to scream?"

"Yes, and very loudly. Can you do that?"

"I guess. I haven't practiced much screaming."

He ran his hand down her arm, the silky blouse and his gloves denying him the softness of her skin. "Guess we'll have to work on that in bed tonight."

She squirmed in her seat, and he had a moment's satisfaction that he could affect her as much as she did him. Taking the reins in both hands, he started Daredevil into a walk. "Now, hold on."

As they moved forward, he ducked beneath branches. Once they cleared the path, the white ghost and horse appeared as usual and Daredevil reared high, much higher than he did for the crowd.

Kat's scream pierced the air.

The white horse and rider pulled to a sudden stop just as Daredevil was about to give chase.

Braeden sawed on the reins, causing Daredevil to sidestep onto the grass toward the ghostly figures.

Kat gasped. "Oh my God. It's Brom!"

# Chapter Fifteen

Kat's cry riveted the ghost's attention. It dismounted from the white horse and dropped the reins. The horse sniffed at the ground as if it would eat.

Braeden struggled to control Daredevil. Finally, the stallion quieted, though he quivered.

Carefully, Braeden jumped down while holding the horse. Every muscle in his body tensed as he turned his back on the ghost. He could only hope this would work. "Would you like to dismount?"

Kat fearfully stared at the apparition over his shoulder but nodded. She fell into his arms and he had to drop the reins to catch her. Daredevil remained where he was, though his eyes were wide and his nostrils flared.

Once Braeden set Kat on the ground, he turned and they faced the apparition together. He lifted the black crepe to better see the ghost. It was much brighter than he'd thought. And a lot more eerie up close. He clasped Kat's hand tightly, suddenly nervous about what the ghost could do to her.

The apparition approached.

"Brom?" Kat's awed whisper caused the ghost to smile before

it reached out a transparent hand to touch her cheek. Her eyes closed and she shivered.

Braeden couldn't stop a ghost from hurting her, no matter what strength he had, but it didn't stop his muscles from bunching or from squeezing her hand.

She opened her eyes to look at him then faced the apparition. "Brom, this is Braeden. One of your descendants. I love him."

The apparition turned as if it understood and stared at him a moment. It wasn't unfriendly but the sightless eyes were still a chilling aspect. Then the ghost of Brom nodded. When it reached forward, Braeden stopped himself from blocking Kat. The transparent hand covered both of theirs, and a bone-deep chill permeated his body.

The apparition floated back and touched its chest, then reached its hands out toward them.

"I think he just gave us his blessing." Kat didn't turn from the apparition to speak.

"Either that or he is asking you to let him go."

She snapped her head up to look at him in surprise before she turned back toward the ghost. "You're free, Brom. As am I. I will live in the present now with Braeden."

The ghost turned toward the church and pointed.

Kat shivered again. "Yes, I burned all my mementos of you including my wedding dress. It is a new time and it is my turn to live and love." She glanced up at Braeden even as she squeezed his hand.

He dislodged his hold and grasped her about the waist. "Really?"

Tears gathered in her eyes. "Really."

Laughter startled them from each other and they looked up to find the ghost of Brom remounted. The white horse reared and an answering neigh resounded behind them. Before Braeden could react, Daredevil was off.

They stood in awe, watching Daredevil race the ghost of Brom and his white horse across the clearing. As Brom's steed hit the bridge, he disappeared into smoke, his laughter fading along with the sound of Daredevil's hooves pounding the earth back to the stable.

With one hand, Braeden unbuckled the straps that held the Headless Horseman frame over his chest. Pulling the frame from his shoulders, he set it on the ground. He took Kat into his arms and brushed the tears from her eyes. His heart constricted at her sadness. "Are you sorry to see him go?"

"No." She sniffed. "I'm happy I finally had a chance to say goodbye."

He hugged her to him as the full weight of what she'd endured fell on him. In his own need for her to love him with her whole heart, he hadn't realized how much she'd been hurt. He hurt for her now.

He lifted her face from his chest, his confidence in his feelings strong. "You are the world to me. You have healed me and challenged me and made me a better person. I love your kindness, your beauty and your strength. Kat, I love you."

Her squeal of delight lifted his heart even as she pulled his head down for a cock-hardening kiss. He tangled her tongue with his, his mind conjuring a way to get her naked in the clearing.

When she needed to breathe, he lifted his head. Movement in the cemetery caught his eye. A figure hovered near one of the graves. Though the moon shed some light, it was difficult to see. Was it the dark rider?

"Braeden?" Kat's voice tugged at his attention.

He sucked in his breath as the figure slowly sank feet-first into the ground. All thoughts of lovemaking fled. He had no doubt what he'd just witnessed.

"Braeden, what is it? You look like you've seen a ghost, which I guess we have, but you didn't look like this."

He continued to stare at the spot, and Kat finally turned to look. "What are you staring at?"

"The Headless Horseman."

She turned back. "Huh?"

He moved his gaze to focus on her upturned face. "Nothing. We better get back to the stable or Ludo will send out a search party." A very real possibility he hadn't considered. Then again, with Kat, he rarely thought straight. He glanced once more toward the cemetery, then picked up the Headless Horseman frame.

Linking his arm with Kat's, he started them on the short walk back to the stable.

~~*~~

She could feel Braeden's gaze on her as she took out the braid he'd made her put in. The man was a contradiction, but she loved that he was just a bit jealous and wanted to keep her to himself. It had been fun dressing nicely for a day, but not doing her work made her uncomfortable.

Braeden didn't take his gaze off her while he unbuttoned the black silk shirt he wore as the Headless Horseman.

As his black tank revealed his muscular arms, she scanned the strength she loved so much and grew too hot. Work could wait for tomorrow, she had other "work" to do tonight. Reaching beneath the waist of her short gown, Kat untied the drawstring and let it flare out. With little hesitation, she pulled the material over her head and dropped it on her chest at the end of the bed. Her stays pushed her breasts up, exposing half her nipple beneath her thin shift.

She glanced down and watched the areolas pucker. When she

looked up, she found Braeden's gaze on her chest. Tingles started from her hard nubs and traveled to the juncture of her thighs.

But then Braeden reached behind his head and she stared as he pulled the black tank off and dropped it on the floor. His naked chest rose as he took a long breath in, and she enjoyed the view of his hard pectorals and washboard stomach above the black leather pants. She could scrub her clothes clean on his stomach.

"I'm going to make love to you, Kat."

His low voice caused her to lift her gaze. His lids were heavy, sending goose bumps along her arms. The desire for her in his eyes was like the winds whipping the sheets on the line, intense and sharp.

She took her own deep breath and buried her hands beneath her clothes, loosening the drawstring that held her undergarment. It fell to the floor, leaving her in her shift and stays. Braeden's gaze riveted once more to her chest beneath the thin material. With daring she didn't know she possessed, she put her hands on her hips and took a deep breath, pushing her already hard nipples up and over the stays to make them strain against the softness of her undergarment. "I hope so."

Braeden moved fast and she stepped back with her hands out to stop him. "Wait." She pointed to his leather pants. "I want those off."

He grinned wickedly. "Then take them off."

The challenge in his stance had her back straightening even more. "Fine."

Kneeling, she unbuttoned the top button and pulled down on the metal fastener. The smell of leather, horse and Braeden was heady, and she wavered as his cock sprang free. Taking his shaft in her hand, she looked up at him and licked her lips.

"Witch."

She stilled and drew back. Witch?

"What's wrong? I was teasing." He stroked her hair to ease her.

Her mind raced. *Of course.* "No, I understood simply by the way you said it." She smiled up at him, aware he could see into the neckline of her loosened shift to her exposed breasts. "But you just made me realize that Dame Vandend is a witch."

"Huh?"

"Don't you see? She is the one who knows Sleepy Hollow is under a curse and when I confronted her about a way to break it, she wouldn't say anything. She's the one who cursed the village! We have to make her tell, or I'm afraid of what will happen to us."

His eyes softened and her heart sighed in response.

"I like how intelligent you are as well as your beautiful body, but I'm thinking since it's late, maybe we should wait to call upon the grand dame tomorrow. Right?"

She nodded and released his hard cock. Tugging the leather of his pants down past his hips to pool at his feet, she grasped his shaft again before he could move and licked the underside.

He hissed. "Two can play that game, woman." He bent over her and untied her stays, which dropped to the floor. The lack of constriction was welcome, as were Braeden's hands as they latched on to her breasts through the thin material of her shift. "I want to taste every inch of your body. I will make you mine tonight."

The rush of blood to her sheath left her lightheaded, and she held his cock tighter before licking the head.

Braeden's hands moved to her hair, encouraging her, so she sucked the tip in and caught the edge with her teeth. She watched, fascinated, as the defined muscles in his thighs tensed and moved beneath his skin with his pleasure. He was hers. He loved her. The warmth that had camped around her heart at his declaration by the church surged to life now. Moving her mouth over his entire shaft, she swallowed, her throat squeezing his cock.

He moaned and his grip in her hair tightened. Tilting her head, she pulled more of him into her mouth until he was as far back as she could take him. She didn't move except to tongue the silky, hard shaft.

"Jesus, Kat." Braeden pulled away before she could react. "You make me so hot for you, I want to bury myself in your body." Gently, he helped her to stand. "I'm not going to rush this. I swear."

She smirked at his need to say it aloud. That she could make this huge man lose control had her feeling rather powerful, until he scooped her up and dropped her on her bed.

"Lord." She exhaled as she settled onto the quilt, the chill in the air defeated by the fire Braeden ignited in her body. As he climbed onto the mattress, he raised the hem of her shift up her legs, caressing her as he went, though he ignored the inferno that built within her core.

Sensually, he moved the soft material up her waist, over her breasts, forcing her to move her arms above her as he lifted the shift from her body and threw it across the room.

"You're totally mine." His look was possessive, territorial. "No more ghosts."

She sobered. "No more ghosts." Lifting her arms to him, she stared into his eyes.

He accepted her invitation and covered her from toe to head, his lips touching hers in a gentle kiss. He pulled back and stroked hair from her face.

"I love you, Braeden Van Brunt, current Headless Horseman of Sleepy Hollow."

His face tensed, more serious than she'd ever seen him be. "I love you, Katrina Van Tassel, proprietor of the Sleepy Hollow Inn. You were made for me."

She raised her brow. "Actually, you were created for me because I was born first and I am much older than—"

Braeden's lips cut off all verbal communication as his tongue invaded her mouth. She wrapped her arms around his neck and lifted her chest to press against his as he leaned on his elbows to keep from squashing her. She wanted him against her. She needed to touch every part of him, and she had to show him her words of love rang true.

He must have sensed her need because he lowered himself to more fully cover her.

She ran her fingers through his hair as his tongue commanded hers while her other hand stroked the deep grooves of his shoulder blades and back muscles and then wandered down to latch on to his taut ass.

He broke off their kiss and raised a brow at her.

She grinned. "I like your butt."

"You do? Well, all you had to do was say so." He lifted himself off her and lay on his stomach.

Surprised by his sudden change in position, she resituated herself to kneel next to him. The view was breathtaking in the lantern light. Small shadows fell in all the right places, wherever sinew met sinew. Could this beautiful man truly be hers? Could she keep him despite their difference in time? For how long?

She ran her hands down his back, reveling in the movement beneath his skin as she touched him. His faced was turned toward her and he watched. She rubbed the large muscles around his spine before bringing her hands down over his rounded butt and onto his tight thighs.

He groaned and she moved back to his butt and kneaded that perfectly shaped area, but it wasn't enough. She needed more. With no warning she crawled on top of him and fit her body to his, her hips just below his ass. She pressed her abdomen against the lower curve of his butt, as if she could crawl inside and be loved forever.

"Shit, woman, you're such a tease." He rolled over, easily trapping her beneath him once again. "I always plan to take my time with you and then you make me lose control."

She wrapped her arms around his neck, pleased to be exactly where she wanted to be. "It has been too long." She opened her legs wider. "Take me now. We can always go slow later."

He raised his brow. "I like the way you think." Lifting his hips, he positioned his cock at her opening. "Damn, you're so wet."

"Just for you, Braeden."

He hesitated. "Promise?"

Her heart crawled up into her throat and her sight blurred as she nodded.

His eyes searched hers, but then the corner of his mouth quirked. "Good." As the word escaped his lips, his cock plunged into her to the hilt.

She gasped in pleasure, tensing her sheath to hold him inside, loving his invasion and never wanting him to go. But he did go as he pulled back, only to thrust forward again, pressing into her, sending exciting pulses racing from her core to the ends of her fingertips nestled in his hair.

As he thrust, she lifted her hips and wrapped her legs around him, her heels resting on the backs of his upper thighs. The added tilt of her pelvis caused her clit to rub against the hair at his base, and his cock slid deeper, as far as it could go.

"Oh yes." Her hands found purchase in his shoulder muscles and she dug in, grinding herself against him.

Braeden's movements grew faster. One hand came up and grabbed her hair, turning her head so he could conquer her mouth as well as her quim. He was everywhere—in her, against her, moving with her.

Kat lost herself to the feel of Braeden's body and the love she had for him as he pumped into her, sending shocks of joy throughout her with every stroke as she held tight.

She moved her feet higher on his butt, to get him as deep as he could go, and his muscles tensed. Her breaths were mere gasps around his mouth as her body tightened in anticipation of his release. His mouth tore away from hers and he yelled, his hot seed filling every tiny crevice not yet taken by him and sending her over the edge into a mutual bliss. "Oh Braeden!"

His movements continued, holding her to her delight a bit longer before he slowed and rolled them onto their sides. It gave her the ability to take deeper breaths, ones she needed after such strenuous lovemaking. She smiled inside. They had truly made love. Her with her whole heart. The sweat on both of their chests proved their need to be connected.

He held her close even as his cock remained inside her, her leg on top of his, holding them together. This was what she wanted for the rest of her life, but how could that be with her village still cursed? What if there was another fight weeks later and Braeden aged ten years?

"Kat, you're frowning." He pulled her closer. "What are you thinking?"

"I'm thinking I don't want this to end. Do you?"

"No. Why would you think that?"

"Because we are in different times. What if we can't lift the curse and we argue and we don't make love?"

He grinned. "You mean have congress with each other?"

"Yes." She wrinkled her brow at the term. Already it seemed old-fashioned.

He tucked her head beneath his chin. "Don't worry, we will figure this out. I promise."

She lay listening to his heartbeat, which she found soothing when the clock in the hall struck twelve. It was Saturday night and they didn't need to make love to stay in Newtime, but she was glad they had.

"Hey." He let her lean back a bit. "If we make love now, we can be sure to keep Sleepy Hollow in Newtime for Monday."

She pretended to ponder the thought. "Hmm, but what if that doesn't work because the new 'day' hasn't started yet?"

"Then we can make love again in the morning just to make sure."

She stared into his warm eyes and smiled. "Fine."

Kat squeezed Braeden's hand as the door opened.

"Oh Kat. I thought you said you don't need me today." Max stood in his breeches and shirt, his feet bare despite the colder air.

"I don't, but I—we came to see your grandmother."

"Oh right." He stepped back, allowing them to come in before he closed the door again. The air in the main room wasn't much warmer. No fire blazed in the fireplace.

"Grandmother is in the kitchen."

She thanked him and watched in puzzlement as he disappeared into his room. Wouldn't he be curious about why they were there?

Braeden bent and whispered, "Stephen charged his book reader. I bet he's reading."

Ah, that made sense. "The kitchen is right through that doorway."

"After you."

She hesitated. All morning she'd been anxious to come, pacing until Braeden had come back from his fruitless search for his latest pumpkin head. He really liked that one and had been so disappointed it was gone. But now that she faced having to convince the old woman…the witch, to tell her how to lift the curse, she couldn't help but be nervous about the success of the venture.

"Kat?"

She looked at Braeden and found her backbone. He was worth whatever terrible event she might have to participate in to keep him. That Dame Vandend had divulged that much did give her some control. Straightening her shoulders, she led the way into the kitchen.

As they entered, the change in temperature was immediate. The kitchen, warm and cozy, held Dame Vandend, who sat in a comfortable chair, her feet resting on a small bench. In fact, it was so warm, the window to the backyard had been opened a hand's width to allow fresh, cool air in.

Kat studied the woman for a moment. The old lady in front of her wasn't her idea of a witch. Maybe she was wrong.

"Yah, Kat and the Newtimer. To what do I owe the pleasure of this unannounced visit?"

Braeden stepped forward and bowed, taking the woman's hand. "Ah, madam, I do believe you already know the answer to that question." He gave her old knuckles a squeeze before he moved to the side of the window and leaned his shoulder against the wall, folding his arms across his large chest. His stance told them he expected some answers.

Dame Vandend twitched in her seat and turned her head to face Kat. "You have a handful in that man. Are you sure you can handle him?"

"I handled Brom, didn't I?"

The old lady chuckled. "Yah, you did that, but you were supposed to stay a maiden." She lapsed into an awkward silence.

Kat pulled a chair out from the wooden table and made herself comfortable. So that was why Dame Vandend had called her a maiden. She thought Kat still was, so the chance of her making love to Braeden and keeping them in Newtime would be small. Thank the Lord she hadn't waited until she and Brom had wed.

She had one answer now but she didn't plan on leaving until they had them all. It was the last day of the festival, and if the lovemaking session she and Braeden had engaged in this morning satisfied whatever curse had been leveled on the village for another day, then she wanted it to be a productive day. Not that she minded staying abed with him until noon, but since the curse hinged on her somehow, she planned to discover what she could do to lift it.

She glanced at Braeden. He watched her, brow raised. Could he tell what she was thinking?

He returned his gaze to the old woman, who wouldn't look at either of them.

"I didn't know it would work," Dame Vandend whispered, her voice hoarse, as she continued to avoid eye contact with either of them.

When Braeden remained silent, Kat couldn't wait any longer. "What do you mean?"

The old woman finally looked at her, a bit of fear in her eyes.

"The curse. I was visiting Sarah Prudett." She shrugged. "I was just curious, with all the talk of witchcraft and such."

"So you learned how to curse the village from her?"

"Yah. But I never would have thought of such a complicated curse with so many details and requirements." The old woman's eyes lit with excitement, her eyebrows twitching. "It was very smart. I just added my own touches, like making the Van Brunt descendants very, very strong to cause problems with courting."

Braeden's eyes widened before he scowled. He was obviously trying to figure out what his family had to do with it.

They were, however, making progress toward their goal. All Kat wanted to know was how to lift the curse, but since the old woman was at least talking, she didn't want to stop her. "So you had help?"

"Help?" She laughed. The truth be told, it sounded more like a cackle to Kat and she barely kept herself from putting her hand over her heart. She could suddenly believe Dame Vandend was a witch.

The old woman continued. "No, he didn't help except to tell me what he wanted and get me what I needed, like a lock of your hair."

Kat gasped and grabbed her braid where it lay on her left shoulder. "My hair? Who wanted a lock of my hair?"

"Not who. What. For the curse he designed. I needed a lock of your hair because you are the pivot point."

Kat looked at Braeden with concern and he met her gaze, subtly shaking his head. Her panic calmed at his confidence. "So who designed the curse?"

"Ichabod."

"Why would Ichabod curse me? We were friends. He even gave me singing lessons."

The old woman's laughter this time was purely evil, and Kat shivered.

"Friends? That isn't what Ichabod felt. He thought you would marry him and your family's farm would be his. He'd been biding his time, looking for the right moment to ask you. He had to be sure Brom wouldn't influence you, but then Brom chased him off. Humiliated him. He wanted revenge."

"*God in de Hemel.*" Kat stared at Dame Vandend in shock. All these years they had been caught in Oldtime because Ichabod felt humiliated? "But Ichabod died years ago. Why are we still cursed?"

The old woman smirked, turning her worn face into something resembling a frog. "Because he had children."

"What?"

"I was paid for my curse. Ichabod did well for himself and continued to pay me. When he passed, he left instructions for the next generations and so I have grown as rich as King George."

Kat stared. Every villager's life had been put on hold for revenge and greed? It was too much to stand. The curse needed to be lifted. Now.

She started to rise but Braeden's expression stilled her. Taking a deep breath, she sank back to her seat. Anger at the woman's selfishness and being unable to express it had Kat digging her nails into the chair beneath her.

Braeden looked at the run-down kitchen, and she saw what he saw. He spoke. "Then why don't you use the money?"

"Maxwell. It is for him to have so he can live in comfort when he finds a woman I can approve of. For now, this is enough. If we lived better, then people would talk."

Kat shook her head. The woman's thinking baffled her. "But Max wants only to be in Newtime. He won't even look at a woman in that way because his mind is on the progress and evolution America has come through."

Dame Vandend frowned. "Yah. I know. I must get his mind off Newtime."

"Don't you see? You can't. He belongs in Newtime. He is intelligent and already knows so much about it that he will never be satisfied with Oldtime. We must make it possible for him to live in Newtime, or you will never see him marry. If I can help make that happen then you must tell me what I can do."

Dame Vandend frowned and studied her hands. She remained silent a long time.

Kat clasped her own hands together, despite how sweaty they were. When the old woman shook her head, Kat wanted to scream.

"If the curse is lifted, I will not last very many more years."

"But if you do last a lot longer, what will happen when you die and you take the solution to the curse to your grave?" Kat barely kept herself from growling at the woman.

"I can tell you before then."

"But how old will Max be then? Thirty? Forty? Alone?"

The old woman's face fell and Kat's hope rose.

The sly witch then looked toward Braeden, her expression shrewd. "I could tell if I was compensated for my words."

Braeden answered her directly, his gaze hard. "No. You will not gain more money with this immoral curse you have brought upon these people. Does your greed know no bounds? You will tell because you know it's the right thing to do. Remember, if the curse involves Kat then she must also be young enough to fulfill her part of it."

"Oh." The old woman was clearly startled, so focused on her own world she neglected to realize that despite being in Oldtime, her fate was still connected to others. "Very well."

Kat's heart pounded with anticipation and nervousness. What would she have to do? Swallow a toad? Jump in Cramer's brook fully clothed and stay there all day? Catch a bat? Could she do whatever it was? She glanced at Braeden and despite his relaxed expression, she could feel his tension. "Thank you. Now what must I do?"

"First, you must fall in love."

She gazed at Braeden and smiled. "Fine. What else?"

The old woman smiled wickedly. "Then you must get the unanimous consent of the village to marry, and then marry."

That was it? She studied Dame Vandend. Why did she look so smug?

Braeden's stare at the witch was hostile. "And if we get the consent of the rest of the village to marry, you will also agree?"

The old woman's shoulders sagged. "Very well. I will agree."

The sound of reins hitting a horse outside startled all three of them. Braeden turned toward the window just as black forelegs rose before it and then a blur of black moved past. Braeden was out the back door and after the rider before Kat reached the opening, but he stopped at the old fence the rider had jumped over, the black horse galloping headlong into the forest.

Braeden watched a moment longer before returning to the house.

"Did you see who it was?" Kat studied his serious face.

"No, the rider wore a black hood, but I noticed other things that clued me into the identity. We will talk privately about those."

She glanced over her shoulder to see Dame Vandend had risen from her chair and listened intently.

Kat nodded once to show him she understood. She stood aside to allow him into the kitchen again. "Whoever it was, they heard what it would take to lift the curse."

"Yah." The old woman cackled. "I may not be the only one unwilling to move into Newtime."

Gritting her teeth in frustration, Kat gave the woman a frown. "You keep forgetting this is in the best interest of Max. You do at least care for him, don't you?"

Braeden touched her shoulder and gave it a slight squeeze. "I think we are done here. Let's go." He turned toward the witch and nodded once. "Have a nice day."

As they strode home, Kat couldn't help but ask Braeden about his final comment to Dame Vandend.

He chuckled. "It's a common expression in Newtime, and I know she is worried she may be living in that time period soon, so I decided to give her something to think about."

She still wasn't sure she understood, but she didn't mind. Just being able to walk the lane with their arms entwined had her feeling better. As they passed by Hans and Ludo's place, she noticed the older man's dog gnawing on something. Pulling Braeden closer to that side of the lane, she stopped.

"What is it?"

"I don't know. Wait." She laughed as relief flooded through her. "It's the bucket that Max tripped over. Hans' dog took it."

Braeden's eyebrow rose. "And that's a good thing?"

"Oh yes." She smiled at him as she urged him to continue their walk home. "That means when the bucket disappeared, it wasn't a ghost or a bad omen of things to come. Just a dog being a dog. That's very important here in Sleepy Hollow."

"I have noticed strange occurrences seem to be the norm here."

She squeezed his arm. "Of course. That is part of the charm."

"Kat."

Something in the tone of Braeden's voice caused her to stiffen. "Yes?"

"The lifting of the curse is dependent on us getting married."

Oh Lord, she hadn't even thought about how he might feel about that. He said he loved her, but many a year could go by before he might feel inclined toward a betrothal, if he would be interested at all. She kept her comment neutral. "I know. That is an important commitment."

He stopped them and stepped in front of her. "You know I love you, and you have said you love me."

She nodded, her throat refusing her the ability to speak.

"You need to know I have never felt this way about any woman. In fact, you're the only woman I've been able to have a relationship with beyond sex."

He glanced away and her heart lurched. She waited for him to explain there was a problem. She could sense it coming and she wanted to stop him, but no words would form.

# *Chapter Sixteen*

Braeden ran his hand through his hair, which made her more nervous. He stared hard at her. "You know who I am. You like me." The intensity of his gaze when he said those words was almost too much to hold. "But you know I have this issue with my strength. That witch in there cursed me as well. If the curse is lifted, I have no idea what my physical abilities will be like then. I could become as weak as Ichabod Crane even. I-I don't want—"

She lifted her free hand to touch his face. "You're worried if we were to marry that I would no longer find you physically attractive."

He nodded, his relief at her understanding palpable.

Her own relief was far more substantial. She loved him for his caring heart far more than for his substantial muscles. "What about me? I know nothing of Newtime. If we do break the curse, you may grow cross with me for not understanding certain things or for behaving incorrectly. Your brother has told me of your success. You are an important man."

He smiled, a gentle look entering his eyes. "For such strong personalities, it appears we both have our insecurities. I can promise to be patient with your learning curve, if you can promise to tell me if my body no longer attracts you. Will you do that?"

She touched his face, undone by his insecurity. "I will."

Braeden lowered himself to one knee in the middle of the dirt road. "Katrina Van Tassel, will you marry me?"

Her eyes watered as she gazed upon the man that was her heart. "Yes. Definitely yes, Braeden Van Brunt."

He stood, picked her up and twirled her around. "Yesss!!" His shout echoed in the trees and a flock of birds took flight.

Her heart filled with joy as she laughed.

When they stopped spinning, he set her gently on her feet and cupped her face. "I love you, soon-to-be Mrs. Van Brunt." Before she could reply, his lips were on hers, tasting her, claiming her as his. She wrapped her arms around his neck and kissed him in return with all the love she had for him.

He broke away suddenly, and she held on to keep from falling. "What is it?"

"I need to get you an engagement ring."

"Well yes, but—"

He unhooked her hands from around his neck and held to one as he started to propel them toward the village. "I need to get one right now. Come on, we have to hurry. I want to run into town and be back in the village before nightfall."

Kat's mind spun at his insistence and hurry, but she didn't bother to try to understand. The fact was, the man she loved wanted to marry her and that was all she cared about.

Kat fiddled with the beautiful diamond on her left hand as she waited for Braeden to finish dressing. It was a large octagonal stone with an intricate gold filigree around it that sparkled with diamond chips. Braeden informed her it was an authentic Victorian-era ring he'd discovered in an antique shop. His thoughtfulness about what she might like touched her, and she cried when he put it on her finger. She would never stop touching its beauty.

"Are you ready to face the crowd?" Braeden stood by the reception desk. His black jeans and gray long-sleeved chamois shirt made him look even bigger than he was and gave him presence. They would need that today.

"Yes, I am." She smoothed the folds of her long skirt. It was her best one. She wanted the village to see how important their vote was today.

Braeden wrapped her shawl around her shoulders. He pulled on a black leather jacket of a similar look to those she'd seen on Newtimers who rode the motorized bikes. He looked rather intimidating, and she liked that.

Opening the door of the inn, he allowed her to pass before ducking his head and following her. "Why are you smiling?"

She laughed. "Because you're quite good at bending under that door. I like that you're comfortable in my inn."

He grasped her arm in his and lowered his head as they walked to the village square. "I'm very comfortable in you too."

Heat rushed to her cheeks and she grinned, but as they drew closer, her happiness faded and she squeezed Braeden's arm harder.

There was no hesitation at all this time. A wide gap opened in the circle as they approached, but her papa stepped in front of them. He stared at Braeden a moment and nodded once before he hugged her to him. He whispered in her ear, "We believe in you."

She squeezed him back before taking Braeden's hand again to move to the middle of the circle, the speaker's place. They could do it. They had to be confident. She scanned the faces of those in the circle, mentally noting who might need convincing that they remain in Newtime and who would be willing. She was disappointed Nora wasn't there, but her daughters were. That surprised her. Nora would have been her biggest ally next to Max.

Braeden raised their joined hands and the sunlight glittered off her new ring. "I have asked this wonderful woman to be my wife, and she has agreed."

A cheer arose around the circle and Kat smiled, pleased so many were happy for her, though when she glanced at Jurgen, his scowl made his feelings clear.

After the noise died down, Braeden continued. "However, there's one issue standing in the way of our marriage and you can help. We have discovered how to lift the curse from Sleepy Hollow and keep the village in Newtime forever."

Many started talking at once. Kat strained to focus on different conversations. When Braeden moved to speak again, she held him back and pulled him down so she could whisper in his ear.

"What?"

"Let them chew on this a bit longer. They need to discuss it before we tell them more."

He nodded and waited until she nudged him. He raised his hand. "The curse can be lifted if Kat and I marry, which we wholeheartedly want to do." He gazed at her for a moment with so much love that she had to swallow hard. Her mother sighed and linked her arm with her husband's. "However, everyone in Sleepy Hollow must agree to this marriage because it will not only join Kat and I, but it will permanently join the village with Newtime."

"Whoop! I say go for it!" Max's jump in the air and strange expression didn't sit very well with the rest, but others did appear to be in agreement. However, many were not.

Ludo's dad spoke up. "We don't know anything about Newtime. How will we fit?"

Max answered, a bit calmer. "I can teach everyone. I have been following all I can and I can help."

"And," Kat paused until she had everyone's attention, "you already know quite a bit because we have interacted with Newtimers since the curse began. We know what kind of clothes they wear, what countries exist and some of the inventions they use. What we don't know we can learn with Max's help and Braeden's help. Besides, I don't think there's any rush."

"I say no!" Jurgen raised his fist. "This isn't right. It's not the way things are meant to be. All the signs are clear. Dame Van Brunt's fence fell down for no reason. My garden was trampled by the black rider. The black rider didn't even appear until *he* showed up." Jurgen pointed at Braeden. "Makes me wonder why. Could a ghost be coming back to take revenge on us staying in Newtime when we shouldn't, like today?"

Murmurs ran through the circle. She caught Dame Vandend smiling. Kat pulled Braeden down again. "We can't let this continue or more things will suddenly portend the worst."

He agreed, but before he could speak, someone shouted out that the Headless Horseman's pumpkins had all disappeared since Braeden had arrived.

Jurgen gloated. "Is this true? Your brother's pumpkins never disappeared, nor your grandfather's. Have all yours disappeared?"

Kat cringed at Braeden's fisted hand, a sinking feeling tightening her belly as he answered, "Yes, that's true, but I found the batteries of one."

"You found them?"

The female voice sounded loud in the utter silence after

Braeden's admission. All eyes turned to Liesbeth. When she noticed, she stepped back and tried to hide behind Max.

He turned and brought her forward to face Kat and Braeden, but he held her hand "Liesbeth, if you know something about the pumpkins, it's very important you tell everyone."

She wouldn't look at anyone, so Max lifted her chin. "Please, tell us."

Her gaze was so agonized Kat wanted to turn away, but the young woman's response was far too important.

Liesbeth continued to look at Max. "I was collecting them so I could give them to you for your birthday. I thought if I gave you something from Newtime, you would notice me as more than a friend."

The village was silent as Max's eyes widened. "You mean you took them for me?"

She nodded.

Kat tensed. *Please, Max, see how much this girl cares for you. Open your eyes.*

"And you did it because you like me?"

The woman blushed and lowered her eyes as she nodded.

"Right." Max's befuddled expression would have been laughable if his understanding of the situation wasn't so critical to Liesbeth's heart.

Kat tried to step forward but Braeden held her back and shook his head.

The silence was deafening while Max looked at Liesbeth and perhaps for the first time saw her for the beautiful woman she had come to be. He lifted her chin again. "I didn't know. I'm humbled and…very, very glad." His broad smile caused the poor woman to sway, but he held her up like a gentleman and put his arm around her waist before speaking to everyone. "I guess those missing pumpkins have no bearing on Braeden being a curse. The way I see it, we should all vote yes on this marriage and lift the curse."

Kat's heart soared as she heard conversations agreeing and witnessed heads nodding until Jurgen's voice broke through again. "But what about the black rider? He only rides when Braeden is here."

"That's not true." Kat spoke quickly, not willing to let the tide turn again. "I was almost run over by the black rider during Oldtime. That could very well mean the rider was aware Braeden and I were falling in love and was trying to stop the curse from being lifted."

"And as for Dame Van Brunt's fence," Braeden paused, "I discovered it didn't simply fall down. Someone kicked it until it broke."

Jurgen scowled. "How would you know that?"

Braeden stared hard at the man. "Because the shoe print was left in the soft wood where the rail was split in half."

People started whispering again and looking at Jurgen's feet. Kat took the opportunity to try to use reason. "I say it is time we joined the rest of the country. Let our young find their way in the current world to live a full life instead of growing old, alone, in Oldtime after we are gone. This is our only chance. I am the one who must marry, and I will marry no other than Braeden Van Brunt."

Braeden squeezed her hand while they watched many nodding and talking excitedly. Dame Vandend sat sullen on her bale of hay, but other than that, it looked as if they might get the vote they needed. Kat's only question was Jurgen and his friends. She scanned the crowd where he'd been standing but he wasn't there. As she searched the rest of the circle, she spotted smoke rising from Jurgen's furniture shop.

"Fire!" She pointed and people quickly turned.

Her father yelled out "bucket line" and people scattered.

Kat grabbed Braeden. "You should man the water pump. No one else has your kind of strength."

"Got it." He ran for the pump as she raced for a bucket. She'd just reached her yard when a hand closed over her mouth with a piece of cloth and everything went dark.

Braeden pumped as fast as the villagers could put the buckets under the spout. He didn't see Kat but the bucket line was long. The place going up in smoke was Jurgen's. It was ironic that he was trying to save Jurgen's shop, but a fire was a fire and could spread. Besides, he doubted there would be a fire engine rolling up to help any time soon.

At a brief pause, he whipped off his shirt and soaked it to cool his heated body. While the pump wasn't difficult, the repetitive motion was muscle-numbing and he was thrilled when they called a halt. Word came back that the building was a loss but the fire was out and wouldn't spread.

Hours of pumping had taken their toll and he soaked his shirt again. As he covered his torso with cold water and wiped his face, he heard the sound of horse's hooves.

He spun to find the black rider heading straight at him, but this time he could see the face clearly since the hood was thrown back. He wasn't surprised to see Nora, but what concerned him was the fear on her face.

She stopped feet from him. "You have to help Kat. Irwin has taken her! Jurgen tried to stop him, but he's been shot."

Braeden looked over the people standing around and all the

pieces clicked into place. The fire was a distraction. Throwing his wet shirt on, he grabbed the saddle. "Hold on to the pommel, I'm coming up." He mounted Gunpowder and took the reins. "Where?"

"The stables. You can talk to Jurgen. I think he has an idea where Irwin might take Kat."

"Thanks. Now hold tight." Braeden kicked the beast into a gallop and raced down the dirt road. Nora squealed and grabbed the pommel tighter. He rode into the barn and dismounted in a heartbeat, leaving Nora to slide from the horse's back by herself. His stride took him to the man who sat against a tree out back.

When he stood before Jurgen, he clenched his fists, wanting more than ever to grab the man by his collar and yank him to his feet, but even he could see the growing blood stain on Jurgen's shin. That had to hurt like hell. Good. He kept control of his anger and his voice. "Where's Kat?"

"Irwin took her. He plans to wait somewhere until late tonight and then cross outside of Sleepy Hollow. You've got to save her! If she crosses after midnight, she will turn to ash unless you two had congress already today."

"Ah, fuck."

Jurgen's face paled as his last hope slipped away. "Go! But watch out. Irwin is mad and he has a gun. He's spouting about Ichabod's revenge and he's staying on this side of Sleepy Hollow until midnight because he wants to watch her dissolve. The bastard." Jurgen's face fell in defeat. "I never wanted to see her hurt." He lifted his gaze. "I love her."

"Yeah, so do I." Braeden turned to find Nora standing with Daredevil.

"I could only get the reins on him. I can't lift the saddle."

"Ludo usually does that for you, right?"

She blushed. "Yes."

He grabbed the reins and mounted bareback. "Don't worry, I'll get her back. Just tell me where to look."

After Jurgen gave him three possible places based on Irwin's ramblings, Braeden rode as if Brom's ghost were racing them. Daredevil seemed to sense his urgency and they whipped between trees and flew over rocks. After looking in the first spot, an abandoned cabin, he felt the chill of the night air. He'd taken his watch off when he pumped the water but he'd stuffed it in his back pocket. Letting Daredevil walk toward a small stream to drink, he pulled it out. It was already after eight and he had two more places to check, *if* Jurgen was right.

Braeden refused to contemplate possible failure. He'd not found Kat just to lose her. That was not an option, but shit, he'd had no idea Sleepy Hollow was so big. Not knowing exactly where he needed to go didn't help either. "Come on, Daredevil, we have to find her." He didn't blame the villagers for fearing to go near the boundaries after dark. From what Nora said, no one knew precisely where the lines were and so stayed inside at night.

After another hour, Braeden exited a cave made from boulders low in the ground. A partial moon made the outside lighter than the interior of the cave, but not by much. He still had one place left. Pulling out his watch, he grimaced. It was almost ten. Not only did he need to find Kat and take care of Ichabod, he also had to make love to her by midnight. He'd settle for no sex and wait a year as long as he knew she was still alive, but even as he willed himself to make that sacrifice, he refused to accept it. The last place was an old schoolhouse. She had to be there, and he had to find it.

He stroked Daredevil, the strong horse starting to show signs of weariness with the unusual amount of exercise. "Not much longer. We're going to find her."

Daredevil nickered in response and Braeden smiled. "I wish you could tell me she will definitely be there. You were in the original story, so you should know."

The original story. "Of course. Ichabod was the old schoolmaster in that story and Irwin would know that. Thanks, Daredevil." He patted the horse, who seemed to perk up at the praise. "To the schoolhouse!"

Daredevil took off like a cannonball from a cannon, reminding Braeden of the story Irwin had told him about the real Headless Horseman. When he finally found the half-gone school building, he sensed Kat's presence though there was no light shining from inside. Relief at finding her flooded his limbs, causing him to stumble as he jumped from Daredevil's back. Shaking off his emotions, he crept toward the building. The back half had caved in, though the front looked as if it still stood intact, despite the weathered wood.

"Who's out there?" Irwin's nasal voice sounded loud in the darkness.

Braeden dropped into a crouch.

Kat's voice came clearly from inside. "Irwin, how many times do I have to tell you? There are no ghosts out there. Why don't we go back to town? You'll feel safer there."

"I'm not stupid. I know there are ghosts out here. I listened to the tales from my grandfather about how Ichabod fought off the Headless Hessian and escaped capture."

"Irwin, that was Brom acting as the Headless Horseman. There is no such ghost."

Though he now knew Kat was incorrect, Braeden just hoped he wouldn't see proof of that tonight.

If Irwin was afraid of ghosts, he could work with that. Quietly, he removed his shirt. After tying the sleeves, he filled it with leaves.

Twice as he did so, Irwin yelled out and Braeden stopped. When he was done, he tied the bottom of the shirt. Thankfully, he had a large shirt, so it did look like a headless torso.

Climbing up a tree just out of sight of the doorway and Irwin, Braeden set the torso on a limb, but when the branch moved, it began to fall. He grabbed the shirt just in time, his heart racing at the possibility of being shot from the tree before saving Kat. Shit.

If he had a rope, it would make his plan a lot easier. He looked at his boots, but he wasn't sure the laces would hold. Ah, but his belt. In no time, he secured the torso to hang from the branch and climbed back to solid ground. He crept around the back of the schoolhouse. As he came up on the right side, he caught sight of Kat between the slats of the wall. She was tied but he could see her working at her ropes while Irwin stared outside. *That's my girl.*

Continuing to the front edge of the building, he took a deep breath. Hefting a rock he'd found on the ground among the leaves, he threw it hard. It hit the trees and fell into the leaves, making a good loud noise. Daredevil neighed in response.

Irwin stuck his head out the front door and froze at the sight of the torso.

Braeden lost no time. Jumping onto the porch, he tackled Irwin from behind. He pulled at the gun in the man's hands and twisted. Irwin squeezed the trigger as Braeden slipped it from his grasp and the gun exploded.

Kat screamed and Daredevil charged. Braeden barely had time to knock Irwin out before Daredevil's hooves hit the porch. Braeden plastered himself against the wall as the horse barreled by. "Daredevil!"

The stallion slowed and turned. "It's me. I'm okay. Are you?" The horse snorted, bouncing its head up and down, still prancing a bit. Braeden swore it understood every word he uttered. Daredevil calmed and walked back, showing no sign of injury.

"Hey, who's out there?"

At the sound of Kat's voice, Braeden ran inside.

"Braeden!"

He turned to find her lowering a mean-looking piece of wood with nails protruding from it. She'd escaped her bonds. "Ah Kat, I thought I would lose you." His heart threatened to beat outside his chest as his fear overwhelmed him.

She dropped the board and he grasped her to him like a lifeline. If he'd lost her, he'd lose his reason for living.

Irwin moaned, reminding him he still had clean-up to do. As much as he didn't want to let Kat go for a moment, he disengaged from her. "Let me get him tied up and on his way to the village. Ludo will take care of him. Stay right there?"

She nodded and he went outside, making short work of tying Irwin to Daredevil. "Take him home, boy."

He patted the horse on the rump and Daredevil snorted before trotting off back toward town.

Braeden pulled his watch from his pocket. Pressing the light on it, he stilled. It was 11:33 p.m. He rushed back into the schoolhouse.

Kat brushed dust and cobwebs from her skirt. He grabbed her hand and pulled her outside. She stumbled, so he scooped her up in his arms.

She laid her head against his shoulder. "I'm sorry. My legs aren't working properly yet after being tied for most of the day."

"That's okay. For what I want to do now, you won't need to stand for long." Finding a relatively clear area, he set her against a tree, then kicked and pushed as many leaves as he could into a pile. He came at her with a purpose. "Strip."

"What?"

"Take off your clothes and hurry. We need to make love in the next twenty minutes or you will disappear from me for another year and I can't…"

"Oh Braeden. I didn't realize it was so late." She'd already untied her skirt and as it fell, he spread it over the leaves. When he looked back, only her shift remained and he divested himself of his jeans, underwear and shoes. "Come here."

She wobbled over on unsteady legs and he lifted the light fabric from her body. She shivered, the cool air making her nipples hard and erect. He wanted to love every inch of her, but that would have to be later…again.

He grabbed her to him and held her tight. He'd almost lost her forever. The reality struck him so hard his eyes watered. "God, Kat. I don't ever want to let you go."

She mumbled against his chest and he loosened his hold. "What?"

"I said I don't want to let you go either, Braeden. I want to make love to you. Now."

He gently laid her down on their makeshift bed. The limited moonlight reflected in her pale hair, making it almost glow. A dark mark just beneath her right eye caught his attention. He dropped down to inspect. "Did he hit you?" Fury washed over him.

She touched the spot with her fingers. "No. I did that trying to get away from him. Knocked my face on the saddle."

His body shook as the unneeded adrenaline rush sped through it and his respect for her rose another notch. She was no coward. He loved that about her. That and so many other things. He softly kissed the bruise. "I will never let anything happen to you again. I promise."

She raised her arms to him. "I know."

Her gaze proved her words and his heart swelled with her confidence in him. Accepting her invitation, he lay over her and cradled her face between his palms. "I will never let you go." Lowering his lips to hers, he poured all his love for her into his kiss.

Kat grasped him to her, proving her feelings were the same. The adrenaline that coursed through his veins coupled with his fear of losing her had him ravishing her mouth, desperate to have all of her.

She must have felt the same way. She pulled on his hair, forcing his face closer. He resisted, fearful of hurting her. He lifted his head to press kisses down her neck. "It's okay, Kat. I'm here now. I'll always be here."

She clawed at his naked back even as he encountered tear tracks on her cheeks.

"Please, Braeden."

The request was all he needed. He rubbed his hard cock along her moist entrance.

Her legs opened wider. "Darn it, Braeden. Now!"

Smiling inside at her spirit, he positioned himself between her open thighs and plunged into her, his lips claiming hers again.

Her body molded to his, letting no space between them as he pumped his cock into her tight softness, her moans filling his mouth and her scent overwhelming him.

His heart hitched. *She's all right.* The litany in his head ran on and on in rhythm with their lovemaking. *She's all right. She's all right.* Until her sweet surrender sent his thoughts soaring and left nothing but ecstasy behind.

## *Newtime—Tuesday Morning*

Kat and Braeden stood in the circle with the rest of the

village. As the previous morning's meeting had never finished, the meeting resumed, though in quite a different tone. Jurgen, hobbling in on crutches he'd made for Max just a week earlier, apologized and urged everyone to vote in their favor. He admitted to setting the fire as a distraction. He also revealed that Irwin had told him he would take care of Braeden, showing him the gun. Jurgen had kidnapped Kat to make sure Braeden followed, but when he heard what Irwin planned to do with her, he had tried to stop him.

Jurgen's tale had a number of people shaking their heads, but Kat publically forgave him. The villagers could be far too judgmental, and she wanted Jurgen to find someone else to love. That wouldn't happen if they all treated him as an outcast.

Jurgen left the center of the circle and approached, staring at Braeden. "I'm sorry. I couldn't accept she was in love with someone else."

Braeden extended his hand.

The man stood still a moment, obviously surprised, before shaking. Afterward, he looked at Kat. "Do you want to speak now?"

She was about to answer when another person made for the center of the circle. She grinned. "I guess I will have to wait until Nora is done."

"Nora?" Jurgen looked back before hobbling into the line of people.

Nora addressed them, her confident stance portraying she was proud to be there, so her words were a bit of a surprise. "Since we are confessing today, I also need to confess."

A number of people nodded. Kat glanced in question at Braeden, but he simply smiled.

"As many of you discovered yesterday, I am the black rider."

A murmur ran through the crowd and Kat turned to Braeden. "You knew? How?"

He lowered his head. "Her rose scent, her shoe size and her motivation."

"Huh?"

He ignored her and watched Nora.

The woman held her hands up for silence. "As you can see, I am not a ghost, nor was I trying to make it appear that Braeden had brought bad luck. In fact, my goal was the opposite."

"What was your goal?" Max yelled.

Kat rolled her eyes. That man needed Newtime and he needed it now.

Nora shook her head at him. "I would tell you if you would stop interrupting."

The villagers smiled knowingly, allowing Nora to continue.

"My goal was to make Braeden stay. We need to be in Newtime. My daughters," she pointed to the two almost-grown, pretty women, "will want to marry and have families one day. There are no men in this village of an age with them, except Max, whose only focus is Newtime, and now possibly Liesbeth."

The young woman blushed but Max smiled proudly.

"I want a future for my girls. I want to see them have a happy life like I have had or like I have now." She turned and focused her attention on Ludo. "I have been lucky in my life to fall in love twice, first with my husband and now with Ludo Van Ripper." She reached her hands out toward him.

The man strode forward to take them with no hesitation.

"I love you, Ludo. And I want everyone to know it. No more midnight courting."

He gazed at her, surprise as well as a hint of uncertainty on his face. "But you could find someone better in Newtime."

"There can be no better man than you in any time."

"Ah, Nora." He pulled her against him and kissed her.

Everyone clapped and Kat brushed happy tears from her eyes. She glanced up at Braeden to see a smug smile on his face. "You knew that too?"

He nodded. "As an outsider, I noticed different things than those of you within your circle."

"So why did you run down the Newtimer?" Janna asked.

Someone else joined in. "And tramp through Jurgen's garden?"

"And listen at my window?"

Kat added her question as well. "And why did you run me down when I came home one evening from giving Dame Van Brunt a ham and Hans Van Ripper's dog a bone?"

Nora addressed Kat first. "I'm sorry, Kat. Running so close to you was an accident. Gunpowder was spooked and I was trying to control him when we bounded out of the woods and there you were. I ran close to Braeden to try to keep him from leaving Sleepy Hollow. I didn't realize he planned to return. I trampled the gardens of those who wouldn't accept that the curse needed to be lifted."

"And you were coming to my aid," Braeden's voice was loud, "when Jurgen's men knocked me out."

"So you listened at my window to help lift the curse." Dame Vandend stood, a strange occurrence for her, so everyone's eyes were on her. "You all want this Newtime," she spat. "You will be sorry if you lift the curse. Mark my words."

Nora whirled around, pinning the old woman with her intent stare. "Why, witch? Do you plan to lay another curse on this village?"

The entire village went silent, the chickadees the only living thing daring to make a sound.

Dame Vandend scanned the crowd before her gaze settled on her grandson. She seemed startled, as if she'd forgotten he was there.

"Is this true, Grandmother?" Max took a step forward, his disbelief heartbreaking for Kat to watch.

The old woman avoided his gaze and shrugged. "I'd never harm you."

"That's not what I asked."

Dame Vandend sat on her hay bale and waved her hand to the side. "You want Newtime, you can have it."

Max's hurt was obvious and Nora took the opportunity to step back to the edge of the circle to comfort him. She nodded to Kat.

Without hesitancy, Kat and Braeden stepped forward. "I think we should take a vote. Will you all approve my marriage to Braeden, thereby keeping Sleepy Hollow in Newtime forever? If you approve, please raise your hand."

Kat's heart raced as hands went up all around them. They turned together to check and as she scowled at the witch, the woman raised her hand. Even Jurgen's arm raised along with his followers. Relief filled her heart as Braeden squeezed her waist.

Nora called out, "How do you two vote?"

Everyone laughed and Braeden grasped her hand in his and raised them together. "It is unanimous! We will marry and Sleepy Hollow will stay in Newtime."

Cheers erupted and even a few hats flew into the air.

Kat turned to Braeden with tears in her eyes once again. "I love you."

"Good. Because we are going to get married right now."

"What? But I don't have a dress. We haven't been engaged but a day. There is no supper planned. Braeden, your family isn't even here."

"Katrina Van Tassel." He pulled her toward him and wrapped his arms about her waist. "I'm not waiting one more minute to be your husband. I will never take the chance of losing you again. This wedding will satisfy the curse in Oldtime, but we will have to marry again in Newtime under the laws of the country now. Then you can have a beautiful dress and an amazing reception and all my family will be there. So in essence, you will have two weddings. Okay?"

"Fine."

"Good." He kissed her deeply, then raised his head. "To the church! We're getting married right now."

Kat grinned as the men grabbed Braeden and propelled him toward the path to the church while the women pulled her back to the inn. In no time she was dressed in a beautiful chintz gown of tiny pink rosettes on an ivory background, her hair raised high upon her head and flowers in her hand.

Nora finished pinning up the hem of the skirt. "This looks much better on you than it would have on my daughter."

"I feel terrible taking the gown you made for one of your daughters. Are you sure, Nora?"

The woman laughed, more carefree than Kat ever remembered seeing her. "Definitely. Thanks to you, I will be able to purchase ready-made dresses for both my girls in Newtime."

Kat gave the woman a tearful hug and they left the inn arm in arm.

The ladies walked her to the church. A group of geese couldn't have been louder. It was so different from the first time she'd come to the small church to be married. That time, she'd been waiting for a groom who never showed. Now her groom, obviously impatient, waited for her.

As they came to the entrance of the church, she lifted her face to the sky. *Thank you, Brom, for letting me go and giving me such an amazing husband.*

A chill swept through her but she smiled. He'd heard.

With a full heart and a light step, she floated forward, anxious, after more than two hundred and forty years, to finally begin her new life as Katrina Van Brunt.

# *Epilogue*

Present Day

Braeden pressed his wife against the door to the hotel suite. The low-cut neckline on the white satin gown revealing her ample cleavage had given him a day-long hard-on. As beautiful as she was, he liked her better in nothing.

"Braeden, someone will see."

He chuckled against her neck as his hand squeezed the breast he craved and pushed it up toward the opening of the dress. "What will they see, but the tails of my tuxedo?" He continued to squeeze and work her breast until the nipple popped above the neckline. His mouth, already close, couldn't resist, and he tongued the hard nub.

"Oh Braeden. I'm getting wet for you."

He jerked his head up. "Where did you hear that expression?"

"Why? Is it not appropriate?"

He leaned his forehead on her chest and talked to her breast. "Yes, it is if your goal was to make me so hard I will lift this dress to your waist and take you here in the hallway."

Her intake of breath told him his idea had increased her excitement, and he forced deep breaths through his lungs to gain control of his desire. When he could speak again, he lifted his head. "Just tell me who told you."

"Marilyn."

That cooled him like nothing else could. "My brother's wife?"

Kat nodded.

Okay, there were some places a man never needed to tread, and into his brother's bedroom was one of them. Stepping back, he glanced over his shoulder to be sure no one was in the hall and then stepped to the side to slide in the room key, all the time keeping his gaze on the one nipple peeking over the top of her wedding gown. If she thought being ravished by him in the hallway was hot, he couldn't wait until she saw the bedroom in their honeymoon suite.

He opened the door before he scooped her into his arms. "Wife! Welcome to your honeymoon." Stepping across the threshold, he kicked the door closed behind them.

She stared wide-eyed at the floor-to-ceiling windows in the main area. "By the saints, this is too much." She looked worriedly at him. "Is this expensive?"

Only Kat would think about the expense. He let her feet down and held her in front of him while he whispered in her ear, "Yes, and I can afford it."

She turned. "But the wedding was so big and the dinner and now this? Are you sure?"

"I'm sure." He was very sure. He'd spent years amassing a fortune, only spending it on Reed and a bit on himself. Now Reed didn't want his support anymore, so he was free to spend it on what was most important to him, his wife, and what pleased her. The honeymoon suite was for him to pleasure her. After being home for only a few weeks, he was as anxious as she was to return to Sleepy Hollow. By then, the cellular tower should be finished and they could slowly bring everyone up to speed. "Did you want to look?"

She nodded, so he guided her to the window where they were

able to view the Hudson River and the Catskill Mountains. It was the view he'd been reminded of by the painting in her parlor.

"Braeden, it's beautiful. Is Sleepy Hollow down there?"

He wrapped his arms about her waist. "Yes." He pointed. "Just to the right of that bridge."

She sighed.

"You miss it already?"

"Yes. Is that wrong?"

He turned her in his arms. "Nothing is wrong if it's how you feel."

He lifted the comb from her hair and watched as the lengthy silkiness fell to the side. "This little comb kept me connected to you throughout the year. I think we need to put it in a special place."

She smiled shyly. "I'm glad you took it. Grandmama would have been pleased, and it is nice to have something of the old with me."

"And I'm happy that Irwin is safely institutionalized." He kissed her forehead. "I doubt he'll ever convince anyone that he's sane."

Kat picked at the sleeve of his tux. "It is hard to understand all of the laws at once. You will have to be patient like you promised."

"You have taken in a lot in just a few weeks. We will make it easier for the others by going slower. I'm sorry I rushed you, but I wanted you to be legally mine as soon as possible in Newtime."

She brought her gaze back to his. "I know. It has been very interesting, and I love your family. I like Reed too. I'm so glad he remembers you and you can be real friends again."

"Me too." Having Reed and Stephen as his best men had been perfect. He couldn't have asked for anything better. "So do you want to see the rest of the place we will call home for a week?"

"Yes." Her smile was wide and happy. He never wanted that to change.

Walking her to the bedroom, he opened the door and watched her face.

She hesitated before taking a step. "Oh Lord. Braeden, there are mirrors everywhere."

"The better to see you with." He grinned devilishly and as she turned, she blushed.

"You want to see me?"

His cock took notice of the possibilities of the room. Mirrors on the ceiling over the bed, on the closet doors, along another wall and from what he could see, a few in the bathroom as well. "I want to see us. I want to see you come as I pump into you. I want you to see me as I thrust inside you. I want to watch you lick my cock. I want to see every angle."

Kat swallowed hard and her chest rose, her shy nipple having retreated back into her dress, disappointing him.

He stepped closer, backing her up to the mirror on the wall. "Now where were we? Oh yes. I believe I was paying homage to your nipple." Without further preamble, he pushed her breast above her neckline again, much like he did when she wore her stays. He took her hands and held her wrists together above her with one hand while his other kept her breast where he wanted it. Lightly, he scraped his teeth across it and nipped.

Kat's moan had Braeden's cock growing harder. Thank God they had a week because he planned to love her until she couldn't walk. Having finished with that nipple, he tried to get the other breast released, but the neckline wouldn't budge.

"Braeden, unzip the back of the dress. I have a surprise for you underneath."

Needing to taste her nipple motivated him more than his curiosity, so keeping her hands raised, he moved his other hand behind her and did as she bid. The white gown floated to the floor around her, leaving her in the sexiest pale-blue corset and gartered stockings he'd ever seen. The corset pushed up her breasts but left them exposed. Her mound of curls between her legs was covered with a small triangle of cloth and he glanced in the mirror to see the thong string peeking out from the top of her rounded ass.

Braeden groaned and his balls tightened in anticipation. "Shit, Kat. You're too sexy."

"I hope so. You looked so dashing all day in that tuxedo. I couldn't wait to get here."

He caught her gaze and held it. He kept forgetting that though his wife was from the 1790s, she was no innocent even if not very experienced. What he loved about her was her willingness to explore. He pushed her back up against the mirror and proceeded to suck on her other breast as he'd wanted to do. He pulled at the nipple with his teeth and mimicked the action with his fingers on the other one.

"Please, Braeden. I need you now."

He growled against her skin and dropped her hands. Throwing off the tuxedo coat, he undid the tie and ripped the button from the shirt while she worked on his pants. When his cock sprang free, he slowed, his control at last within his reach. Kicking off the shiny black shoes, he stepped out of his pants and pulled off his socks.

Kat's eyes gleamed as her gaze roved his body and he growled again. "Now." Picking her up, he gently tossed her on the bed on her stomach, then pulled her hips up to place her on her hands and knees.

"Braeden. What are you doing?"

He took a few deep breaths. "You wanted me to take you now, right?"

"Yes."

"Look in the mirror, Kat."

She turned her head toward the closet mirrors and stared.

He watched as she viewed his long cock just inches from her ass. Her gaze swept up to his and then she looked at herself, her luscious breasts hanging beyond the corset, her nipples hard and pointing toward the bed. When she licked her lips, his hold on her hips tightened.

"Watch us, Kat." He made a show of moving the thong string to the side and slowly touching his head to her opening. She was so wet that his cock slid along her, coating him with her juices. His ass tensed. "Now, Kat?"

She met his gaze in the mirror. "Now."

He pushed into her to the hilt, pulling her hips back against him.

"Yessss."

Her hiss caught his attention and he looked into the mirror to watch her face. Then he bent over and lifted her up to kneel. "Put your hands around my neck."

She did, causing her to arch slightly away from him and tighten their connection.

He grasped one breast in his hand as his other moved down to touch the place where they joined. He watched on the other wall mirror, fascinated by their connection. "Tell me what you want, Kat. I'll make you happy any way you want."

"Touch me."

"Where?"

"On my…" She licked her lips again and he sucked on her neck until she spoke. "On my clit and my nipple."

His cock surged within her at her words and he quickly obeyed. He played with her clit, stroking her juices from her pussy over it by dipping his finger inside with himself. He held her up with his arm as his finger played and plucked at her sensitive nipples and he licked and sucked at her shoulder until he felt her tighten around him.

"Oh God, Braeden!" As she came, he watched her body convulse against him, even as he felt her try to suck him into her vortex, but he held on, grasping her breast and pressing her clit to her body and against his pelvis.

As she calmed, he set her back on her hands and turned her head toward the mirror. "Watch."

She did, and he pulled out of her to thrust back in. His own view was the best, but from the side angle, she could see him take her. He pumped back and forth, holding her hips even though she met every thrust. Her wet sheath stroked him, sucked him, until he wanted more and more. He drove into her, slamming against her ass, his balls hitting her as they met. Her pussy contracted on him, grasping him as he pulled out, and on his inward thrust, it sent him over the edge.

He yelled in triumph at having claimed his wife forever.

When their breathing had slowed, he pushed her forward and rolled them onto their sides. "I love you, Kat." He grasped her about the waist, pulling her ass snugly against his pelvis.

"I love you too, Braeden."

He grinned. "Do you want your wedding present now?"

"Wasn't that it?" She sounded drowsy but he had news that would wake her.

"No. That was just the beginning of the week. I'm thinking of keeping you in here and not letting you out until it's time to go home."

"Really?" Her voice perked up a bit.

"You like that? That's my girl. We'll take it an hour at a time. With something special at midnight."

"Oh, I like the sound of that."

"So do you want your wedding present or not?"

She moved his hand from around her stomach to her breast. "Yes, I'm ready now. What is it?"

He watched her face in the mirror, her eyes were closed, but from her heartbeat, he could tell she was excited. "The land the village of Sleepy Hollow is built on is ours."

Her eyes flew wide before she separated them and rolled over to stare at him. "What? How can that be?"

He smiled. "Actually, it's a wedding present from Brom."

"Braeden. Tell me." Her tone was demanding and he laughed.

"I'm trying, but you keep interrupting."

"Fine."

His heart warmed with love for this beautiful woman and he smiled into her eyes. "Brom purchased the land while he was alive and it has been handed down all these generations. My father gave it to me at the wedding. It's now ours, so no one will have to leave the village until they want to or if they choose, not at all."

"Oh Braeden." She wrapped her hand around his neck and pulled him closer. "I will forever be grateful that you were forced to play the 'stupid Headless Horseman'."

"And I will forever be grateful I walked into the Sleepy Hollow Inn and begged an irritated woman for a room, any room."

"I'll have you begging for more than that in a minute."

He raised his brow. "Stranger things have happened."

She smirked. "But only in Sleepy Hollow."

If you enjoyed this story, a short review is always welcome.


For updates, sneak peeks, and special prizes, sign up to receive the latest news from Lexi at http://eepurl.com/D3MqT

Read on for a taste of **Masque** (http://www.lexipostbooks. com/masque/)

# Chapter One

## Cape Breton, Nova Scotia

People. Living, breathing people.

Synn MacAllistair grasped the embrasure of the parapet, his heart thudding as he stared at the vehicle crossing the stone bridge over the moat. It came to a stop at Ashton Abbey's massive gate.

He waited. The great iron grille, chained and padlocked against intruders, would be considered a significant deterrent to entering. *Open it. Damn it, open it!*

The vehicle remained stationary. No one exited the large red monstrosity.

Impatiently, he pushed away his hair as the breeze whipped it across his view. What were they waiting for? If they needed an axe to break the chain, he'd gladly provide them with one.

Another smaller vehicle rolling parallel to the west wall caught his attention. It crossed the bridge and parked behind the larger one. More people?

A man stepped from the small conveyance and shuffled to the gate. Synn leaned farther over the battlement, anxious to see if their time had come. The joyful sound of clanking chains floated up to him on the breeze.

*Finally! About bloody time.* He swallowed hard to keep the yell of triumph from escaping his throat. No need to scare their new guests.

The man below hurried back to his transport and, without hesitation, backed across the bridge and left faster than he'd arrived.

Synn peered down at the red vehicle, still as a brick, its black windows making it impossible to see inside. A door opened and a woman burst onto the cobblestone entrance. She bent over and spoke to someone else still inside. Her blonde hair hid her face, but her ass, covered in men's trousers, was small, her legs lanky. A woman? A woman dared enter a haunted abbey? He tried to grasp the concept.

His plan was to convince a man to enjoy the pleasures of the flesh, but there had to be a man to convince…unless a couple entered the Abbey. Couples enjoyed the Pleasure Rooms as well. If he could persuade a couple to participate in the Masque then his companions could still be freed.

Peering hard, he watched and waited. After what seemed another decade, a door on the other side of the red contraption opened. He held his breath, willing the occupant to have broad shoulders, a beard, anything to indicate a man.

A long, slender leg stretched out, a black high-heel shoe of delicate design at its end, and a feminine hand grasped the side, but remained stationary.

He growled with frustration. "Bloody hell. What am I supposed to do with two women?" He hadn't expected women. The Abbey overflowed with spirits. Only men should dare enter. How were blasted women going to help him? He paced away from the wall, but quickly returned. Could there be more people inside the vehicle?

He waited, his patience long gone, not that he ever had much, but damn, it'd been a hundred and fifty years. That would strain the patience of an archangel, something he definitely was not.

He glared as the leg moved and within a moment's breath, the woman unfolded herself from the conveyance.

Synn stared, frozen in time for once, drinking in a beauty far surpassing any painted Aphrodite he'd ever gazed upon. Her long, wavy brown hair captured the sun, shining like fine brandy. Her figure, as lush as any Greek goddess, swayed sensuously in her short dress. Her arms were bare and the smallest of noses held her dark glasses in place. He stepped back, away from the crenellation, his heart racing, his mind whirling with ideas.

He paced the length of the wall. A vision was about to enter his stone prison. A woman fit to be worshiped with every salacious touch he'd ever learned. His cock hardened beneath his pantaloons. Amazed, he stopped and looked down at it. After so many years of having no needs—for food, for sleep, for relieving himself—the last he'd expected to feel was the need for a woman. He shook his head. It defied logic. But if his body could respond, then he could participate, guide a woman through the Masque.

The creaking hinges of the gate brought him back to the wall to see the backs of the two women entering the Abbey courtyard. Two women. Vivid memories of his happier days with the prince caught him by surprise and gave him hope. As he strode across the wall-walk and down the stone staircase, his mind raced with possibilities. One after another they were discarded as he floated to the landing on the second floor. But a new plan began to form as the great pine doors opened.

If she hadn't been in heels, Rena Mills would have jumped over the threshold as she and Valerie pushed open the twelve-foot doors of Ashton Abbey. Their creaking sound didn't bother her. In fact, she'd be sure those hinges never saw oil for the rest of their days. They made a perfect first impression for a haunted bed-and-breakfast.

Valerie shook her head. "You love that noise, don't you?"

Rena grinned sheepishly as she stepped into the two-story stone entry the size of her parents' house and spread her arms wide. "It's perfect. I can't believe it. I'm actually going to make this happen. Can't you see it, Valerie?"

Her friend raised her eyebrow. "If you say so."

"I do." She examined the stone floor beneath her feet before touching a wall. The hard rock under her fingers was cool and rough. Her stomach somersaulted as success filled her veins. She could do this. Ashton Abbey resembled a castle and tourists would love staying here. All she needed was a little plumbing, a little electricity, a functioning kitchen, and a few ghosts. "Seriously, Val. You can see the potential, right?"

Valerie gave her a hard look. "You don't have to do this, Ree. You don't have to prove anything. That jerk is full of himself. So all your success has come while working at your family's company or at Bryce's. That's simply because you are a good event planner. Look at me. I've worked for my dad's company all my life. That doesn't mean I don't know my shit."

"It's not about Bryce. I have to prove this to myself." She wished Valerie could understand.

Her friend threw up her hands and stalked away. The woman was too confident to have any idea how it felt to be unsure. Rena sighed. The fact was, her ex-fiancé had a point. All her jobs had been obtained through her parents or him. After two months of being out of work, this was her only option. Now she had to make her new haunted abbey into a successful bed-and-breakfast, not simply to prove she could, but because she had every last penny on the line.

As she perused the large entry with its double staircase leading to the next floor, her jubilance returned. The abandoned building was so much more than she'd expected for the price. She looked up at the semicircle windows near the ceiling, which let in sunlight, but she didn't see any spirits. "I hope the real estate agent hadn't exaggerated about the ghosts. If this place hasn't sold because it's haunted, then I better see some dead people pretty darn fast."

"Uh, Rena?"

She glanced behind her to see Valerie had stepped into the next room. Turning, she strode through the doorway to find a grand dining room with green-and-gold paisley wallpaper. She stopped and smiled. "Oh, this is too good to be true." Valerie had pulled aside one of the curtains from the fifteen-foot windows to let in the sun, and it reflected off an elegantly set table.

"Over here." Her friend stood at the head of the table, a deep frown on her face.

"What is it? Did you find something?" She started down the length of the long table set to feed twenty-four. Her stomach twitched with excitement at the sight. She stopped to look at the place setting Valerie stared at. "What am I looking for?"

Valerie shook her head. "Do you see anything unusual here?"

She peered at the setting. The silverware had an elaborate P etched into it, but other than the fact it had multiple plates as if set for a formal occasion, she saw nothing out of the ordinary. "No. Should I?"

Valerie sighed and crossed her arms over her small chest. "How long has this place been empty?"

She shrugged. "I don't know. Over a hundred years or so? From what I hear, colored lights can be seen shining from the windows at night, but there's no electricity. I guess the Abbey got lucky with ghosts and I'm going to make that work for us."

"And is there a caretaker of some sort?"

"There is one family here who has taken care of the grounds for eons. I can't remember their names, but it's an old widower and his son. Why?"

Valerie dragged her finger across the plate. "Do they take care of the inside as well?"

"No, we are the only ones to enter inside these walls in a hundred and fifty years. Isn't that amazing? Why, what are you getting at?"

Valerie lifted her finger in front of Rena's eyes. "Then why is there no dust?"

Her brain came to a halt as she grasped Valerie's point. Taking another look around the room, she saw no cobwebs, no dust, not even a chair out of place. She returned her gaze to Valerie. "Clean ghosts?"

Valerie raised her brow. "Did you read about that in your research?"

Rena picked up the plate and examined it, not comfortable meeting her friend's eyes. "No, but I didn't exactly do research. I watched a few shows on television and discovered people will pay to go to a haunted hotel. There has to be an explanation. Maybe someone has been living here and no one realized it."

Valerie crossed the room to the windows. "You mean behind the padlocked gate?"

She joined her friend, puzzled, ready to believe in ghosts who cleaned. "What are you looking at?"

"These curtains. If they're a hundred years old, shouldn't they be dry-rotted and in shreds?"

A shiver ran across Rena's skin. "Oh, damn. This is stranger than a simple haunting." She ran her hand along the forest-green velvet of the curtain. The material, strong and thick, had a beige cotton backing. This didn't make any sense. She turned to examine the rest of the room. The chairs around the massive table also had velvet in their backs. She stepped closer to one and ran her hand over the material. The softness was irresistible…and new.

She paused. "It's as if time has no meaning inside these walls. I wonder if the place is bewitched as well as haunted!"

Valerie gave her one of her deprecating smiles. "And why is it haunted?"

She grinned. She couldn't help it. The more she saw of the Abbey, the more convinced she was that she could make it profitable. "It had something to do with the Red Death that swept through this town around 1861. I read that it could take a life within thirty minutes of exposure."

"Hmmm, that would explain a haunted town." Valerie ran her hand along the fireplace mantle. "But why is the Abbey the only place haunted? There has to be more to it than that. Maybe a monk bargained for a life and they all ended up dead?"

Even more sure now than the night she'd watched the documentary on haunted hotels, Rena headed for the door at the end of the room, the clacking of her heels echoing across the room. "I don't know, but I plan to find out. I will need a history of this place to put up on the website."

Valerie followed. "That will work. It's a good thing you're rid of Bryce. He'd find a reasonable, logical explanation for this and take all the fun out of it."

Rena stopped in her tracks, causing Valerie to bump into her. "Ugh. Thanks for ruining my mood again, Val."

"Hey, it's true. You are so lucky to be rid of him. Are you ready yet to tell me why he broke off the engagement? There's no one to overhear but the ghosts."

She faced her friend, aware that her heartache shone in her eyes, but it was too raw, too humiliating still. "I can't. Not yet. Okay?"

Valerie gave her a quick hug. "Of course. But remember, I'm your best friend and you will have to tell me eventually."

She nodded, but her excitement for the Abbey had left. "Why don't we bring our luggage in and find bedrooms? If we have to buy blow-up mattresses, I'd rather know now instead of tonight when the place is pitch black and all we have are our lanterns."

"You got it. And maybe we'll run into a ghost in the process."

Valerie's smile was contagious and Rena grinned, her upbeat spirit making a quick return. "We better, or this haunted bed-and-breakfast idea will be a complete bust."


Synn ducked around the doorway as the ladies turned toward the entry once again. He let the slender blonde pass through, but he couldn't resist touching the other one. Lightly, so as not to frighten her, he brushed his fingers across her bare shoulder.

"What?" She turned, looking about.

The scent of dusky, tart pomegranate wafted by his nose. His body responded with an overwhelming need to touch her again. He craved her smoothness like a pickpocket coveted a half-dollar. When had he last craved anything? He tamped down his own interest. It was of little importance. This woman would be their freedom.

"Rena, are you coming?"

With her smile wide and full of joy, she followed after her friend. "You are not going to believe this, but a ghost just touched me."

That she hadn't run in fear confirmed his belief she could be the answer. Rena. He liked her name.

Her hips swayed with her quick pace, her energy palpable. Would she have that kind of liveliness in bed?

As she crossed the threshold to the outside, his gut tightened in panic. She couldn't leave. Not now!

Synn ran to the open door and stopped, the memory of his last venture outside freezing his limbs in place. He couldn't leave the Abbey or he'd cease to exist. He needed to calm himself. Too much was at stake.

The women pulled belongings from their conveyance. They should have allowed the servants to do that kind of work. When they turned to enter again, he blended back into the wall, his stomach relaxing at their entrance.

The blonde dropped her bags. "Okay, I'll take the stairway to the left and you take the one on the right."

Rena glanced upward. "Great. If you see anything unusual, yell. I want to see a ghost."

"Believe me, you'll know if I see one."

As the two ascended the grand stairways, Synn followed. He glanced around, surprised Mrs. McMurray hadn't appeared yet. Not that he minded. Their two guests seemed to be open to the spirits who lived here, but he hoped they could settle in first. At least until he introduced himself, and the way he wanted to introduce himself had his cock paying attention.

Rena headed down the hallway on the second floor, opening doors and looking inside. Her mumbled words made her opinions of each room clear. Everything from "hideous" to "extraordinary" passed by her lips. Lips, full and red, with no rouge, begged for a kiss.

When she had passed judgment on all the rooms, she returned

to the one second from the stairs. He tried to ignore the fact she stood outside the bedroom next to his. It appeared fate continued to play with him.

He followed her inside as she gave the bedroom a thorough inspection. He could not fault her taste. Decorated in pale yellows and deep purples, it suited her. When she moved next to the large four-poster bed, he couldn't resist standing behind her, inhaling her unique scent. Her hand touched the quilt, and he ran his fingers along her bare arm, wanting more than anything to turn her around and kiss her.

She stilled but didn't pull away. "Is there someone here?"

He remained silent, but placed his hands upon her arms and let his breath brush by her ear.

A shiver ran through her body and Synn grinned. A responsive woman was exactly what he needed. Triumph filled his heart and he brought his chest in contact with her back.

Her breathing grew rapid, but from sexual excitement or at being touched by a ghost? He bent his head to kiss her neck when a scream rent the air.

"Reeeennnaaa!!!"

She pulled away and ran across the inside balcony that connected the two stairways on the second floor.

Irritated, he tried to ignore his reborn need for a woman. Adjusting himself within his pantaloons, he followed. Who was causing problems now?

Rena came to a halt before an open doorway. Inside, the blonde stood with a candelabra held before her like a Roman shield.

"What is it, Val?"

She pointed to the corner of the room. Before the open wardrobe doors stood Mrs. McMurray. Synn silently sighed. At least

Mrs. McMurray was a kindhearted soul who wouldn't hurt a three-legged cat.

Rena clapped her hands as she joined her friend. "It's a ghost. A real, live ghost."

She probably wouldn't appreciate him correcting her oxymoron, so he remained silent and invisible. He leaned against the doorframe behind the women, but where Mrs. McMurray could see him. The older woman's expression turned from concerned to relieved.

Rena approached her. "Hello. I'm Rena and this is Valerie. We are pleased to meet you."

Mrs. McMurray gave her guests a deep curtsy.

Rena turned back to look at Valerie and smiled. She had the whitest teeth he'd ever seen. She mouthed the words "she has no legs", her eyes wide with surprise.

Valerie glanced toward the older lady and sucked in a breath before nodding.

Facing Mrs. McMurray again, Rena addressed the spirit. "Can you tell us your name?"

Mrs. McMurray shook her head then lifted her gaze to him. Her pleading look had him cursing inside. He had wanted more time, but he couldn't ignore his friend's request. She wouldn't be able to vocalize until closer to the full moon. Blast.

Allowing himself to materialize, he answered for her. "Her name is Mrs. McMurray."

## Paranormal Romance

Masque

Passion's Poison

Pleasures of Christmas Past (A Christmas Carol Series: Book 1)

Desires of Christmas Present (A Christmas Carol Series: Book 2)

*Coming Nov, 2016*

## Sci-fi Romance

Cruise into Eden (The Eden Series: Book 1)

Unexpected Eden (The Eden Series: Book 2)

Eden Discovered (The Eden Series: Book 3)

Eden Revealed (The Eden Series: Book 4)

*Coming 2017*

## Contemporary Cowboy Erotic Romance

Cowboys Never Fold (Poker Flat Series: Book 1)

Cowboy's Match (Poker Flat Series: Book 2)

Cowboy's Best Shot (Poker Flat Series: Book 3)

Cowboy's Break (Poker Flat Series: Book 4)

Christmas with Angel (Last Chance Series: Book 1)
Trace's Trouble (Last Chance Series: Book 2)
Fletcher's Flame (Last Chance: Book 3)
*Coming October, 2016*
Logan's Luck: (Last Chance Series: Book 4)
*Coming Soon*

# About Lexi Post

Lexi Post is a New York Times and USA Today best-selling author of romance inspired by the classics. She spent years in higher education taking and teaching courses about the classical literature she loved. From Edgar Allan Poe's short story "The Masque of the Red Death" to Tolstoy's *War and Peace*, she's read, studied, and taught wonderful classics.

But Lexi's first love is romance novels. In an effort to marry her two first loves, she started writing romance inspired by the classics and found she loved it. From hot paranormals to sizzling cowboys to hunks from out of this world, Lexi provides a sensuous experience with a "whole lotta story."

Lexi is living her own happily ever after with her husband and her cat in Florida. She makes her own ice cream every weekend, loves bright colors, and you will never see her without a hat.

www.lexipostbooks.com